Dennis Boyle is a practicing criminal attorney who has prosecuted and defended more than two hundred trials, including many murder trials. He is also a hunter and outdoorsman who is familiar with the north woods where this story takes place. He has also studied werewolves extensively and read many books and novels about werewolves, although he has never met one.

I would like to dedicate this novel to my wife, Darla, without whose encouragement and support, this book never would have been written.

Dennis Boyle

THE BEAST OF WINTER HAVEN

AUSTIN MACAULEY PUBLISHERS™

LONDON * CAMBRIDGE * NEW YORK * SHARJAH

Ordering Information
Quantity sales: Special discounts are available on quantity purchases by corporations, associations, and others. For details, contact the publisher at the address below.

Publisher's Cataloging-in-Publication data
Boyle, Dennis
The Beast of Winter Haven

ISBN 9798889106012 (Paperback)
ISBN 9798889106029 (Hardback)
ISBN 9798889105084 (ePub e-book)
ISBN 9798889105077 (Audiobook)

Library of Congress Control Number: 2023923109

www.austinmacauley.com/us

First Published 2024
Austin Macauley Publishers LLC
40 Wall Street, 33rd Floor, Suite 3302
New York, NY 10005
USA

mail-usa@austinmacauley.com
+1 (646) 5125767

Chapter 1

It was cold and a light snow was falling, giving the forest a peaceful, yet foreboding appearance as Cynthia Johnson waited for the meeting. She had been told to travel to the parking area adjacent to a trailhead about ten miles outside town. She had been to the trailhead before and had hiked on the trial on warmer summer days, but now the area was desolate. Snow slowly drifted to the ground, silently providing the forest floor with a new white blanket.

Although it was past midnight, the snow-covered ground reflected the moonlight, illuminating the forest to a minor extent. At the same time, the light quickly faded into the darkness of the mixed conifer forest. The oaks and maples had months ago lost their leaves, and the black branches stretched out like spindly arms seeking an embrace.

Her car was twelve years old, and gas was expensive, so she had turned off the engine for a time. She wore a heavy winter coat, and the cold felt good on her cheeks. She enjoyed the silence of the forest on these cold winter nights. She imagined she wouldn't be alone for long. It was five minutes past the appointed meeting time, and her suitor should be along any minute…unless he changed his mind.

No, that wouldn't be possible. He wouldn't set up this meeting and then miss it; that would be just too cruel. He would be along any minute.

As she sat in the driver's seat, she thought she heard a noise, perhaps a dead branch snapping. Then she imagined she saw some movement in the mountain laurel. Maybe it was the wind, but when she looked more closely, there was no wind. The chilly air was completely still. There was no more movement in the mountain laurel. She concentrated to see if she could see or hear anything, anything at all, but she couldn't.

Then she saw a face, or the outline of a face, to her left. It was there for a moment and then it was gone. It was not a human but she couldn't say what it was. She thought it might be her imagination. The deep forest has a way of playing with a person's mind. As she searched the forest, she could see nothing more.

After a minute, she decided it was her imagination. She tried to concentrate on the man she would meet. He had perfect teeth and piercing blue eyes. He was twice her age, maybe more, but she liked mature men. Anyhow, it was getting cold now, and it would be a good idea to roll up the window and start the engine to warm the car. She also reflexively locked the doors. There was nothing to be afraid of, but there was no harm in locking the door, either.

Cindy had once been a beautiful girl. She had been elected to the homecoming court in high school, and everyone wanted to date her, although few had the courage to even ask. She had a sparkle in her eyes in those days, together with a beautiful smile. People said she had a 'cute' figure. But all of that was ten years in the past, and those years had not been kind to Cindy.

Possessing what she thought was beauty, she saw little need to study in school and no need to work hard at anything. She would marry and marry well. Her boyfriend was Drew Anderson, quarterback for the football team. He was good-looking, very good-looking, or so they said. People were sure he would have a career in the NFL and make millions. What's more, they were in love, and she would be his celebrity wife.

She became pregnant just after Christmas her senior year, a couple weeks before he was offered an athletic scholarship at a university three states away. When she told him of the pregnancy, he accepted the news solemnly, as he should have. They talked about what to do. He wanted to get married—at least he said he did—but he also said there would be 'difficulties', and she knew there would be, but youthful enthusiasm and dreams lifted her spirits far above any difficulties her parents could see or warn her about.

She was five months pregnant when she graduated, looking forward to a July wedding. There would not be a honeymoon, but at least she would be married when her son was born. As the date for the wedding approached, she became concerned at Drew's lack of interest in the wedding. He seemed unable to even commit to a date for the wedding. Finally, he told her that he needed to concentrate on football that summer.

His scholarship and their future, he told her, depended on his football career. Marriage would have to wait until the next year. He loved her. He told her so. She knew he did. He wanted to be there for the birth of his son, and she knew he would be there. Drew spent nearly every evening with her that summer before leaving for college, and when he left, he told her he would email her every day, and he did, for three months.

Her son, Andrew, after his father, was born in September, but Drew couldn't make it for the birth. There was a big game that weekend and he had to be there—because of his scholarship—even though he wasn't going to play. When he came home for Christmas to see 'his son', he spent only twenty minutes with Cindy and Andrew. He told her that he never loved her, that he had outgrown her, and that he was too young to marry.

Drew spoke of his college career and his football career. She cried. She cried a lot, but Drew didn't seem to care. He had another girlfriend, one worthy of his new station in life. He assured her that he would support his son. For some reason, she believed that promise.

Nine years had passed since that promise. Life had not developed as Drew thought it would. The truth was, he wasn't that good at football or at college, either. His success in a small, rural Pennsylvania high school never translated to success in college, where other candidates for the quarterback position were stronger, faster, and smarter. By his junior year, an injury disqualified him from the program, and he lost his scholarship.

He did not return his senior year to finish his lackluster academic career in a major that held no promise. He never thought about calling Cindy or visiting his son. Cindy attempted to collect child support but Drew moved from job to job and from state to state. 'Support' was sporadic and always behind. In the past nine years, Drew's most significant employment had been as a manager in a discount shoe store. That job had lasted eighteen months.

After high school, Cindy never pursued any education or training. Raising the baby had taken nearly all of her time. Plans A, B, and C had been to marry well, but the beauty she had in high school faded, and she discovered there were other beautiful women out there. The baby did not add to her appeal. She started drinking and smoking to help her deal with things, but the drinking and smoking did not have a beneficial effect on her pretty face or figure.

She put on weight as the years passed, and her face and the rest of her appearance looked more haggard. She used other drugs, cocaine mostly, when it was offered to her, but no matter what, she couldn't keep up with the younger girls. She had a son, and her son needed her. She tried to be a good mother. Dating was difficult, at least dating good guys who were interested in a future together.

She always put her son first, however. She hoped that her some would grow up to be handsome and intelligent. He would go to college. He would be hardworking. Most of all, he would be respectful of women. She might not accomplish anything else in life, but she would raise a successful son. When she was old, he would take care of her.

Now, nearly a decade later, she didn't think much of dating anymore. She supported herself and her son by working at a local bar/restaurant, each week being more or less like the one before.

So, she was more than surprised when a good-looking, obviously wealthy stranger began talking to her at the bar where she worked and seemed interested in her. He spoke with a soft, engaging voice and asked her a lot of questions about herself. He had a southern accent, which sounded like honey, and was old-fashioned in his attitudes. The stranger came back a couple more nights, and she began to look forward to his visits.

One night, they laughed and they talked for more than two hours, but after only thirty minutes, she knew he was special. He hung on her every word, told her she was beautiful and was interested in her life, even her son. He didn't talk about himself, as most men do. He made her laugh and smile, and she felt better about herself than she had for many, many years. By the end of their third conversation, she would have done anything for him.

Now she found herself waiting alone in a secluded parking lot in a state forest in the middle of nowhere, waiting for him to arrive. They had made plans to meet at 12:00 a.m., but it was now nearly 12:30. It was cold and her heater didn't work well. It was an odd place to meet but she wanted…no, she *needed* him to meet her. She would wait, even if it took all night.

Where was the handsome stranger and why had he picked this remote location to meet? Maybe he was married. She understood that and was willing to accept it. At least she understood his need for privacy.

Although she had closed the windows, she thought she heard the sound of a footfall in the snow, a slight crunching sound, close to the car. She smiled, thinking it would be her companion, but then realized that no vehicle had pulled into the parking area. She nevertheless turned her head, hoping to see him. Before she could focus on anything, a big hairy hand burst through the driver's side window and seized the car door in its large black claws, tearing it from its hinges.

It threw the door across the parking area like it was an old license plate. Another arm reached in and seized her by the throat. She tried to scream but couldn't. She tried to breath but could get no air. Its fingers, or rather claws, closed on her throat, cutting off all air and slicing into her neck.

As it drew her toward him, she looked into two beady eyes and the largest set of fangs she had even seen. She smelled rotted blood and death. She resisted with all of her strength, but she was powerless; she was like an insect caught in the unrelenting grasp of a predator.

Cindy knew there was nothing she could do and that she was going to die. She couldn't run. She couldn't fight. She thought about begging for mercy, but there was no mercy in the eyes that now faced her. Blackness began to seep into her vision, narrowing her focus. In her last moments, she glanced at the wallet-sized photo of Andrew she kept taped to the dashboard. In it, he was wearing the typical little league baseball uniform millions of other elementary-age children wear every year. He wore a baseball cap and was all smiles as he held the bat in a swinging pose.

Cindy smiled at her son. He was so handsome. Then the photo disappeared in a splash of blood and gore. The end, in a way, was merciful, or at least more merciful than those who first arrived at the scene might have suspected. First responders and police would find a scene worse than that from a horror movie. The dismembered body, which no longer looked human, lay in a pool of blood, but at least Cindy died quickly.

The fangs sunk into her shoulder and face as a clawed hand snapped her neck. It was over before she fully realized what had happened. The blood and gore, her severed head, her viscera spread over the entire interior of the car— that all came after she died.

Chapter 2

The attacker spent about an hour with his prize, relishing his power. There were two different emotions struggling within him. The first was the immense joy of the kill. For a hunter, there is nothing more satisfying than the subjugation of the quarry. There are multiple examples in nature: the cat and the mouse, the coyote and the sheep, and the human hunter and whatever animal he decides to kill. It was no different for the creature. He enjoyed killing his quarry. He reveled in the fear he had inspired and the life he had ended.

There was nothing personal about the death of this woman. He was a predator and she was prey. The creature could no sooner feel bad for this woman than a wolf could feel sorrow for the caribou it killed. It was all part of nature, the creature told himself. After the death, he took some time to tear apart the victim. He did so because he had to—it was nature, or at least in *his* nature. As he randomly flung body parts around and blood spread over the snow, he marveled at the carnage he had created.

He ate her heart and part of her liver. He doubted anyone would notice the missing organs with the rest of the mess he left behind. Besides, they would not need the heart or the entire liver to determine a cause of death, would they?

Another force inside of him wrestled with the visceral joy he experienced, and that was the need for self-preservation. He knew he had to escape before he was seen by anyone, and he had to be careful not to leave any unexplainable evidence behind. If he stayed too long, he risked discovery. This one was dead, and now the stalk and the kill were over. There had been others in the past—at least a hundred. There would be others in the future. Now, he had to get away.

He had miles to travel across the mountains, and so after making sure he left no evidence behind, he set off into the forest on his way home. A light snow had fallen, and his tracks would eventually be covered. He was safe. He would soon be home.

The next morning, a passing motorist saw Cindy's car parked in the parking area. The driver's side door was missing and things didn't look right. When the motorist pulled into the parking area, she saw the blood and gore around the car. Since there was no cell reception in the remote area, she had to drive another five miles before she called 9-1-1. She reported what she had seen to the dispatcher but refused to return to the scene to meet with the state troopers who were being dispatched.

The state police didn't have the option of driving away as the motorist had. The first two troopers who arrived sealed off the crime scene and called for detectives. The lead detective was a thirty-year veteran of the force, Detective John Jones. He arrived about an hour after the initial call had come in and was overwhelmed by what he saw. The veteran detective had seen a lot of murder in his day. He seen all manner of death, people shot and stabbed.

He had seen human beings hit by tractor-trailers and run over by trains. He had been to the scene of a murder where a man had killed his wife and nine-year-old son with an axe. This was different than any of those murders, and worse by far.

The victim—possibly a Cynthia Johnson, age twenty-six—had been completely mutilated. What kind of a sick bastard could do something like this? There wasn't even enough left for a next-of-kin to identify, not that he would ever show any of this to anyone else. God, it made him sick to look at it. The head was not attached to the torso. One leg and one arm were missing. The other leg had been severed below the knee, leaving only part of a jagged bone.

No one could even tell if the entire body was present. It appeared as though much of the abdomen and one of the thighs had been eaten. There appeared to be bite marks from some animal on the body, something with well-developed fangs that tore chunks of flesh away.

The crime scene technicians would later recover DNA from the interior of the car. Some of the DNA appeared to be from some type of canine, perhaps a wolf. There was also hair recovered from the interior of the car that was tagged and placed into evidence. Technicians at the state police lab could not extract any DNA from the hair. When it was analyzed at the State Museum, scientists could only say it was consistent with that of a wolf.

An early theory that emerged during the investigation was that the death was the result of animal attack, but the theory was quickly rejected. There were no large predators in Pennsylvania capable of inflicting these types of injuries. There were black bears in the area, but black bears are normally not aggressive toward humans. Black bears had been known to attack people, but there were no recorded cases of a black bear attacking a victim inside a vehicle.

In addition, the bite patterns and tooth marks were not consistent with a bear attack, and the hair and DNA samples recovered ruled out a bear as the culprit. A wolf seemed to be a more likely suspect, but wolves had been hunted to extinction in the Eastern United States more than one hundred years ago. Coyotes, a smaller cousin to the wolf, inhabited the forest, but an adult coyote weighed at most fifty or sixty pounds—too small to inflict the massive injuries Cindy had suffered.

There was also the problem of the vehicle. Whatever had killed the victim had killed her in her car. Either she had opened the door to her attacker or the attacker had opened her door to kill her. An animal such as a bear or a wolf could not open a car door, and it seemed unreasonable to believe that Cindy would have opened her door with a vicious animal outside. The door had not only been opened; it had been torn from its hinges.

No animal in North America, except maybe a polar bear or an Alaskan brown bear, could inflict such damage, and there were no such animals within thousands of miles of the murder scene. In the end, the theory of an animal attacker was ruled out. Cindy was killed by a two-legged predator responsible for almost all violent deaths to humans: another human.

This was not going to be an easy investigation. It would most likely either be quickly solved or not solved at all. Law enforcement professionals refer to this type of murder as 'disorganized'. The amount of violence employed would normally indicate a deep-seated anger, hatred even, of the particular victim. These types of murders are normally committed by someone who knew the victim well, someone motivated by emotion.

Typically, murderers in these cases turn out to be husbands or boyfriends. The killer usually leaves lots of forensic evidence. In this case, however, there was no identifiable human DNA evidence left behind nor any other clue. The lack of forensic evidence seemed at odds with the disorganized nature of the murder. Detective Jones had his team look into the victim's background. They quickly determined that she had been a high-school dropout with no significant steady employment. She had a child out of wedlock when she was young.

She had dated a lot of guys, too many guys to have anyone stand out as a likely suspect. In the end, they could not identify any potential suspect. The young woman did not seem to have any enemies. There were no former psychopathic boyfriends. The police were not able to identify anyone who might have wanted Cindy dead.

The other possibility was that Cindy had been killed by a serial killer. If this were the case, then Cindy was likely selected at random, and her killer could be anyone and anywhere. The media loved serial killers. The public was afraid of them. Detective Jones hated serial killer cases. He needed to get ahead of this and quickly. A serial killer on the loose could destroy his career.

Chapter 3

While Detective Jones was still at the crime scene, David Krell, a former police detective who now worked as a private investigator, was making his way home after a night of surveillance. He had been following a suspected unfaithful husband for a domestic relations attorney. The husband told his wife that we would be snowmobiling with some friends at a local state park. Because of the distance, he had said he was going to spend the night at a hotel near the park.

The attorney suspected that snowmobiling was not the main reason for the trip. It had been a successful night for Dave. Successful because he would be paid and, almost as important, successful because he had photographs. This was one of the aspects of his job that he enjoyed. He had been trying to catch this particular cheating husband for weeks without success. On this particular night, he decided to try something different.

Dave had tried following this guy on two previous occasions but lost him. This time, he decided to stake out an isolated motel called the Twilight Inn, which was not far from the park where the husband would allegedly be snowmobiling. Following a target, particularly a cheating husband, is difficult—especially in isolated rural areas where there is little traffic. Once the target discovers that he or she is being followed and starts to take evasive action, the opportunity to follow the target to his or her ultimate destination is gone.

Surveilling a building, like a motel, is usually more fruitful. It is easier to arrive undetected at a location where the target and his lover are going to meet, and then simply hide and wait for the meeting to occur. Dave's previous attempts to follow the target had generally led in the direction of the Twilight. Tonight, he decided to rent a room himself and then spend the night in the back of the van with his cameras. It had been a long night.

The target arrived at about 11:00 p.m. Dave photographed him entering room 36 with a key at 11:14 p.m. At 11:36 p.m., a much younger woman arrived and entered the room. The blinds were drawn, so Dave was not able to see what was going on inside the room. But he *was* able to photograph the young woman leaving the room at 5:05 a.m. the next morning. As a bonus, the took a photo of the middle-aged man kissing the woman in the doorway as she left. It had been a very successful but long night. It was now time to head home to bed himself.

It was a long drive home, and on the way, he decided to stop and relieve himself and stretch his legs in the cold, crisp morning air. Dave walked up the logging road, no more than fifty yards, just before the sun came up. The sky was becoming lighter, even if the sun had not yet cleared the eastern horizon. It had snowed for much of the night, and a light snow still fell. The northern mountains were beautiful under a blanket of newly fallen snow. More than a hundred years ago, the old growth white pine and hemlock had been cut to be replaced by hard woods: oak, cherry, ash, beech, and birch.

During the summer, their dense foliage obstructed the mountain views. In the fall, the colorful leaves brought tourist 'leafers', as they were called by the locals. But during the winter, the leaves were gone, the birds had left, many of the animals had hibernated, and a strange peace descended upon the high mountains. It was the peace of a deep sleep.

The wind was picking up, and Dave's light jacket offered little protection against the elements. There were maybe three or four inches of new snow on the ground. He had been out of his car about fifteen minutes. It was time to head back to the car, but his peripheral vision caught movement on the side of the logging road, and he waited to see what it was. Deer still fed, and coyotes and foxes still hunted rodents during the winter. Dave supposed it really wasn't that peaceful, after all. Life and death struggles continued even in the dead of winter, but in a quieter way.

As he watched, something stepped from the forest onto the logging road. At first, his brain had trouble processing what his eyes clearly told him was there. It was a creature like none he had ever seen before. It was huge, over seven feet tall, and walked on two legs. Its arms were thicker than a telephone pole with long claws at the end of each finger. Long hair, brownish or blackish or grayish, hung from the creature, except for its face.

Dave only had a second to view the creature before it turned and looked at him. The two beady black eyes that sat above a protruding snout glared at him with hatred. The creature wrinkled its lips, showing a full set of fangs, and let loose a bloodcurdling cry. There was nothing beautiful about the creature. Its hair was matted and caked with something, maybe blood. Saliva fell from its fangs. Dave took a step back, and then two, as the creature appeared to be trying to decide what to do.

Dave took a third step back. As a private investigator, he always carried a firearm. Today, he had a pistol, a Smith and Wesson .357 caliber revolver—six shots from a relatively powerful handgun, but handguns are made for self-defense, primarily against humans at close range. They weren't designed to stop a heavily muscled animal larger than a bear—at least not reliably so. He took another step back. The truck was no more than thirty yards away now, the creature seventy or eighty yards in the other direction.

Dave took one more step back, keeping his eyes on the creature the whole time, hoping he could make it.

He took another step toward the truck. The creature continued watching him. One more step. Part of his mind was screaming for him to turn and run; another part told him to move slowly, to not do anything sudden or precipitous. For the moment, the latter part of the brain held sway, but just barely.

Dave had now closed half the distance to his vehicle and then two things happened almost simultaneously. The creature charged at a full run, and Dave drew his pistol from its holster and aimed at the creature. *Bang…bang…bang.*

Dave was an excellent shot and all three shots hit the creature in the center of its chest, but it kept coming.

When the animal was no more than twenty feet away, Dave knew that he would not kill it. With his last remaining bullets, he dropped his aim and shot for the creature's knee.

He squeezed off two more shots, and with the second shot, the creature screamed and collapsed. The scream, however, was a scream of anger or hatred, not pain. After it fell, it tried to get up but could not. It began dragging itself toward Dave.

Dave turned and ran for his truck. His flight instinct had overcome his fight instinct but now he knew he had time to run. He jumped into his vehicle, started the engine, and drove off. Only as he drove off did he take time to look back at what he had seen. To his surprise, the creature was once again standing on two legs. It just stood there, unmoving.

A couple miles down the road, Dave began to shake. There was something new in the North Woods. Something new and something dangerous. Whatever it was, it was big and strong and malevolent, almost like a mythological monster, but it was no fairytale. Dave had saved himself but he had not won— he had only barely survived. Next time, if there was a next time, he would be more prepared, but even with better preparation, he doubted he would survive.

Chapter 4

As the pickup truck drove down the road, the creature cursed his own carelessness. How could he step into a clearing without first checking to see if any humans were present? He had become complacent as he moved farther away from last night's killing, and he had allowed himself to think about things other than his survival. By the time he realized the human's presence, he had already been seen. Almost as bad, he had been indecisive in dealing with the threat.

He could have jumped back into the forest and disappeared. The human probably would not have told anyone what he had seen, and even if he had, no one would have believed him. He could also have attacked. He could kill the threat and carry the body with him, dumping it someplace it would never be found.

The human's movement toward his truck made the creature react. He decided to kill the threat and hide the body. As he charged, he could see the human draw a revolver. The creature laughed as he thought of the human's futility in trying to defend himself. The first three bullets struck his chest but did no damage. His body would expel the little lead bullets over the next couple of days. No problem.

Then the human shot for his knee and, much to the creature's surprise, actually hit his right knee. The creature collapsed and the human was able to make his escape—only the second time a human had gotten away from him. His knee would heal, and it would do so quickly. For the next couple of days, however, he would be injured. For now his rapid gait had now been reduced to a slow walk. He would not make it home before more humans began to stir.

As Dave drove away, he tried to figure out what had happened. Even worse, how could he tell anyone what had happened? Many people claimed to have seen Bigfoot in the North Woods; some even claimed to have photographs, but the respectable folks in the area knew these sightings came from drugs or alcohol or mental illness. There was no Bigfoot; there never had been. If he told people he saw one and shot it, no one would believe him.

He was a private detective who worked for local attorneys and often had to testify in court. If he started making outlandish claims, he would lose his credibility, and no one would ever hire him. He could already hear the laughter as he imagined himself in the witness stand.

"So, thank you for your careful observations in this case; now tell us about the time you shot Bigfoot."

And yet he couldn't ignore the danger to the community. This was not some peaceful, comedic creature that just wanted to be left alone. Bigfoot or Sasquatch was usually described as a large, ape-like creature that ran or hid whenever humans were nearby. This was a vicious, dangerous carnivore that was certainly capable of killing a man. It was not only capable of killing a man; it seemed as though it lived to kill people.

It had no fear and worst of all, it seemed impervious to pain. He'd fired three rounds into the animal's chest but it hadn't slowed down. Dave had only escaped because of his lucky knee shot. The creature had to be destroyed, and there was only one person Dave could think of who would hunt this creature.

Edwin Reynolds sat at his desk. He had spent the past forty years as a lawyer, but now he did not have any work to do, or at least not much. He wondered if this day would be his last. He reached into the top left-hand drawer of his desk and pulled out the Smith and Wesson .357 magnum he kept there. Its weight was reassuring in his hand. He opened the cylinder and saw the brass shell casings with their silver primers in the stainless-steel cylinder. He snapped the cylinder shut and sighted down the barrel.

He liked the revolver. To people who spend a lot of time with guns, the weapons develop personalities. There was the old twelve-gauge double-barrel given to him by his father. As a child, he carried that heavy gun through forests and fields in search of squirrels and rabbits and the occasional pheasant. That shotgun carried with it memories of simpler, happier times.

His .300 Winchester magnum had been with him when he had shot elk and bear. It, too, had been there when he needed it, and the memories of those hunts were bound to that rifle.

The .357 was different. It had been in his desk or by his side for decades, but he never shot anything more than a target with it. It was not as efficient as the newer semi-automatic pistols. It carried only six shots, far less than the fourteen carried by many of the newer pistols. The design was antiquated, not that much different from the old Colts that cowboys and gunfighters carried after the Civil War. Maybe that was why he liked it; it was old and antiquated. Maybe like him, it had lost its usefulness.

But it still worked. At least it worked well enough. Each shell contained a bullet composed of 158 grains of copper-jacketed lead. A single squeeze of the trigger would send that bullet out of the six-inch barrel at over 1,400 feet per second. It might not be reliable enough to kill a deer at fifty yards, but at point-blank range, it would destroy a human skull and the brain inside. Six years before, he had been one of the leading trial lawyers in the nation.

He took only the biggest cases, and he always won. His own personal office occupied the entire top floor of one of Philadelphia's highest buildings. He flew around the country in his own private jet, stayed in the best hotels, and ate the finest food. He could have anything he desired, and he indulged in whatever he wanted. Although he had always loved his wife, the allure of younger, more attractive women who would do whatever he wanted had taken him to places he never should have gone.

There was no one to say 'no' or to even question his decisions. He spent hundreds of thousands of dollars every year with nothing to show for it, but hundreds of thousands of dollars meant nothing when he was making tens of millions. His mansion on the Main Line had cost $15 million, but that was only one of several homes.

His life could not have been more blessed.

That was before everything had unraveled. That was before the investigations and the lawsuits. They say that lawyers have no friends, and Ed found that out quickly. Leaders of the bar and friends who were judges had abandoned him almost immediately. Attorneys he worked with more closely gave him the benefit of the doubt for a couple of months, but the relentless reporting of his fall got to even his closest 'legal' friends, and he was soon all alone.

The suits against him multiplied. In the end, he avoided a criminal indictment and was able to keep his law license, but the suits had taken everything he owned.

Now, rather than the office on the top floor of a skyscraper in Philadelphia, he worked out of a converted garage attached to a vacation cottage in the Poconos. Clients were few and far between. Worse than that, however, was the humiliation. And so, every day, he sat at his desk and took out the revolver and held it in his hand, wondering if that day would be the day it happened. Would this be the day he put the .357 Smith and Wesson to his temple and ended it all?

In some ways, it would be so easy, a momentary squeeze of the trigger, and then oblivion. There might be a momentary burst of pain but then all of his pain would be gone. The revolver was efficient enough. It would do what he asked.

And yet, for over seven hundred days, he had always placed the revolver back in the drawer and closed it. Today, he heard his wife banging around in the cottage, cleaning it. She had become a recluse since the media started the very public chronicling of his downfall. Some of her friends had been supportive, or so she thought. In reality, they were just the bored spouses of other lawyers searching for gossip.

The need to live on a budget and the loss of the country club membership struck her particularly hard. She needed him and he could not abandon her. He had already caused her an enormous amount of pain; he couldn't abandon her to a life alone.

He also worried about the effect his suicide might have on his grown children or his grandchildren. It wasn't that he was particularly close to them. Ed had made sacrifices along the way, and some of the things he sacrificed had been his son and daughter. He knew them more through the pictures that adorned that office in Philadelphia than from the time he spent with them growing up. It was only after his life crumbled that he saw their achievements, but it was too late to salvage the relationships he had thrown away.

A lifetime of accumulated mistakes created overwhelming regret, but Ed knew he had caused a lot of pain, and justice—something that seemed so important forty years ago when he began his legal career—required him to suffer the pain he now felt. This day, he would not place the muzzle of the revolver to his head and squeeze the trigger. He might tomorrow or the next day, but for now, he would continue another day or two.

He could always shoot himself later. After examining the revolver for a few more seconds, he put it in the drawer and closed it.

He picked up a client file, a DUI with a preliminary hearing set for the following Thursday. There was no need to review the file and nothing much would happen at the hearing. It was completely routine, but he couldn't think of anything else to do. As he flipped through the file, there was a knock at the door.

It was Dave Krell, the man he considered his best friend. He used to have a lot of friends, but the number had dwindled to one. Even his wife was now a stranger. They talked, at times, but she was always distant. He had given her the lifestyle she always wanted, but then he had taken it all away. She stuck by him, probably more out of obligation than anything else. Dave, however, stayed with him through the whole ordeal.

Their friendship dated back thirty years, to a time when Dave was Detective Krell of the Scranton Police Department. In a single evening, he went from being a law enforcement officer to being an accused criminal. He had just left a local bar, conferring with one of his sources. It was 11:09 p.m. when he saw two individuals behaving strangely in an alley. Detective Krell suspected a burglary and went to investigate.

When he yelled for the two suspects to stop, one reached into his jacket, toward his belt. The detective fired a shot quickly into the abdomen of the suspect. At the same time, he saw something shiny in the hand of the other suspect and fired another round, which caught the second suspect in the throat. He immediately called for backup and an ambulance. One suspect died at the scene. The other died two days later in the hospital.

The problem was that the first suspect had been unarmed. Dave had no idea what he was reaching for. The second suspect had been armed with a cell phone. Detective Krell had made a split-second decision, but it had been the wrong decision. The smell of alcohol on his breath didn't help his cause, nor did the fact that it was later discovered that he had known one of the suspects, an African-American teenager who had filed a suit against him alleging police brutality from one of their previous encounters.

Because the shooting was an officer-involved shooting, the investigation into what happened had been turned over to the state police. The police chief directed Detective Krell to report to the local hospital for a blood-alcohol test. He had decided to go home instead.

He was placed on administrative leave pending the outcome of the investigation. This was kind of like paid time off and Dave didn't mind. He was not concerned about the investigation. He believed in the 'brotherhood of the badge' and the 'thin blue line'. If anyone would understand the split-second decision that had to be made, it would be his fellow officers in law enforcement.

Unfortunately, they proved to be far less understanding than he had anticipated, and after his first interview with the investigators, he decided he'd better hire an attorney. He picked an attorney recommended by the Fraternal Order of Police, but things went from bad to worse. The attorney tried to offer Dave's retirement in order to avoid prosecution, but the district attorney rejected the offer. The case became a high-profile political affair.

After three months, the FOP lawyer told Dave that he was about to be indicted for two counts of third-degree murder. The lawyer told Dave he had negotiated a plea agreement for two counts of manslaughter. Patting himself on the back, he told Dave that the sentence would be five to ten years. He was confident that Dave would be out in five.

That was when Dave first met Ed. He couldn't afford Ed but Ed had decided to take the case anyhow. From the first meeting, Ed believed Dave and told him he would represent Dave at trial. Ed threw everything he had into the case and focused on the spit-second life-and-death decisions that all of us, for our own safety, require the police to make. It had been a tough case but Ed had made a compelling defense.

Even as the jury retired to deliberate, no one knew what they would decide. After three days, they found Dave not guilty of all charges. If not for Ed's efforts, Dave was convinced he would have gone to prison. Dave did not have much time to savor his victory. Three days after the jury acquitted him, the police department fired him. They did not fire him for shooting the suspects; they fired him because he had failed to take the blood-alcohol test. They called it 'disobeying a direct order'.

His police career was over, but his new career as a private detective was just beginning. He would use his knowledge of police procedure and his experience as a skilled interviewer to turn the tables on his former comrades. Dave's friendship had been forged in the stress of that trial.

Dave was now in an obviously agitated state as he sat across from Ed at his desk. He seemed nervous and scared and had trouble talking. Every couple words he would stop as if he didn't know whether he wanted to continue or not. But continue he did.

"It was big, real big. I shot it. I shot it in the chest. It kept coming."

"What did you shoot?" Ed asked, but Dave seemed not to want to answer that question.

"Come on," Dave replied. "We need to go get it. It's dangerous. It'll kill someone if we don't go."

"Go where?" Ed asked.

"After it."

It was cold out, and Ed did not look forward to hiking through the woods in the dead of winter. Years of friendship, however, required Ed to go, even if he didn't understand why, and even if he didn't want to. Finally, he said he would go back with Dave and see what was there. As he got up and put his coat on, Dave insisted he take a rifle. More to humor Dave than for any other reason, he went to his gun room and picked up the .300 Winchester Magnum. He grabbed a handful of cartridges and stuck them into the pocket of his parka. It was bitterly cold out, and Ed would have preferred another cup of coffee to the freezing temperature.

By the time they got back to the logging road where Dave's encounter with the animal had occurred, it was already past noon, and four inches of new-fallen snow had erased any evidence that might have been there. Nevertheless, they went to where Dave had said he first saw 'it', but he still wouldn't say what it was. Where it had first appeared, however, was a trail, probably a game trail. The trail seemed to head toward town, a distance of about seven miles through the mountains.

More curious than anything else, Ed decided to follow the trail to see what Dave might have seen. Together the two men moved somewhat briskly along the trail, carefully looking for any signs as they went. A 'sign' was a clue left by an animal or a man as it moves through the forest. It may consist of a footprint or a depression in recently fallen snow that covers a footprint. It could be a broken branch, a twig snapped from a tree, a piece of hair or wool from a coat or a sweater.

Sometimes it is the absence of evidence that provides the clue. Trails in the woods, particularly when covered by snow, are difficult to follow. A slight gap between two trees could indicate the trail. A rock wall, a cliff, or a river could indicate that the tracker took the wrong trail, and he may have to turn around and follow his trail backward till he finds the correct trail.

After following the trail for about a mile, they began to find signs. At first, they saw slight depressions in the snow. As time went on and they drew closer to their quarry, Ed was able to tell that the right foot seemed to be dragging. Whatever they were following, it was injured, and they were gaining on it. Infrequently, they would see a slight pink discoloration in the snow, evidence that their quarry had taken a break and blood had soaked into the snow.

They followed it up the side of one mountain, across the top of that mountain. The top was covered with mountain laurel, a bushy plant that does not lose its green leaves in winter. Visibility was limited to no more than a few yards. The footprints indicated they were following something large—Ed guessed it might have been a bear. Even with his rifle at the ready, he didn't want to run into a bear at such close quarters, especially one that had been wounded. They moved slowly to avoid an ambush.

Finally, the mountain laurel opened up to reveal a steep downhill slope to a small stream. The open side of an opposing mountain greeted the two men. The bottom of the opposing slope was heavily wooded, but directly across from them—in an opening in the woods on a small field of white snow—stood something that defied explanation. Although it would have taken at least an hour to get to where the thing stood, it was only about nine hundred yards away in a straight line across the mountains.

Its appearance defied description. A lifetime as a hunter on four continents had not prepared Ed for what he was looking at. It was big, seven feet or more, and walked on two legs. Its body was covered with hair. It moved steadily up the mountain with a slight limp. The entire body appeared to be covered with long hair. It wasn't a bear. It wasn't like any animal that lived in the North Woods. In fact, Ed wasn't even sure it was an animal.

"Shoot it," Dave whispered into Ed's ear.

Ed leaned against a tree, turned the magnification setting on his scope to twelve power and tried to rest the crosshairs on the creature. Nine hundred yards, more than half a mile, was a difficult shot under ideal conditions, and conditions were not ideal. It was cold, and the wind had picked up. He did not have a solid rest for his rifle. With each beat of his heart and with each breath he drew, the crosshairs would sweep across the back of the creature.

Even worse, the creature appeared to be somewhat human. It walked like a man. It seemed to have intelligence. What if it was a man in a monkey suit? Or was it simply a man whose appearance was obscured by weather and distance? What if it was someone trying to play some kind of joke? What if, after he shot, he discovered he had killed someone? He wasn't prepared to commit murder.

"Shoot it," Dave said a little louder.

"I can't," Dave replied. "I don't know what it is."

Dave became more animated, trying to convince Ed that no matter what it was, it had to be killed. Ed tried to explain that he couldn't kill a man for no reason.

As they talked, the creature seemed to sense that it was being followed. It turned and looked directly at them for a moment, then dove into the heavier vegetation at the side of the clearing. It moved quickly through the brush. It was coming down the mountain, toward them.

Chapter 5

The creature, whatever it was, now moved rapidly, closing the distance. Once it moved into the brush, the most Ed and Dave could see was a flash of fur here and there. The sound it made grew continuously closer. They started back to Ed's truck but there was no way they would make it. The creature was traveling three or four times faster than them, and the distance to the car was too great. The hunters had become the hunted.

Without a good option, all they could do was retreat as rapidly as possible. Dave led the way. Ed kept his rifle at the ready. They moved as quickly as they could, but by now the sun was setting. A modest wind developed, causing the branches of trees to clash together. The rapidly diminishing daylight and the increasing noise caused by the wind made it difficult to know what was out there. Was the creature closing on them? Was it going to jump from behind the next tree? Or had it given up its pursuit?

Intelligence and instinct are the two pillars of survival in the wild, but they frequently lead to different reactions. For the two men, instinct told them to move as fast as possible, to get as far away from the danger as possible. Neither man understood what they faced but both knew at the depths of their beings that it was a great danger. Intelligence reminded them that they were armed, that they could protect themselves and that, no matter what, they could not outrace the creature in any event.

Intelligence won, but just barely. They moved through the forest as quickly as they could, but they kept a careful watch around and behind them. They did not panick. Several times on the trip back, they paused because of a possible movement or a potential ambush.

The creature also faced the same internal battle between instinct and intelligence. He lived only so long as his existence remained a secret, and these two humans now knew of his existence. Self-preservation, the greatest of all instincts, counseled that the threat be destroyed, and for a time, instinct prevailed.

It moved silently down the slope, its sore knee healing and becoming more flexible with each step, and with each step, it gained on its new prey.

But humans were not like other prey. In fact, they were the greatest predators on earth. Although they might appear puny and weak, the firearms they carried could kill him. Three slugs from the pistol were still lodged in his chest. They would come out and the wounds would heal, but they were reminders that he was not immortal. The rifle could do far more damage.

He slowed his pursuit as he cut across the top of the mountain. He could smell their scent and hear their footfalls. They were no more than fifty yards ahead of him, but now he slowed his pace to match theirs, and as he did, his intelligence overtook his instinct.

His existence needed to remain a secret, but even if they told others about him, no one would believe them. For centuries, there had been stories of large, hairy ape-like creatures throughout North America, Europe and Asia— Sasquatch, Bigfoot, the Abominable Snowman, the Yeti. He was not one of them but he considered how anything they said about him would be received. No matter what they said, they would have no proof.

His intelligence told him that if he attacked, he could be killed. Even if he killed the humans, the risk to him would not diminish. Rather than being mere crackpots, the two humans would be victims, and the police would scrutinize the murder scene, interview people, and perhaps come closer to catching him. A clean kill now—when he had no time to plan, to weigh his options and make appropriate preparations—was uncertain.

These two could always be killed later if it became necessary. Now was not the optimum time to act—better to wait and plan.

He followed the humans across the mountain top. They were vigilant but the most they ever could have seen of him was a fleeting glimpse. As he came to the edge of the thick mountain laurel where the trail started down, he stopped and watched the prey descend the mountain. He laughed silently to himself— he had allowed them to live. He had spared them. And yet, they were still ignorant of the danger they were in.

By now, he had regained nearly all his strength. The limp would remain with him for another week or so, but it would not slow him down. The men had at least another two or three miles back to their vehicle, depending on where they parked. He had about six miles to the village. He would make it to his home long before they made it to their car.

He turned, let out a long howl—a sign of his triumph—and then he was gone.

Well, not quite gone. His injury had slowed his progress, and the appearance of the two hunters had distracted him. He was many hours behind schedule as he made his way to his lair. Ideally, he would have entered the town around 4:00 a.m. when nearly all of the townspeople would have been asleep and the streets empty and quiet. He had lost the entire day traveling across the mountains and was now entering the town at 11:00 p.m. The town was still relatively quiet, and most people were at home. He decided to risk it.

While the creature slid through the side streets of the town, careful to avoid any streetlights or other areas where he might become visible, Shelley Connor was making her way home after a night of celebration. She was smart, tough, and attractive—not beautiful, but attractive. She was about five feet six inches tall with a medium build. Her primary issue was her personality, which people described as erratic.

She also drank too much and would, when the mood struck, use some cocaine. She had no friends, and although she had frequent relationships with both men and women, depending upon her mood, none of these relationships lasted much longer than a night. She could never understand why people sucked so much.

Shelley was a lawyer, an up-and-coming lawyer who worked harder than she probably had to in order to build her reputation. When work ended earlier that day, Shelley went to one of the local bars, the Taproom, and began to drink. Seven hours later, in was time for her to leave. She hadn't wanted to go home alone, but there were no guys that interested her in the bar that night.

There was a pretty redhead, but she was oblivious to Shelley's advances and became incensed when Shelly suggested the woman come back to her apartment. By the time she left, Shelley was drunk.

As Shelley stumbled from the bar and headed home, the creature who attacked Cindy was still making its way back to its lair. It would have to pass through the main section of town, but it was certain it could do so without anyone noticing it. When Shelley stumbled into the street, she caught the creature by surprise, and it had sprung into a nearby recess in the walls between two row houses.

It would have stood there perfectly still until Shelley was gone, and then it would have proceeded quietly and quickly to the house where it lives.

Shelley, however, turned and walked toward the recess between the two houses. The creature pulled itself as tight as possible against one wall, but Shelley stopped right in front of him. There was nowhere to hide anymore.

As Shelley walked past the alcove, she thought she saw or heard something in the recess to her right. As she stopped and stared, a large creature stepped into the center of the alcove. The alcohol was slowing her senses and making it difficult to focus. It was a dark night, and the animal stood in the shadows. It appeared to have black fur. She was having trouble discerning its form. The only thing she could tell for sure was that it had stood on two legs.

It seemed very large, taller than the tallest man. But she was not certain of any of these observations. She leaned forward and squinted, trying to get a better look but she could not quite register what she was seeing. Part of her thought it might be some sort of alcoholic hallucination. She closed her eyes and rubbed them, then turned away for a minute to allow her eyes to adjust better to the dark.

The creature had a split-second decision to make. Knowledge of his existence would bring catastrophic consequences. On the other hand, killing this woman might be even worse. It was not his practice to kill people he did not know. Normally, he put significant preparation into his killings to make sure there were no loose ends. If he killed her now, under circumstances he had not evaluated, the killing itself could possibly lead to loose ends.

There might be a witness walking down the street at the wrong time. In addition, this woman could be someone significant, and her murder could launch a major manhunt.

As he pondered what to do, the human bowed her head and started to rub her eyes. The creature quickly took a long step toward Shelley and then immediately turned and sprang down Main Street into the dark. When Shelley looked again, the creature was gone. She wondered if it had ever been there.

Minutes later, the creature was in its lair. It had been a terrible two nights. A routine hunt had led to him being witnessed and shot by one man. He had then been observed by another person too close to his lair. He needed to be more careful.

Chapter 6

Cindy's murder made the front page of newspapers a hundred miles away, but the publicity did not aid the police in their quest to solve the crime. There were tips, of course, but most of the calls provided nothing more than speculation. The investigator, State Police Detective Jones, was under ever increasing pressure 'to do something'. He interviewed Cindy's sometime-boyfriend, a guy with a record of misdemeanor assaults and a solid alibi for the night in question.

He had actually been arrested for DUI in a town thirty miles away and was sitting in the county jail when the crime occurred. Interviews with Cindy's mother and her co-workers yielded no information. Crime Scene Investigators sent out from the state capitol found a few strands of what appeared to be animal hair, but they were unable to tell what kind of animal it came from, and in any event, it was impossible to say if the hair was connected to the crime.

Jones had spent thirty years on the force and had settled into a comfortable career as a criminal investigator. The state police only had jurisdiction in counties where there was not another police force. This jurisdiction was concurrent with that of the the local municipal police department, but for major crimes like murder, the state police normally led the investigation. Unlike big-city police departments, murders were rare, and even then, they were normally not complicated.

The vast majority of Detective Jones' experience involved barroom fights that had gotten out of hand or domestic abuse that had gone too far. The suspects he arrested were normally apparent when he arrived at the scene of the crime. He had surprisingly little experience when it came to real murders.

A search of the various law enforcement data bases in the Northeast did not reveal any crimes with similar *modus operandi*. Jones contacted the FBI's Behavioral Analysis Unit and talked to one of the profilers about the case. He had sent his report to Quantico, Virginia, for analysis, but there was insufficient information for the unit to provide any meaningful analysis.

The level of violence suggested a crime of passion, and the amount of blood and the failure to clean it up showed a lack of forethought. They suggested the suspect might be someone close to her, but it was only a guess. A wrong guess, as later events would prove.

The coroner had concluded that the victim died of blood loss from the deep lacerations she suffered. It didn't take a medical degree to figure that out. Detective Jones knew the cause of death the minute he glanced at the corpse. He wanted to know what the murder weapon was; that would have been more useful to the investigation. On that point, the coroner was much more circumspect. It did not appear as though a knife had been used.

The cuts followed an almost uniform pattern. In most cases, there were four parallel cuts an inch and a half to two-and-a-quarter inches apart. They ranged in depth from being superficial to about three inches deep. Then there were the puncture wounds. They appeared to have the pattern of elongated bite marks, but they were two-and-a-half to three inches deep. It was almost like the perpetrator wanted the attack to appear as though it was an animal attack.

"Could it have been an animal attack?" Jones asked the coroner.

"No." The coroner's response was direct. The lacerations were too deep, and the puncture wound pattern did not match any known animal. The killer had to be human.

Just to make sure, Jones contacted the Department of Fish and Game. The supervisor in charge of large predators for the region, mainly bears, coyotes, and bobcats, agreed. There was no animal in the area, and probably none in North America, that could have inflicted the injuries Cindy had suffered before and after she died. Perhaps a grizzly bear, but there were no grizzlies within two thousand miles of where the attack had occurred.

Although it appeared to be an animal attack, there were simply no animals that could have inflicted the injuries she suffered.

There was a call from a local cryptozoologist who had some theories about the perpetrator. He had collected a file of sightings of unknown animal species in the region, and another file of known animals that were not native to the region but that were nevertheless seen by 'responsible people'. Jones met with the 'scientist' mainly because there were no other leads. When the cryptozoologist arrived, Jones was surprised.

The man looked like someone you would see on TV. He had perfectly cut hair, a perfectly tailored suit, and spoke with a perfect mid-western accent. Dr. Jason Miller, as he introduced himself, had a Ph.D. in biology and had devoted his life to the study of unknown animal species. He was the author of over twenty books and had hosted three different television shows, all of which involved the search for mysterious creatures.

In fact, his most successful show, which had run for three seasons, was entitled *Mysterious Creatures*. Maybe his experience in showbiz explained Dr. Miller's near perfect complexion and presentation.

Dr. Miller and Detective Jones first talked about the sighting of animals that were known to exist but were not native to the region. There were a surprising number of sightings of wolves and mountain lions. However, the experts from Fish and Game assured him that mountain lions had never been common in the state, and that the last known mountain lion had been killed in 1885. The last known wolf in the state had been killed in 1895, but a wolf had been killed in state the 1990s.

Wolf and mountain lion attacks on people, even in regions where the animals were common, were extremely rare, and the injuries inflicted did not match either of these animals. Besides, wolves or mountain lions would not have been able to tear the car door from its hinges.

The amount of violence inflicted on the dead girl was astounding, but not beyond the capabilities of a human murderer. The human body was remarkably resilient and difficult to dissect. With a little planning, however, a body could be turned into very small pieces. With the use of some as-of-yet unidentified tool, a human perpetrator could easily have inflicted the damage Cindy suffered. The door was another matter. Tearing a car door from its hinges was beyond the capability of any human.

Not even Arnold Schwarzenegger in his prime could have pulled a car door from its frame. Some tool had to have been used, but Jones had examined the door and seen no evidence of any tool marks on the door. The bolts holding the door to the frame had been pulled out of the frame but, again, there was no evidence as to how it could have happened. To Jones, this was the biggest mystery.

The other file contained 'reliable reports' of UFOs, alien creatures, and Sasquatches. Dr. Miller focused upon the possibility of a Sasquatch attack first. As Dr. Miller explained to the astonished police detective, Sasquatches were generally known to be peaceful animals; however, there were instances of extreme violence by the creatures.

There was an incident near Mount Saint Helena in Oregon, where one or more Sasquatches had attacked a mining camp, forcing the minors to flee. There was another incident in Portlock and Port Chatham, Alaska, where Sasquatches or some similar creature had driven the local inhabitants from their towns. Dr. Miller explained that he believed a rouge Sasquatch to be the most likely culprit.

Pennsylvania was a little outside their traditional range, but there had been sightings in the region in the past. Also, a Sasquatch did possess the strength to inflict the damage Dr. Miller observed from the crime scene photos.

Dr. Miller covered his Sasquatch theory without a single question from Detective Jones who, in truth, was speechless. From the Sasquatch theory, Dr. Miller suggested the second most likely culprit for the murder: interdimensional alien travelers. As he launched into the history surrounding the existence of these creatures—who, according to Dr. Miller, were responsible for the construction of the Egyptian pyramids—Detective Jones stopped his explanation, saying there was someplace else he had to be.

Dr. Miller said that he understood and offered to schedule a follow-up meeting. The detective told Dr. Miller he would be in touch. The doctor left a thick file containing evidence for Detective Jones. When the cryptozoologist left, that file went into the trash. Detective Jones did not even make a report of the meeting because he feared someone might read it. There were always crackpots and conspiracy theorists that came out of the woodwork whenever a case that was a little complicated.

And so, within three days of the murder, the state police had exhausted all known leads. If this murder were to be solved, it would take incredible luck, a new murder where more forensic evidence was left behind, or an unexpected tip from the public. Jones was not optimistic. He would respond to media inquiries by saying the case was still open, that promising leads were being pursued, but that he could not provide any more information because it was still an open investigation.

Eventually, the story would grow old and the media would stop calling. It was a tried-and-true method of handling these cases. There were a lot of unsolved murders in the state. This case would undoubtedly join them.

Still, he wondered about the murderer. In the back of his mind, he continued to harbor doubts about whether it was even a human.

Chapter 7

Every human has his or her own particular scent. This is why a bloodhound is able to follow the trail of a single human through a crowd of dozens of people. There are animals with a more sensitive nose than a dog's. A bear's nose is about hundred times more powerful than that of a dog. The creature's nose was even more sensitive than that of a bear. He could detect gender, age, and race. He could gain insight into aspects of an individual's personality. As he walked through the village, his nose was constantly searching for the 'right' victim.

The right victim would be a young female prone to excitement. People who were more excitable experienced greater terror, and the creature fed on this greater terror.

After the sloppiness of the last kill, he had considered relocating but ultimately decided not to, at least not yet. There was a certain pattern the creature followed. Four deaths, and then he would move on. It took considerable planning to live the life he lived, and if he left now, the creature did not have a plan to continue its hunting. His knee had, by now, almost fully healed. There had been no contact from the police and media coverage failed to focus on the truth.

The creature had already identified an appropriate suspect for the crime and, if any attention did come his way, the creature could simply accelerate his plan at that time, although he did not believe it would be necessary.

As the creature walked around town mingling with its inhabitants, he caught the scent of a particular young woman, a sixteen-year-old named Kimberly Smith. She signed her name 'Kimmie' with a circle over the 'i'. Of course, the creature did not know these facts from her scent, but he could tell she was a very emotional girl. He could sense the increase in her heartbeat frequently, and that increase was not related to any form of exercise.

The creature was also able to determine that this girl was sexually active, and he could even identify her boyfriend from his scent on her. The creature then did some other research on this particular human. It was able to determine that she would be lucky to graduate from high school and seemed to have no further ambitions or plans. Her mother was divorced from her father and worked in a Walmart twenty miles away. Her father currently lived in Virginia and had not seen her since she was five.

Few people would miss this girl when she was gone. Her personality and her background doomed her.

With the first victim, the creature had to lure her to a secluded location. For Kimmie, he did not need to lure her anywhere. It turned out that there was an old, abandoned cabin about three miles from town, and her thirty-five-year-old boyfriend met her there a couple times a week. The boyfriend would arrive around 4:30 p.m. and build a fire in the fireplace.

She did not have a car, so she would walk to the cabin, arriving a little after 5:00. Because days in northern Pennsylvania were shorter in the winter, it was normally dark by the time she arrived.

There was nothing romantic about the rendezvous. The cabin had been abandoned some years ago and was nowhere near livable. The furniture, at least what was left of it, was musty, filthy, and broken down. The floorboards were rotten and covered with dirt. Spiderwebs, left over from the warmer days of summer, clung to every corner. Kimmie and her boyfriend shared this little love nest with other forest dwellers, primarily raccoons, but there was a nest of snakes hibernating under the floorboards.

They hibernated during the winter, however, so Kimmie never knew they were there. The sex itself was quick and perfunctory. The boyfriend brought an old blanket to lay on the floor on their first meeting. When they were done, he folded the blanket and left it in the corner for the next time. Their encounters were not the mature lovemaking of adults engaged in mutual satisfaction—they did not take the time to slowly excite each other to bring the evening to a crescendo. No, this was a quick meeting.

Clothes came off quickly and the event would be over in ten minutes. Afterward, they would both dress quickly because the fire, although providing some warmth, did not provide enough heat to make the place warm. As soon as the boyfriend zipped his pants and put his coat on, he was gone. If he took more than a half-hour, his wife might wonder where he had been. Sometimes Kimmie wondered if he really loved her.

Three weeks had passed since the first killing, and the creature decided it was time for Kimmie's life, worthless as it was, to end. The creature had no feelings, as such. The night's events would be about his pleasure, and she played a significant role in that pleasure. But it was the role that a game animal would play in a hunt. He wondered if people who worked in slaughterhouses, killing and dismembering cattle or hogs or sheep, felt as he did. He suspected not. If slaughter were as pleasurable to humans as it was to him, everyone would want to work in a slaughterhouse.

The creature caught Kimmie's scent as she neared the forest on the edge of town. The boyfriend had taught her to be careful to make sure she was not followed. She, therefore, took a trail through a ravine, and then followed a small stream to the cabin. Kimmie checked to make sure no one was following her. There was no reason for anyone to follow her, or even be on this trail at night in the winter.

There was no way she could detect the creature that was, even then, stalking her. It stayed far enough away to ensure that she would not see or hear it.

She was glad to see her boyfriend that night, but she told him she needed to talk to him. When she said this, it annoyed the boyfriend. She had nothing to say that he was interested in hearing but he would have to humor her for a few minutes to get the sex. He didn't have all night to talk, however.

Kimmie wanted to talk about the future.

"I've told you, Kimmie, that I love you and that I want to spend the rest of my life together. I would leave my wife right now—tonight—but people would not understand our love," the boyfriend said.

She knew that was true. No one would understand their love. It wasn't fair. They were madly in love—in fact, the boyfriend was the only guy who had ever said he loved her. But people had made these arbitrary rules about age.

"Don't worry," the boyfriend continued, "you'll be eighteen in no time, and then we can run off together." He knew that it would never happen but it was enough to get him sex tonight. A few minutes later, they were both naked. A few minutes after that, they were intertwined in an act of sexual intercourse. A few minutes after that, they were done and getting dressed again. The boyfriend walked out the front door and got into his old, beat-up pickup truck and drove off.

Kimmie remained behind to warm herself by the fire for a few minutes before she left. Her mother was working that night and Kimmie would eat cold pizza when she got home.

The creature had watched the entire encounter through a broken window. He marveled at the human obsession with sex. They seemed to spend an inordinate amount of time pursuing sexual activity. Sex itself is procreational in nature; the purpose of sex was to reproduce the species. Throughout the animal kingdom, all animals engaged in sexual intercourse, but it was always directed at reproduction.

The creature found it odd that humans always wanted to have sex but went to great lengths to avoid reproduction. Of course, he had once spent a lot of time pursing sexual activity but he had largely forgotten its allure. There was something much better than sex, a far better release, and the creature was about to experience that feeling once more.

Kimmie left the cabin through the front door to begin her journey home. She was thinking about the boyfriend and whether he really loved her when a pungent odor assaulted her. She had never smelled something so terrible. It smelled like something had died, only worse. Kimmie looked around and caught sight of the most horrible thing she had ever seen.

It looked like a human, or like a monster, or like a human monster. It was big—bigger than the boyfriend—with ugly black hair. Its face looked like that of a wolf, but it stood and moved like a human.

Kimmie unleashed a bloodcurdling scream, and then she screamed again. Her bowels and her bladder let loose as she screamed a third time.

It was better than the creature had hoped. The creature enjoyed screams, and this girl screamed very well. Her fear was total, as was the creature's pleasure. Kimmie turned and started running for the road, which was hidden by a couple of rows of pine trees. In just a couple bounds, the creature was once again in front of her, between her and the road. She screamed again and turned, then began running in the opposite direction.

The creature jumped in front of her again. This time, he knocked her down, just to see what she would do. She got up and ran in yet another direction.

She could not get away. They were in an isolated location. The creature played with her as a cat would play with a mouse. Sometimes, he would let her run a little farther, giving her the illusion that she might be able to escape. Only after she began to develop some hope of escape would he intervene and crush that hope once more. After twenty minutes, she quit trying to escape. She was exhausted, lying on the ground, sobbing uncontrollably. Kimmie no longer had the ability to scream. All she could do was beg for her life.

The creature was growing bored. He reached down and grabbed the girl with its black hands and claws. He grabbed her by the throat and lifted her completely off the ground. As she gasped for her breath, the creature took one of his claws from his other grotesque hand and slit her stomach from her breastbone to her pelvis. She felt her intestines spill out of her body, onto her legs and feet. The creature then tossed her through the air.

Her spine smacked against a tree. She was still conscious when he walked up to her broken body and lifted her once again by her head. In a quick motion, he snapped her neck and then sliced her throat with one of his claws. She was dead by now, mercifully. The creature relished the utter destruction of Kimmie's body. As with the first victim, there were body parts all over the place. There was no snow falling this night, and so the creature's presence would not be hidden under a layer of new-fallen snow.

He, therefore, took some time to brush out footprints and remove other evidence of his presence. He could not remove all evidence of his presence, but he didn't have to. This had been a good night. There had been no errors like on the previous hunt. The creature made his way quickly and quietly back to his lair.

Chapter 8

Detective Jones had been sickened by the first homicide but this one was worse. Part of it was the fact that a sixteen-year-old girl would never have a chance to experience life, but the bigger part of it was the fact that she had been tortured for an extended period of time. There is a natural tendency among police officers, prosecutors, and even defense attorneys to dehumanize victims. The victim is not dehumanized because no one cares.

Rather, it is a defensive mechanism deployed by the brain to allow people who deal with the worst catastrophes to survive. If Detective Jones had to face the inhumanity, he dealt with routinely without separating himself from it, it would have killed him. Therefore, he viewed the first victim, Cynthia Johnson, simply as Victim 1. Kimberly Smith, he saw as Victim 2. He hoped there would not be a Victim 3.

Victim 1's death had been violent but quick. The crime scene for Victim 2 revealed that she had been alive for some time, running from one spot to another before she was killed. This was purely an act of torture.

Another difference between Victims 1 and 2 was that the medical examiner in Victim 2's case had been able to recover usable DNA—and even better, the DNA matched a known sample. The sample belonged to a local school janitor named Brian Parra, who had been convicted fifteen years before for a third-degree sexual assault. The facts of that case were not as serious as they sounded. He had dated a sixteen-year-old girl when he was eighteen.

At the time, he received probation, but the conviction had landed his DNA in the national database. Now that database pointed toward Parra as the suspect in a murder case. The working theory was that he had raped and killed Victim 2. Since the body had been similarly ripped apart and the laceration and puncture wounds were the same, he became the prime suspect for Victim 1, as well.

The state police had to react quickly before it became known to the public that the victim was Kimberly Smith. Two troopers were sent to the high school to pick up Parra and transport him to the police barracks for questioning. During the twenty-minute drive, Parra attempted to engage the troopers in conversation but they did not respond. When he arrived at the barracks, he was taken to an interview room and left alone for another twenty minutes.

He wondered why he was there. Were they going to ask him about the Smith kid? Had she said something about him? Different scenarios played through his mind as he thought about the story he might tell.

Detective Jones entered the room and took a seat. "So," he started, "tell me. How does a child molester get a job at a high school?"

Parra was stunned. He stammered for a few moments but never answered.

"That's really not why I'm here. We know you changed your name and lied on the application. We're here to talk about Kimberly Smith—you know her, right?"

"I've met her," Parra responded.

"I mean, knew her," Detective Jones said. "When was the last time you saw her?"

"I don't know. I guess a couple of days ago," said Jones, trying to find a safe answer.

"How about last night?" Parra sensed he was in trouble. He said nothing.

"Ms. Smith was murdered last night. The medical found your semen in her. It looks like she was raped and killed. This is your opportunity to try to explain what happened, but I really don't care if you want to talk or not." Jones leaned back and waited.

"Kimmie's dead?" Parra seemed shocked. The detective had to admit it was a good act.

"You were with her. You know. She was raped and murdered. You were there."

"No. I mean, I met her, and we had sex. It was consensual," Parra started to explain.

"It wasn't consensual. You know that. You know a sixteen-year-old can't consent. Now tell me what really happened." Detective Jones's voice was steady, inviting Parra to explain further.

"I mean, I would never hurt her. We were together last night in an old, abandoned cabin a couple miles outside of town. I left her there at about 6:00 p.m. She was okay when I left."

"Why didn't you drive her home?" Detective Jones asked.

"I didn't want anyone to see us," Parra replied. He hung his head in shame as he heard the words he had just spoken.

The conversation continued for another hour. Parra denied knowing Cynthia Johnson. He said he had never heard of her. On the night of her murder, he said he was in Buffalo, New York, with his wife. Her mother had been hospitalized at that time and the couple had driven to see her. He said his wife could verify that he was with her.

They had checked into a local hotel in New York, and he offered to provide the credit card receipts for the trip. Parra also remembered that he had signed in the visitor's log at the hospital early the next morning. He was sure there were video cameras that could prove his alibi. Detective Jones made careful notes. It would be a simple matter to prove or disprove the alibi.

At the end of the interview, Parra was arrested for the rape and murder of Kimberly Smith. The rape was easy to prove. The DNA test and his confession would seal his fate. The murder wouldn't be a huge leap. He was there, and that would probably be enough. With the announcement of the arrest the next day, the community would rest a little easier. A lot of the pressure on Detective Jones would also disappear. But the murder of Victim 1 had not yet been solved.

Chapter 9

Winter Haven was blessed with beautiful views of scenic mountains and a friendly, rural population. It had been founded in the late 1800s as Rossville, apparently named after someone named Ross who must have had some local notoriety no one could remember. It had mostly died out with the end of the logging boom before World War I, but was reborn in the 1950s as the new—to Americans—sport of skiing took off. Two of the mountains on the south side of town had steep north-facing slopes with more than a thousand feet of vertical elevation. These slopes proved to be perfect.

In addition to the small permanent population of the town, the ski resort drew people from all over the Northeast and far beyond for work and recreation. Its world-class slopes and short flights from New York and Washington drew thousands of millionaires and multimillionaires to the town. In fact, during the winter months, the population of the town more than doubled. Over the past decade, condominium prices had soared to the point where almost none of the locals could afford to live in their hometown.

It was starting to create labor problems, as well. The ski resort employed over a thousand minimum-wage employees, but the town lacked housing these employees could afford. They now sometimes lived five people to a one-bedroom apartment. Rising housing prices and labor shortages were a topic for another night, however. On this night, the local elite had gathered for a fundraiser to support the local hospital. Invitations were limited and highly prized. It provided the town's elite the opportunity to mingle with some of the wealthy visitors.

Its real purpose, however, was to tap into the bank accounts of the rich and famous to fund community improvements without overly burdening local taxpayers. The town boasted some of the best emergency services in the state, a world-class library, and taxes that were among the lowest in the region.

Edwin Reynolds, Esquire, was present, although he was not sure why. Because of the issues with his firm, he was no longer among the local elite. He suspected that someone had failed to remove his name from the prior year's invitation list, and that was how he was invited. Ed thought he should be there. His wife did not feel the same obligation to go. Ed's plan on this particular night was to arrive late, shake a few hands, tell a few jokes, have a glass or two of free wine, and then slip out quietly in the hopes that no one would notice.

As soon as he got there, the mayor, Blaine Harris, saw him and came over to say hello. The two had known each other a long time and had once been friends. Maybe they still were, but Blaine, being a politician, was careful to distance himself from Ed, especially in public.

As Ed and the mayor spoke, an out-of-state potential doner came within range of the mayor.

"Charles Hunt," the mayor interrupted, "this is the local attorney I was telling you about."

"Ah, yes," Hunt said, turning toward Ed. "The mayor tells me you are quite the hunter."

Ed had been to enough of these events to know that the type of people who attended swank, expensive, black-tie events tended to disapprove of the sport of hunting. Their knowledge of the outdoors was confined to a few hours on the ski slopes and the view from a private jet as it descended into the airport. They were usually more inclined to give money to save the whales or polar bears or lions, or whatever other animals public relations firms could use in a television commercial to evoke an emotional response. He didn't know where this conversation would go.

"An interesting topic on which to base an introduction," Ed said, holding up a wine glass. "Tell me, Mr. Hunt, what brings you to our small town?"

Charles smiled. "That was an artful dodge, but you needn't worry about my hunting inquiry. I am a hunter myself, and I was asking the mayor about the local hunting opportunities. He told me you were the person to talk to." His honeyed Louisiana accent was disarming, but Ed had been around the block often enough to not be disarmed.

"But to answer your question," Charles continued, "I am thinking of investing in the new expansion of the ski area. You see, I own a major international resort company with operations all over the world. The ski area here might be a good addition to our portfolio. Before I actually invest in a company, I like to spend some time examining it. Part of my due diligence, I guess you would say, is actually immersing myself in the company I am targeting. That's why I'm here."

The explanation made sense. By this time, the mayor had drifted off, looking for other millionaires to engage.

Charles continued, "But there is something else I'd like to ask you about, since you're a hunter. Tourist industries can be terribly finicky, and whenever a tourist destination experiences any sort of bad news, it can destroy the business. You heard about the murder of that poor woman out along the highway, and then the murder of the teenager? Some people are telling me it was an animal."

"So, quite naturally, I inquired as to whether there were any animals locally that might have been responsible for her death. You know, perhaps a bear or a wolf, or some type of large cat. So, tell me, do you know of any animals locally that could have killed these women?"

Ed took a sip of his wine as he gathered his thoughts. "I really don't know anything about the murder, but in my experience, people are mostly killed by other people." Ed then noticed Hunt was using a cane. "Did something happen to your knee?"

Hunt chuckled. "A minor injury," he said. "It should heal in a day or two." He said no more about his injury or how it occurred.

Ed decided to switch the subject again. "So, where have you hunted, Charles?"

"I have hunted mostly in Europe and Central Asia, mainly for mountain-type game—you know, the wild sheep and goats of the world."

Charles turned out to be both extraordinarily gracious and very knowledgeable about hunting—more knowledgeable than Ed. "Have you ever hunted predators?" Ed asked.

"I have taken a European brown bear in Russia and a leopard in the Central African Republic, but the truth is, I prefer the prey species. To me, there is nothing more exhilarating than spotting your quarry at some distance, then stalking it to within range and administering the final kill. Truth be told, I feel a bit of a kindred spirit with the predator. They, like us, hunt the prey animals."

Charles looked away for a second as if staring at something far off. "Yes," he continued, "I have hunted predators," but he seemed saddened by the admission.

"That's an interesting viewpoint," Ed said, paying particular attention to Hunt's demeanor. "I have always found predators to be more cunning than prey animals and a much greater challenge to hunt. Take the wolf, for example. I have hunted caribou and moose in the tundra of Northern Canada and Alaska, in barren ground where the vegetation was no higher than a shrub. During a week's hunt, I have seen hundreds of caribou but never a wolf."

"And yet, there were wolves everywhere. There would be fresh wolf tracks every morning, and we would hear their howls every night. But when morning came, they vanished."

"Were you ever able to get your wolf?" Hunt asked.

"Not yet," Ed replied.

"Well, I actually came here for the skiing," Hunt said as he turned to engage a young woman who had approached. He was witty and charming but seemed somewhat mysterious, which only added to his charm. Hunt was the talk of the event. Everyone wanted to meet him and everyone seemed to have some information about the rich, handsome, mysterious stranger. He was unmarried, that much was clear, and it sparked a lot of conjecture as the available women in the local elite plotted different strategies to ensnare him.

Most of the men wondered about the source of his apparent wealth. The other topic of conversation at the event was the recent gruesome murders. A few of the attendees at the event knew of Cindy Johnson. One or two remembered her from school. But what had happened to her? There were some who knew people in law enforcement, and one of the guests had a niece who was a paramedic and had been at the scene of Cindy's murder.

'Murder' did not seem to be the right word. Murders were committed by humans. Whatever had killed Cindy could not possibly have been human. Only a savage animal would rip apart a human body the way Cindy had been dismembered, and only a large, powerful animal could rip apart a human. Bears, however, hibernated for the winter. Ed listened to what everyone was saying, but he didn't mention what he had seen the day after Cindy's body had been discovered.

Some people suspected a rogue bear that had come out of hibernation with a taste for human flesh. It seemed an outlandish theory, but it was possibly plausible. Bears could come out of hibernation early, and black bears had, on very rare occasions, been known to hunt, kill, and eat humans. But no one had ever heard of a bear tearing off a car door.

Another group of partygoers thought the culprit must be human. A deranged, violent, and probably mentally ill person must be responsible. It could even be cult members, like the followers of Charlie Manson in the 1970s. Some people thought the cult must be Satanic. No one believed the killer could be a local; it must be someone from somewhere else. The skiing community drew a wide range of people from across the country.

The killer must be one of them, but no one knew which one. And then there was the third group, those who suspected alternative explanations—people susceptible to conspiracy theory and wild speculation. The possible explanation they came up with ranged between mountain lions and wolves, creatures long-since extinct in these forests, and Bigfoot or space aliens. Ed was amazed at how quickly and easily people could leap from one or two known facts to a universe of conjecture. Listening to them gave him a headache, and after an hour, he made his way to the front door and attempted to sneak out.

As he walked to his car, he heard a voice call his name. He turned to see that Charles Hunt had apparently followed him from the party and was walking toward him as fast as his injured knee would allow.

"It was certainly a pleasure meeting you," Hunt said. "I enjoyed our conversation, and I hope we can continue it in the future. I have the sense that we have much in common."

Ed felt a bit uneasy but he found it difficult not to be drawn in by Hunt's obvious charm. "Sure," Ed replied, not knowing if he meant it or not. Charles looked as though he wanted to continue the conversation right then and there, but Ed opened his car door and slid into the driver's seat. It had been a long day and he was very tired.

Chapter 10

Three evenings later, on a Tuesday, Ed found himself walking up to Charles' house on Third Street, just on the edge of town. It was a rented home, not quite a mansion, with a front door that opened onto a town street and a rear door that opened into a rear patio area with a pool house. Beyond the pool house was an expansive area of federal and state forest that went on for miles. Ed had been invited for dinner. The invitation had been directed at Ed and his wife, but Ed's wife had other plans for the evening and did not accompany him.

As Ed reached for the doorbell, the door opened, and a tall man invited him in. He wore a perfectly tailored tuxedo and looked like he might be a bodyguard. Ed tried to engage the man in conversation but he was completely unresponsive. The inside of the home looked like something out of *Country Living*. The tall man led Ed to a library of some sort, and there was Charles, bent over a roaring fire.

He was dressed like he had just stepped off the cover of *L.L.Bean*. Although Ed was dressed casually, the same as Charles, he somehow felt underdressed. Charles took Ed's coat and offered him a seat at one of the two oversized, log-framed chairs that looked into the fire. As the tall man left the room, Ed asked who he was.

"Oh, Samuel. Samuel is my manservant. He is the son of one of my father's favorite servants, and when I turned eighteen, I inherited Samuel. He is like a butler, and he has other tasks he performs for me," Charles replied.

"He doesn't seem very friendly," Ed said.

"Don't take it personally. He never has spoken much. Sometimes he doesn't even speak to me for days at a time. Since we've come here for the winter, he has changed. I can't explain how but he is different."

Dinner was running a little late. The chef that Charles had hired for the evening needed some spices and had gone to the store to retrieve them. In the meantime, the host suggested a drink, and Ed accepted a very good cognac, the same as Charles was drinking. "So how is it that a lawyer becomes a big game hunter?" Charles began the conversation.

"Oh, I don't know. The same as anyone else, I suppose. I grew up around here and learned to hunt from my father when I was a boy. As I achieved some success, I started hunting in more exotic locations, first out west and then in Alaska. From there, I started hunting in Africa and Asia."

"As a lawyer, then, can you give me your take on those young women's murders?"

Ed thought for a second. The easy answer would be to say that he did not know anything about the murder. In addition to being an easy answer, it was also the correct answer. "Well," he said. "I do not know much about the murders. I hear they were quite savage. I have no idea what to make of it."

"I might know something about the murders," Charles said in a quiet voice. "I am not sure what to do, but there have been similar murders in other places I have visited."

"So, you think these murders have something to do with you?" Ed asked.

"I can't think what," Charles said. "But they do seem to follow me. I hate to say this, or even think it, but sometimes I wonder if Samuel is involved. I mean, I know I can trust you because you're a lawyer, but Samuel has an odd family history. I can remember him ever since I could remember anyone. He's obviously mixed race."

"His mother was the daughter of a voodoo priestess, if you believe in such things. No one ever mentioned his father. But his family was always involved in animal sacrifices. I don't know what else they were involved in, but sometimes it scares me."

"Have you thought about going to the police?" Ed asked.

"With what? Suspicions with no evidence about the person who has been closest to me my whole life?" Charles had a point. The meal was excellent, as Ed had expected. Over dinner, as Samuel lurked in the background, the conversation turned to business. Charles explained his interest in the ski resort. Skiing and snowboarding were sports that typically appealed to a wealthier demographic, which was good.

However, these sports were in a gradual state of decline, as were virtually all outdoor activities. Some said it was millennials causing the problem. Charles, however, believed that there were plenty of millennials, as well as other age groups, that could be lured back outside. The thrill of the sport, together with the comradery the sport would create, could turn the slow, steady decline around, if it were properly marketed.

Charles thought that the ski area's close proximity to the major metropolitan areas in the Northeast was also a strength. There were many millions of people within a two- or three-hour drive. If the resort were properly marketed, if the right incentives were offered, then this would be an excellent investment. There were still negotiations ahead, and he didn't know if it would work out, but he was optimistic.

As Charles spoke, Ed kept glancing at Samuel. When he had first answered the door, he'd seen that Samuel was a large man, but now he realized just how big he was. He dwarfed his master. He stood at least six foot six inches tall with a massive chest and wide back, rippling with muscles. His skin was dark. When he walked, he lumbered as a large animal might. He said nothing, but Ed thought he detected a certain amount of menace in his demeanor.

Ed thought back to the creature he and Dave had seen the day after the first murder. Ed tried to superimpose this human over the vision in his memory. They seemed to move in the same way. If Samuel had a thick coat of hair, he could have been what Ed had seen.

But Ed pushed the thought out of his mind. The thing they had seen that day was injured. Dave had shot him in the knee, and it was injured and limping when Dave had seen it. Also, Dave had shot the thing three times in the chest with a .357 magnum. He would not have missed. No matter how big or strong he was, the powerful revolver would have killed him, or at the very least put him in the hospital. He hoped the police would solve these crimes soon.

Chapter 11

Dave was aware of Parra's arrest, but he was also certain the police had the wrong person in custody. He believed the creepy janitor had molested the high school student but he could not have murdered her. His friends in the department told him of the carnage at the crime scene. Dave knew it was not the work of a human. He also knew it was not the work of a human because he had seen the monster.

Ed had also seen the monster but not in the up close and personal way that Dave had. Lately, Ed was becoming iffy about what he had seen. He would use phrases like, 'It was too far away' or 'I'm not sure'. That was bullshit. Ed knew what he saw; he just wasn't willing to admit it.

There was a quirk to Dave's personality that he kept largely hidden from the world. He believed there were many things going on in the world that the government wished to keep hidden. He has read firsthand accounts of aliens and viewed video footage of the aliens filmed by people with no reason to lie. When evidence of these anomalies in normal belief systems arose, why were people so reluctant to believe it?

Perhaps this creature he saw was simply one of these anomalies. But what could it have been? The truth was all over the internet. Google might have the answer.

As he suspected, the internet was full of explanations of unexplained phenomena. There were sightings of a Bigfoot in Pennsylvania but it was not close to his area. Besides, he had been out traveling around the secondary and logging roads, looking for the telltale footprints of a large creature. He had found nothing. So, he began looking for an explanation for the lack of footprints, and he came across some plausible explanations.

The most promising was the 'Michigan Dogman' or the 'Beast of Bray Road', a creature said to look very similar to the creature he had seen, and which lived in the Midwest, not that far from where he was now. These creatures were shapeshifting, wolf-like creatures. If the creature Dave saw could shift shapes, that would explain the lack of physical evidence so far.

As he continued his research, Dave came across a truly bizarre article about an incident in the Balkans. The article contained a photograph of an unusual skull with an elongated snout and long canine teeth, like a wolf but with an enlarged cranium like a human. It had been discovered by a Bulgarian farmer, Trayche Draganov, while plowing a field near the village of Novo Selo in Macedonia. At some time in the distant past, someone had severed the creature's head from its body and buried it in an iron box, which had been chained shut.

This was apparently the traditional way of dealing with werewolves in Macedonia. There were pictures on the internet of both the iron box and the very strange skull. The pictures show either the skull of a wolf with a greatly enlarged cranium, like the skull of a man with a protruding nose and the large teeth of a wolf. It was difficult to rationalize.

Werewolves had been a feature of Macedonian folklore since prehistory; thousands of people had been killed in attacks from these beasts over the centuries. In a letter to his tutor, Aristotle, Alexander the Great, wrote of a particularly dangerous race of what he described as dog-headed men that he reported to be fierce in battle. Only with great effort were the Macedonians able to defeat these creatures. Alexander reported that several of these beasts had been captured in battle.

There were rumors that they still stalked the hinterlands of the Balkans, and that villagers hunted down and killed these creatures in the traditional manner. In fact, as Dave continued to research this topic, he was surprised to learn that lycanthropes—people who could transform themselves into animals, primarily wolves—had truly ancient origins. Some of the most celebrated scholars in antiquity wrote of these creatures as if they were real.

No less a figure than Herodotus, the 'Father of History', wrote of a tribe known as the Neuri that transformed into wolves for several days each year. According to Herodotus, this tribe lives to the northeast of Scythia, a land occupying the steppe region of Ukraine and Russia. While it may be easy to dismiss these stories as myths, they were written in the same work that contains much of our understanding of ancient history.

In fact, the more Ed studied, the more he realized these stories were widespread throughout ancient civilizations. Nearly all ancient cultures believed in lycanthropes or, as they are now known, werewolves.

The most compelling case was that of Gilles Garnier, a reclusive French serial killer who lived in the later sixteenth century. In the town of Dole in the Franche-Comté Province of France, as many as forty people were killed and some were partially eaten, beginning in 1572. The murders were horrific, with bodies being ripped in half and limbs torn from torsos.

The murders continued for months until, eventually, a hunting party came across what they thought was a wolf eating a recently killed boy. When they approached closer, they saw that it was actually Garnier eating the dead boy. He was captured and tried before a court.

According to the surviving court records, Garnier confessed to the murders and to being a werewolf. As he explained in his confession, he was a hermit who lived in the forest. He survived by gathering plants and hunting animals. As he grew older, however, he was less able to hunt the animals because of the pains in his joints and the weakness of his muscles. He knew these were signs of old age, and he suspected he would starve to death during the winter.

Garnier had lived alone from a young age and he suspected he would pass without anyone noticing. Then one day, he came upon another person in the forest. This person had the form of an old woman, much older than himself, but he suspected that she might be a witch. They talked for a couple of hours. Before he departed, this old woman gave him a potion that he could take to restore his strength. She told him that it would allow him to hunt again.

Garnier took some of the potion the next day and, to his surprise, it turned him into a wolf. He was able to run through the forest faster than he had ever imagined possible, and seize boar or stag in his powerful claws and tear out their throats with his fangs. The potion had a side-effect, however. It gave him an uncontrollable desire to eat human flesh. From the first day he took the potion until his capture, all he wanted to do was eat humans.

What separated Garnier's case from that of other recorded werewolf cases was the fact that Garnier actually stood trial for his crimes. There were other werewolf cases throughout Europe, but this seemed to be the only case where a defendant actually stood trial in a court of law. In addition to Garnier's confession, fifty witnesses testified against Garnier. Some had seen him in human form but many had seen him in his transformed state as a werewolf.

In the end, the judge convicted Garnier of being a 'loup-garou' and sentenced him to be burned at the stake on 18 January 1573. It was not the first or last werewolf killed in France.

The literature also suggests that most of the Hollywood conventions about werewolves were not true. They did not change only on full moons; lycanthropes seemed to have a fair ability to change forms at will. Their movements were not restricted to night. Some of the earlier sources about the Vikings called berserkers suggested that they not only wore the skins of wolves but actually became wolf-like in form during battles. They had the strength of many normal warriors and were impervious to injury or pain, at least to a point.

There was another thing that Dave learned. Although they were difficult to kill, they were not impossible to kill. There was no need to use a silver bullet. This legend seemed to come from another French werewolf, the 'Beast of Gévaudan'. This creature was a real animal, although there was some debate as to whether it was merely an extremely large wolf or a supernatural being.

For several years, it had eluded hunters and French soldiers sent to kill it, until June 19, 1767, when a hunter named Jean Chastel shot and killed it. Later reports indicated that Chastel had used a large-caliber bullet cast from a silver Saint Mary's medal. This appeared to be a later literary invention. In reality, Chastel had used a standard lead bullet to kill the beast.

Stories and reports of werewolves or other shapeshifting beings had diminished over the years but they never went away completely. Dave wondered if perhaps the reports of Bigfoot or Sasquatch might actually be sightings of a werewolf. It explained why physical evidence was so rare—the creatures turned back into men or women. It also provided evidence for the existence of werewolves—the creatures people were seeing were werewolves, not Sasquatches, as they suspected.

Now, he would find this werewolf.

Chapter 12

At the end of every evening after the ski resort closed, members of the ski patrol would make one final run down each of the slopes and trails to make sure there were no injured or helpless skiers left on the mountain. It was one of the more enjoyable jobs for the members of the ski patrol—a last, solitary run down the mountain. One of the newer ski patrollers, Katie Neuman, volunteered to sweep the westernmost trail on the mountain, Gun Powder Trail.

She carried a handheld radio, and ski patrol protocol dictated that if she ran into anything unusual, she would call it in. If she didn't see anything, she would simply return to her apartment at the end of the run.

Katie had done this run every day for the last two weeks and was familiar with every aspect of the trail. A light snow fell as she started down the slope. The trail head at the top of the mountain was about forty feet wide and maintained that width through the forest for about two thirds of the way down the mountain. Then for a distance of about two hundred yards, the trail narrowed as it snaked between a stone wall on one side and a steep cliff on the other.

If one skied off the side of the trail, he or she would encounter a steep drop of about twenty feet—not usually enough to be life threatening but certainly enough to break an arm or a leg. On the other side of the trail, a small rock wall about twenty-five feet in height kept skiers on the trail. The slope of the trail at that point, however, was nearly flat with only a slight dip in elevation. The result was an easy run through a potentially dangerous obstacle, something that thrilled a lot of skiers.

As Katie entered the narrow part of the trail, she skied out toward the steep drop-off, looking for ski tracks that might have carried a skier over the side. She skied slowly so she could maintain a careful watch. Nearly all of the slope was lit but on the narrow trail, the lights were farther apart, and shadows obscured areas of the trail. She never knew what hit her.

One minute, she was skiing slowly down the mountain, looking for signs of distress. The next, she was flying over the side of the mountain in the arms of…something. She felt a heavy coat of fur and smelled the awful putrid breath of whatever it was that held her. It was immense, with muscles as tight as steel cords.

When they hit the ground, the wind had been knocked out of her. She had lost her skis and ski poles in the fall. An immense clawed hand pressed her into the snow. She started to scream but her scream stopped when a set of fangs plunged into her neck, ripping veins and arteries and her windpipe from her neck. She passed out within seconds and was dead within a minute. The creature took another forty-five minutes with her body, tearing it apart until, by the time he was done, it looked more like a pile of bloody clothing than a human body.

No one missed Katie—or, it might be more accurate to say, no one ever looked for her. She grew up in Iowa. Her parents divorced when she was six, and her father only came to see her once or twice after the divorce was final. He had moved on with his new wife and new family rather quickly.

Her mother was emotionally devastated by the divorce and was barely able to function for the first two years. She then met what appeared to be a solid, reputable man with a good job. Sam married Katie's mom, and for the next two or three years, they had an almost normal family. Katie's mom gave birth to a baby boy when Katie was eleven, and that baby became the complete focus of Katie's mother. She seemed to forget that she was a wife or that she had another child.

As Katie entered puberty, Sam took a greater interest in her. Unfortunately, it was not a father's interest in a daughter but rather, an unnatural sexual interest. At first, Katie enjoyed the attention and was complicit in her stepfather's schemes to get her alone so that they could do things together. Eventually, however, she came to realize the wrongness of their conduct and she tried to stop it. Sam also wanted to stop but he couldn't.

Just before her sixteenth birthday, Katie decided to tell her mother what had been going on. Her mother was incensed, but not at Sam. She accused Katie of being jealous and mentally ill. She told the young girl that she was 'trying to ruin everything'. When Sam came home, he, of course, denied the allegations, which Katie's mom didn't believe anyhow. Katie's already unpleasant life got worse after that.

She left home a few months later and never went back. She made her way east by train and by bus, working where she could as a waitress or in some other non-skilled job. She matured into a beautiful young woman and learned how to use her beauty to make her life easier. Eventually, through a series of older boyfriends, she learned how to ski and eventually worked as a ski patroller and a ski instructor, supplementing her income with menial jobs and the gifts of male admirers.

But she couldn't have a real relationship. She drifted from town to town, job to job, usually moving for no real reason. Sometimes she just decided to move. On the night that Katie was literally torn to pieces, no one missed her when she didn't return to her apartment. When the landlord entered her apartment the next month after she had failed to pay her rent, all of her personal property had already been removed.

It appeared as though she had simply skipped out on her lease. Her car, with all of her personal possessions in the trunk and the back seat, was found at Logan International Airport in Boston the next spring. No one knew when the car had been parked, how long it had been there or where Katie had gone. She became another of the thousands of young women that disappear every year in the U.S.

No one ever went looking for her.

Chapter 13

Although there were three victims, the residents of the town and the police knew of only two. Two was more than enough, however, to frighten the community and disrupt the tourism industry, which was the life's blood of the town. The state police had arrested a suspect, but there were rumors that they had the wrong person. Meanwhile, the creature still had a 'Phase II' of his plan to implement, but it was not time just yet.

That was the established pattern to his killings: four victims, three months, and then it would take some time off before moving to another location. There would be no more killings for eight or nine months. In his new location, he would select another four victims, kill them over the next three months, then he would move again. After each set of murders, the creature needed to tidy things up so he could leave without any loose ends. This night would be the last night he would hunt in this community.

The first murder had occurred almost exactly three months ago. Now, he wanted only to enjoy the thrill of the hunt and the power of the kill. In a break from his customary pattern, there would be two victims.

Ordinarily, the creature sought out detached and lonely women in desperate situations. It reasoned that their deaths were less consequential than the deaths of younger girls with families that cared, or married women with a husband and children. The creature was, of course, wrong. Every life is precious, but it is also true that some lives are more precious than others. The death of a woman who was a leader in the community or who came from a well-connected family would be investigated much more rigorously than the death of a junkie or a prostitute.

Except for the creature, targeting women with no real family connections was more of a guideline than a rule, and on this night, he set his sights upon two high school friends, one a senior and the other a junior. By all accounts, both girls were going someplace in life, or at least that might have been the plan if the creature hadn't been there. They were attractive, intelligent, and hardworking. There were people who cared about them, and they both had a future.

Under its code, they should have been safe, but their vivaciousness and youth attracted him. The creature could picture the terror in their eyes the moment before they died and feel their warm sticky blood over his hands and face as life drained from them. Then there was the challenge of ensnaring the two of them in a scheme that would bring them to him alone. The more the creature thought about it, the more he realized it had to be them.

In the resort town where they lived, families would come from New York or Philadelphia and stay in their million-dollar condos for a week or two before leaving. Compared to the locals, these folks were viewed as rich and offered a way out for the local high school girls. In reality, these city-dwellers had their own social networks back in the areas they came from, and the local girls offered only a diversion from their normal lives while they were on vacation.

They measured relationships in days or weeks without a sense of permanency. To their temporary girlfriends in this rural area where nothing ever happened, it was more difficult to move on after a 'perfect' boyfriend left.

The younger of the two girls was named Megan Collins, and she had met the most perfect guy ever, at least in her young mind. Benjamin, or 'Ben' as he liked to be called, was tall with an athletic build and an easy smile with perfect teeth. He first noticed Megan as she worked part-time as a waitress in the restaurant in the ski lodge. Before long, he was spending more time in the lodge than on the slopes.

Ben was a brilliant conversationalist, and during breaks or before or after her shift, they would talk, sometimes for hours. She could tell he cared about her, but they only had a week together before he had to leave. Megan thought he would give her his cell number at some point, but he left before she was able to get it.

Megan should have been crushed but she wasn't. She was disappointed, to be sure, but Megan was also smart enough to realize—at least in the deeper, more logical parts of her mind—that it would never work.

Megan was surprised then, when about a week after Ben left, she received a text.

[Hi, Megan—Ben here. How RU doing?]

Megan was elated. [How did you get my number?]

[I have my ways. You didn't think I'd forget about you.]

[I didn't know.]

From there, their budding romance began to flourish. He sent her a couple of candid photos of him on the slopes, taken by a friend. She sent him some photos, as well. Mostly, though, they just talked. Their conversation became more intimate and they began to talk about their future together. First, of course, there would have to be college. Ben would be going to the University of Pennsylvania, an Ivy League college his family had gone to for generations.

Would Megan be interested in going with him? Megan's heart sank as she realized they came from different worlds. Her father had gone to a state college in the south-central part of the state and she imagined that was where she would go.

Ben told her not to worry. His family had 'connections', and he was sure they could get her in. He also explained that finances were not an issue. He was sure she could get a scholarship, and if not, she could get financial help elsewhere. At least it gave her something to dream about, though she was more focused on her life with Ben. He was now officially her boyfriend. On any given day, they would send at least a dozen texts back and forth.

As the ski season was ending, Megan received wonderful news from Ben. He and a friend were going to return to the chalet for a weekend of skiing. Would she be able to see him?

[Absolutely]

[Great. Do you know anyone my friend could meet?]

[Sure. I'm sure my best friend, Danny, will be available.]

[We'll be up on Friday evening by around 7:00. We'll drop our skis off at the chalet and then see you at the lodge, if that works.]

[That works. See you then.]

Except everything didn't quite go according to plan. As Megan and Danny waited at the lodge, Megan received another text.

[Sorry. We made it to the chalet, but Steve's car is having engine problems. We're going to call a mechanic tomorrow, but we can't make it into town.]

[I was looking so forward to seeing you.]

[Me too. Sorry, I don't know what to do.]

[Maybe we could come and see you.]

There was a pause for a few minutes before the next text arrived.

[Great.]

Ben also provided an address for the meeting. It took some convincing, but not much, to get Danny to drive. She was the one with the car. By 7:30, they were headed for the chalet.

The chalet was located on a side road about twenty minutes outside town, and when they arrived, there was a car parked in front of the chalet. The lights were on inside the condo but no one came to the door. Unbeknownst to the girls, there was no one inside. In fact, Ben had completely forgotten about Megan on the drive back to Philadelphia. His photo on the slopes had been taken by a stranger. He did not even know it had been taken.

The texts Megan had received came from an untraceable burner phone. There was someone, or rather, *something*, waiting for Megan and Danny, but it wasn't Ben and his friend.

The creature watched and waited as the two girls got out of their car and walked to the front door of the chalet. They knocked on the door and yelled for someone to answer. They tried to peer through the windows and talked about what to do next. It was humorous to the creature. He crept closer and closer to the two girls. They never even looked in his direction, not that it would have made a difference. And then he was between them and their car.

They still had not seen the creature, but they would as soon as they realized no one was home. It was always delicious to see what humans would do when they first saw him. Some froze. Some couldn't believe their eyes and stood there staring. Most ran.

These two ran. It was the smart thing to do but they still had no chance. The creature gave them a few seconds to run. It was always better to let the prey think it had a chance and then destroy its hope. They made it almost fifty yards before he was on top of them. He first disabled the younger girl. He didn't want her to escape but he didn't want her to die yet, either.

As he caught up to her, the creature struck her in the lower back with his fist, breaking her spine and leaving her paralyzed and sprawling across the ground. Now for the second girl, the older one.

Danny made it almost fifty yards farther than Megan before the beast seized her in one of its powerful hands. It could have snapped her neck in an instant but he held her up by the throat about two feet off the ground. She struggled and kicked and tried to run, her feet spinning in the air. He allowed her to breath, but he restricted her windpipe, making breathing difficult. The beast carried Danny back to where Megan was.

The intent was to increase the terror for both of the victims. Megan was paralyzed and couldn't move. Since she was the most helpless, she would live the longest. Danny could still run.

Well, at that moment she could still run. Throwing Danny to the ground, he seized her by the left ankle and lifted her in the air so that now her head dangled toward the ground. He then sank his fangs into her thigh, crushing the largest bone in her body. As his teeth tore through her jeans and ripped a mouthful of muscle from let leg, the beast tilted his head back for a second to enjoy the fresh blood. Danny hung for a moment by a few threads of meat and cloth before they gave way, dropping her to the ground.

He looked down at her as her life's blood draining from her—he had severed a major artery, and she would bleed out quickly—while he still held part of her leg in his hand. He dropped the leg and then tore the rest of her body to pieces. He finished by feasting on Danny's liver. Megan saw the whole thing, or at least much of it. It was dark, and she thankfully couldn't see everything that was happening. She saw the creature with his powerful back and arms and his sleek, almost shiny black fur.

She could hear bones being crushed and, occasionally, a piece of flesh or bone would come flying her way. There was nothing she could do but watch and cry. A bloody, matted ball rolled her way, coming to rest about a foot from her face. As she looked closer, she could see patches of blonde hair in the bloody mess. Then she saw her friend's eyes. She screamed again and again, but she couldn't move. There was nothing she could do to help her friend or herself.

After the creature finished with Danny, he stood up and walked over to Megan. He looked her in the eyes, and for a split second, she thought she saw something human in his eyes. He cocked his head to one side as if he was listening to her pleas. "Please, please, please," she said, hoping for mercy.

The creature, of course, had no mercy. Megan had no chance of living. He was merely curious. He viewed these victims the same way a wolf might view a sheep, only it was the terror he craved, even more than flesh. The creature wondered if these humans understood their role in the world, the fact that they existed for his pleasure. He supposed they did not.

An hour later, as the creature prepared to leave, the scene he left behind would leave the first responders with nightmares for the rest of their lives.

Blood and body parts were scattered across the front of the chalet. It was impossible to tell which clumps of human remains went with which girl.

Now, it was time to put Phase II of the plan into action.

Chapter 14

Russell Strait had no family or friends. We think that everyone has family, or at least some friends, but that is not always the case. Russ had a biological family. He had a mother, Nina Santangelo, but her motherhood was accidental, and she resented it. She foisted Russ on her mother, who died when he was thirteen. His father, according to his mother, was some guy named Nicolaus Strait, hence the name on the birth certificate, but she was not sure he was Russell's father.

She wasn't even sure that was his name. It might be more accurate to say that his father was some guy, one of many guys, she met in a bar one night.

A more ambitious child might have tried to find his birth father, but from an early age, Russ had no ambition. He wasn't even curious about who his father might be. His mother had been a bitch and he suspected his father was the same. His grandmother, old as she was, seemed to care that he was fed, but she was too old to participate meaningfully in his life. It was all she could do to fight off the cancer that was consuming her body; she had no strength for anything else.

When he was sixteen, Russ dropped out of school and left home. Well, he never formally dropped out of school, he just quit going. He decided it was time to move out and make his own life. When he moved out, it took his mother a week to realize he was gone. In fact, she only realized he was gone because a truant officer from Russell's high school came to check on him. His mother went to his room and found that his things had been taken. She told the truant officer that Russ had run away.

When he suggested reporting the matter to the police, Russell's mother shrugged. She simply sat down, poured herself another glass of cheap liquor and lit up another cigarette. The truth was that she was glad to see him go.

For the past nine years, Russ had bounced from one random place to another. Occasionally, he would be arrested for shoplifting or petty theft, but these charges were always resolved with a short jail sentence, coupled with a promise that he would move on. He picked up a pair of skis along the way, meaning he literally picked up a pair of skis and pole while their owner was in the lodge having lunch.

He took naturally to the slopes and found his life's passion. All the money he earned was used to purchase ski equipment. During the winter, he went to whatever resort was hiring. His career had taken him from the slopes of Vermont and New Hampshire to Vail and Aspen in Colorado. Whenever summer arrived, he would grab a job in construction, if he could, until the next ski season arrived.

Now, he found himself in a small Pennsylvania resort. It wasn't the best place he had ever lived; in fact, it might have been the worst. The slopes were small and not much of a challenge. There was too much ice to negotiate. There were also lots of other instructors, so competition was fierce. It had been a mistake to listen to that guy in New Mexico who told him to come here, but now he was stuck until the end of the season.

The only good thing about the area was the house he had been given, practically for free. The fact that he had this place at all was a bit strange but he wasn't willing to look a gift horse in the mouth. He had been thinking of leaving and going elsewhere when he met a guy, an older guy, at a bar. They talked for a while. At first, he thought the guy might be gay. He wasn't, but by the end of the night, the guy mentioned an unoccupied guest house on his property.

He offered Russ the opportunity to stay there because, as he said, it was better that it be occupied rather than unoccupied. The older guy told Russ he wouldn't charge him any rent, but he might have some things for Russ to do from time to time. Having a place to stay, basically for free, tipped the scales in favor of staying. It wasn't a nice place by the standards of most people, but it was better than Russ was used to.

Normally, he found himself living with roommates who, for reasons he never understood, always grew to dislike him. He was a mooch. He ate his roommates' food and used their stuff. He never understood the issue. After all, he was willing to share whatever he had with them. The problem is that he never bought any food and didn't have anything anyone would want to share. Russ did want to be liked but he had never fit in, not in his family, not in school, not anywhere.

He wanted to have a girlfriend, but here again, he just had never been able connect with anyone. Women seemed to see him as a bit creepy. He wasn't good-looking and had never learned good grooming habits. It may have been his habit of lingering around attractive young women and following them that caused women to see him as creepy, but he was actually just socially awkward. He would never hurt anyone.

Even when a random boyfriend would confront him, his practice was to slink away. A couple of times, he had been punched in the face by chivalrous suitors of girls he would have liked to have met. Even then, he would take the beating and move on. Now, at least, he had his own house, at least temporarily. He had a bedroom, a bathroom, and another room. It came with some furniture and, even better, a forty-eight-inch television and a Nintendo game system.

He didn't have to leave his house. When he was not working, he could now spend all of his time alone playing video games.

Chapter 15

With the murder of two more high school students, the pressure on the police amplified. Everyone now knew that the 'person of interest' the police held was not the murderer. He had sexually assaulted a girl, that much was true, but he probably hadn't killed her. He definitely hadn't murdered the last two girls. He was in jail for those murders, and therefore, had a perfect alibi. On a daily basis, Detective Jones had to explain his lack of progress to his superiors, who had to explain the lack of progress all the way up to the commander of the state police and the governor.

There were threats to fire him but he knew that was not a serious threat. The state police were unionized, and he knew he couldn't be fired, or at least he was pretty sure he couldn't be fired. But there were lots of unappealing places he could be sent and assignments that might be worse than being fired.

The big break in the case came from an unexpected source, as big breaks usually do. An anonymous caller called the barracks and left a message with the trooper on duty. He spoke quickly but said that the killer was Russell Strait. He also gave an address where the suspect could be located. The caller reported that he had been in Strait's apartment within the past forty-eight hours. He said that Strait had told him all about the killings and shown him a fur coat he wore while committing the murders.

The trooper on duty asked the caller to hold for a minute until he could locate the detective in charge of the case but the line went silent. The trooper called back but there was no answer. When the call was later traced, it came back to a burner phone. Cellphone transmission data indicated that the call had been made from Winter Haven, but a precise location could not be identified. The caller would always remain anonymous.

After dressing down the trooper who had taken the call, Detective Jones did some investigation of his own. He soon determined independently that this Strait character lived at the address provided by the caller. He actually lived in a small building on the property of a larger estate. There were no active warrants for Strait but he did have an extensive criminal record, or at least that is what he would report to the district justice when he asked for a search warrant. It was also a fact he would leak to the media at the appropriate time.

A close review of the record, however, revealed that there had been no charges for crimes of violence, only misdemeanor-level theft offenses. Normally, serial killers do not have extensive criminal records so, strangely, the lack of any crimes of violence on Strait's record supported Jones's suspicions that this was the right guy. Besides, they had no one else who could remotely be considered a suspect, and he needed to do something.

The Fourth Amendment to the Constitution provides that citizens of the United States have a right to security in their homes, and that no search may take place without a warrant, based upon probable cause issued by a neutral magistrate. 'Probable cause' simply means reason to believe that evidence is located in the place to be searched. This meant that in order to search Strait's house and find incriminating evidence, the police would need to establish probable cause.

The problem was that they only had an anonymous tip. They had no way of knowing whether the person who provided the tip was reliable or not. Sometimes police can use an anonymous tip to conduct further investigation and find other evidence. Detective Jones had conducted further investigation, but he was not able to find any evidence that supported the anonymous tipster. Throughout his career, Jones had never been one to allow legal niceties—like the Constitution—to impede the capture of a criminal.

There was a murderer on the loose, and Jones had been given the name of a potential murderer. If he could shade the facts just a little bit, he was sure he could get a search warrant for the Strait residence. There were four magistrates in the county. Jones picked the one he thought would give him the least amount of trouble. It was after hours, and Magistrate Carr was a retired state trooper who had worked with Jones.

He was known to be lazy, and at this time of night, he was likely to be drunk. If he had not passed out, he would authorize the search.

Jones had to get Carr out of bed, but after a short explanation, he signed the search warrant, wished Jones good luck, and headed back to bed. If Jones was ever asked, he did not notice the smell of alcohol on Carr's breath. Jones had ordered a team of troopers to the Strait residence—or rather, the pool house outside the main house on the property to be searched. Jones' trip to the Strait house had been delayed slightly by the trip to the magistrate, but he still arrived before the team was fully assembled. They would now wait until the early morning hours before they conducted their raid and searched the house.

On the evening of 13 March, the night before the search, Russ had scored some particularly good cocaine. He was on top of the world when he passed out that night, and he was still passed out when the police raided the guest house at 6:00 the next morning. In his room, they discovered a coat made from the fur of the northern gray wolf that contained the blood of each of the victims. There was a set of mechanical teeth that contained the DNA of several of the victims.

He had lockets of hair and small, worthless pieces of jewelry from each victim in a shoe box in the closet: 'trophies' as homicide detectives refer to them. While the search was being conducted, Russ was taken to a table in one corner of the room and told to sit there while the troopers searched the room. An older cop in plain clothes sat next to him. He told Russ that he was the lead investigator and that they would just sit there until the search was completed.

There might be a time later when it would be necessary for Russ to provide a formal statement, but for now, the police were there to conduct a search. Maybe nothing else would happen if they didn't find anything, he said.

As one item after another was uncovered by the police and brought over to the table where Russ was sitting, he was shocked. He had never seen any of this stuff before. He tried to tell the lead detective that he had never seen any of the items before. "Are you sure?" Detective Jones said as he handed the mechanical teeth to Russ. "Here, take a look. You need to be sure," the detective continued.

Russ took the mechanical teeth from Detective Jones and held them in his hands. The same occurred with the jewelry that was found. Russ picked up a locket and examined it closely. He had never seen it before. In fact, as Jones asked, Russ touched every single piece of evidence as he tried to remember if he had seen it before. Jones then took the evidence back from Russ and placed it into an evidence bag for later processing.

Russ was the only one in the room not wearing surgical gloves.

As the search concluded, Detective Jones advised Russ that it was time to go to the station.

Russ had a right to a lawyer, as one trooper explained, and he had the right to remain silent. Russ thought it would be best, however, if he talked. He had nothing to hide. Besides, he was afraid that if he said he wanted a lawyer, the police would think he was guilty. As they drove to the police barracks, Russell Strait might have been the only person in Winter Haven who did not know that a series of murders had occurred.

He thought he might be suspected of stealing the fur coat and jewelry. In short order, Strait admitted to renting the room where the evidence was discovered. He admitted that he might have known one or more of the victims. He had no alibi for the nights that any of the murdered women had been killed. As the day wore on, he acknowledged that sometimes he blacked out and had no memory of what had transpired the night before. In fact, he said it was possible he had blacked out on the nights of the murders.

Later that evening, even he was no longer sure of his innocence. He was taken from the state police barracks to a district magistrate for arraignment on four counts of capital murder. The magistrate set bail at $10 million, and Strait was taken from the magistrate's office to the county jail to await trial. He knew in the recesses of his mind that he would never see the outside of a prison again.

An experienced, skeptical investigator might have looked more deeply into the case. There appeared to be no motive and no history of violence. No one had ever seen Russ in a wolf coat and, had anyone bothered to check, they would have discovered the coast itself had been purchased for $18,000, more than Russ had ever earned in a year. Had they looked further, they would have discovered that Russ had left no fingerprints at any of the crime scenes.

A close review of the confession would have revealed that it contained no details that would have been known only to the killer—it was vague and generic, normally of little use to professionals. But no one wanted to take a closer look.

Chapter 16

The gossip surrounding the murders and the murder investigations was largely lost on Ed. He was certainly aware that the murders had occurred, but he assumed the police were investigating and would eventually find the murderer. Dave would stop in from time to time to fill him in on the local gossip and any news of interest, but Ed had very little interest in uninformed gossip. Just making it from one day to the next was a challenge for him, particularly when he wasn't sure he wanted to make it to the next.

In the deepest recesses of his brain, he knew that suicide was probably not the answer. He feared the legacy it would leave to his family, and he couldn't stand the thought of his wife finding his body. Maybe he could disappear into the mountains and end his life there without anyone finding him.

The day after Strait's arrest, Ed, as he always did, put on a suit and went to his office to start the day. There was not much to do but he would sit there in his chair and wait for the phone to ring. On this particular day, he didn't have to wait long. At about 9:30 a.m., he received a call from the President Judge's secretary. She informed him that the President Judge would like to see him if Ed had time.

It is always nice when judges and their staff feigned politeness. A request of 'if you have time' from a judge is tantamount to an order. No lawyer would ever think of telling a judge's secretary that the lawyer didn't have time to meet with the judge.

The courthouse was about a fifteen-minute walk from Ed's office. He left immediately and, after a thorough scan by the deputies at the security station, arrived at the President Judge's chambers on the third floor. There he waited for another half hour as the judge finished a pretrial conference with a group of other attorneys.

Tim Watson had been a judge for nearly twenty years. He and Ed had attended the same law school but—although they both frequently told other people that they had been friends in law school—the truth was that they rarely even spoke to each other. It wasn't that they didn't like each other; it was more that they moved in different circles. Ed had been selected for law review, a prestigious honor bestowed only upon the academic elite of the school.

He was destined for greater things: a job in one of the nation's largest and most well-respected law firms or perhaps a clerkship with a federal district or circuit court. The future judge, by contrast, achieved only mediocre academic success. His future lay in practice with his father in the small, rural county where he had been born. As Ed moved up the rungs of success to eventually found his own boutique firm. Tim Watson struggled to do whatever cases came through the door.

He also dedicated all of his spare time to the local Republican Party politics and to ingratiating himself with the chairman. When one of the judges hit mandatory retirement age, the chairman gave the nod, and Tim Watson was chosen as the Republican candidate in the primary. Since the county was about seventy-five percent Republican, his election was assured.

He felt envy at times when he would read about his former law school classmate in an American Bar Association article or saw one of his high-profile cases in the *Philadelphia Inquirer*, but it wasn't a malicious jealousy. In the back of his mind, he simply wished he could have emulated Ed's success.

Recently, however, the tables had turned. Ed had abandoned the high-profile practice or, more accurately, the high-profile practice had abandoned him. It was with sadness that Judge Watson read of the demise of Ed's practice and reputation. There were allegations of impropriety and potentially illegal activity. One of Ed's partners had fled the country, allegedly with several million dollars in client funds.

His other partner was rumored to have also embezzled over $2,000,000 dollars more. That partner shot himself at his desk, and no one, it appeared, could find out where the money had gone.

Professional jealousy had taken over from there as the remaining partners sued Ed for malfeasance. As the senior partner, they said, he should have known what was going on. In truth, Ed agreed with them. He should have known what was going on but he didn't. The disciplinary board filed charges, as well, and an army of accountants examined his books to see if they could uncover any discrepancies.

When it was over, Ed's firm was gone. Now he practiced out of his house in a small town in a rural county in the middle of nowhere. But the judge suspected there was still something left in his old law school classmate.

Ed sat in front of Judge Watson's extremely large desk and stared at the austere men who looked down at him from the portraits that lined the obscenely large office, or chambers, as judicial offices are called. The portraits were of the President Judges that had gone before, back to the years preceding the Civil War. Ed wondered what it might be like to have appeared before one of these judges.

"Ed," the judge began, "thanks for coming. Let me get right to the point. You are aware of the recent murders of a number of young women in the county. Last night, the state police made an arrest. I'd like to appoint you as defense counsel. Now, the county only had a limited budget for—"

One of the cardinal rules of trial practice is to never interrupt a judge when he is speaking, but Ed couldn't help himself.

"But, Your Honor, I haven't tried a murder case in the past two decades. I don't think I'm up to the challenge—"

Now it was the judge's turn to cut Ed off. There is no rule that requires judges to allow attorneys to finish what they are saying.

"Listen, Ed, you can do this case. In fact, I picked you because I think you're the only lawyer in this county that *could* do the case. No one else has your experience. None of the other lawyers have tried as many trials as you have."

The judge's voice softened a bit and he paused for a few seconds before continuing. "If you don't want to do the case, I'm not going to force you to do it. But this kid needs help, and I'm not sure where I'll turn if you tell me no."

Ed sat silently for a few moments. Perhaps the judge was right. This kid needed him. What was equally true but left unsaid was that Ed needed this case, as well.

"Okay," Ed said. After a few more minutes with the judge, Ed left chambers and headed to the county detention center, formerly the jail, to meet with his new client.

Chapter 17

It would be a difficult, probably unwinnable case. But Russell Strait might not be guilty, and no one cared what happened to him. Before wealth and fame, fleeting as they were, the practice of law had always been to Ed about representing those who could not defend themselves. Part of it was religious. Part of it was his upbringing. He, like many of his clients, came from a poor family, the son of an alcoholic who, whenever he did have some money, would abandon his family until the money ran out.

When he was growing up, his clothes were worn out hand-me-downs, given by people at his church. He didn't fit in with the cool kids, or really anyone else, at school. He became used to the slurs and slights from the other kids. By the time he graduated from high school, however, his natural intelligence had carried him to the top of the class. He remembered the other kids from disreputable families, the sons and daughters of single mothers, the kids raised by their grandparents because their parents were not around.

While attending law school, he saw how unforgiving the legal system was and how it crushed the weak and the powerless. The reality of the American legal system is that laws are created to protect the rich and the powerful from the weak and the powerless. When Ed graduated from law school, he decided to dedicate himself to serving the underprivileged. Of course, life had intervened, and he found himself focused on money and reputation rather than the thing that really mattered.

This case might be Ed's chance at redemption.

Fortunately, he wouldn't be doing the case alone. Dave was an excellent investigator and an even better friend, and Ed was sure that he would be able to rely on him. They would probably need more help, but before doing anything else, Ed would need to meet with the client and make sure they could work together. He also needed to know what he was facing. Would Russ say he was guilty and want the most favorable plea available, or would he want to go to trial?

The viciousness of the attacks, at least as outlined in the media, suggested there might be mental health issues to consider. He would also need to make a preliminary call to the prosecutor before he met with the defendant so he could at least hear what the case was about. Ed had tried murder cases before, but that was when he was a younger attorney. In each case, he had a solid defense, and in each case, he won.

But that had been a long time ago, and this case was different from any of those. In the case of *Commonwealth v. Russell Strait*, the defendant, Russell Strait, was alleged to be a serial killer. The FBI defines a serial killer as someone who kills three or more unrelated people. There are actually very few serial killers at any one time in the United States. In fact, less than one percent of all homicide victims are the victims of serial killers. They are notoriously difficult to catch for a variety of reasons.

First, serial killers tend to pick victims they do not know. In most murder cases, the killer is usually someone acquainted with the victim, frequently a spouse or significant other. These killings tend to be unplanned and disorganized, leaving lots of forensic evidence. Serial killers, however, tend to choose victims carefully and at random. Normal police investigative techniques, which tend to focus on people associated with the victim, tend to lead nowhere or to the arrest of the wrong person.

In addition, while it may be a stretch to suggest that all serial killers are geniuses, many have above average IQs. Even those who do not usually study police procedure and know enough to keep from getting arrested. Depending on the victim, a police force may consider a murder to be an isolated event and not look further. If care is taken in the commission of the murders, forensic evidence will be scant.

If the murders are spread out over a larger geographic area, if the killer is cautious about the information he or she leaves behind, and if the killer varies his or her *modus operandi*, the chances of catching the murderer are slim.

As Ed left the judge's chambers, he called Dave and asked him to meet at the jail to interview a defendant in a murder case to which Ed had just been appointed. He didn't tell Dave the name of the defendant or the murder for which he had been charged, but Dave had already heard rumors of the arrest and suspected it involved the recent murders of the young women around town.

Ed also called the prosecutor, Stephanie Cizchak, who was glad to provide a synopsis of the evidence. She said she would send over the entire file, but for the time being, she told Ed that they had fingerprints, DNA, and a confession. It was an open-and-shut case. In order to save the taxpayers money, she said she might consider a plea to four consecutive life terms and spare Strait the death penalty, but she wasn't sure yet. In Pennsylvania, a life sentence means a life behind bars. A prisoner sentenced to life only leaves prison in a casket.

Ed told her he would talk to the client about it. It took nearly an hour before Ed and Dave were admitted to the visitors' conference room and for Russell Strait to arrive. Russ was disheveled and hadn't slept for nearly twenty-four hours. He wouldn't strike anyone as a serial killer. He was shorter than average, maybe five feet four inches. He was not clean shaven and had a bit of a body odor. He smelled of stale sweat, stale beer, and cigarettes.

It was not the smell of someone who had missed a shower in the morning. It smelled like it had been weeks since soap or water had touched his body. He was rail thin, not quite skeletal but not well-nourished, either. He was escorted into the meeting room in chains and his shackles were fastened to the floor. A leather band ran around his waist with a steel ring in the front. A pair of handcuffs held his wrists on either side of the chain.

He looked like he could barely lift the shackles and chains that held him, let alone escape. He sat in front of the lawyer and the detective, gaunt and somewhat despondent. His eyes looked vacant in his hollowed face. The lawyer and the private detective sat across the table from him.

"Russell Strait," Ed began. "I've been appointed by the court to represent you. This is my investigator, David Krell." He paused for a minute, but his client said nothing.

"You understand that you are charged with four counts of murder, don't you?"

Russell's gaze remained fixed to the center of the table that separated them, but at last he spoke. "I didn't kill anyone," he said.

The conversation, such as it was, continued for another hour. Ed hadn't received any information from the prosecutor yet but there had been enough information in newspaper reports to at least give him some idea about the murders. He tried to talk to Russell about the murders but Russell was not much help when it came to preparing a defense. He had no memory of where he had been on any of the relevant dates in the case. Each of the murder victims had been killed on a particular night, and the medical examiner was able to provide a short window of time for when the murder occurred.

Had Russell been able to remember where he was on even one night when a murder had occurred, he could have an alibi that might have cleared him of all the murders, or at least, provided a defense. In Russell's mind, however, every night was pretty much like every other night. He worked when he had work. After work, he went to a couple of bars. He talked to some people. He got drunk or high, and then he went home.

The next morning, he got up and repeated the events of the previous day. This was not going to be an easy case. There was a lot of work to do.

Chapter 18

There was a diner about a block from the jail, and Ed and Dave decided to go there to discuss the case. It was now early afternoon, after lunch hour, and most people had finished lunch and returned to work. They grabbed a booth in the corner of the restaurant where they would have some privacy. Dave did much of his work in local restaurants and bars, pretending to be inconspicuous but eavesdropping on the private conversations of others.

It was rarely a tactic that worked, but it sensitized Dave to the dangers associated with people overhearing conversations. Ed had always been far more concerned with his conversations being overheard and needed no reminder to be careful.

After they ordered coffee and the waitress left, Ed asked Dave if he thought Russell Strait committed the murders.

"No way," Dave responded without hesitation. "I've been doing some research, and I don't think the murderer is even human. You saw what I saw, and you know it."

"Dave," Ed said, stopping Dave before he could go further. "This is a murder case. The cops and the prosecutors have evidence. We have been appointed to represent the person charged with those murders. That means focusing upon Russell Strait." Dave knew that, technically speaking, Ed was right. He was a little disappointed that Ed did not seem to be interested in the creature they had both seen, but he could also tell that this was not the time to put his theory forward.

"Sorry, Ed. I know what you mean. No, there is no way that guy we just met could have organized and committed four murders. Organizing a trip to the grocery store seems to be beyond him."

"I agree," Ed said. "We are dealing with a serial killer. The police have become tunnel-visioned. They are fixated on Strait for some reason, and we will have to find out why. But he doesn't seem capable of being a serial killer."

The two parted ways after lunch. Dave planned to pursue his own theory and find the real killer, even if he wasn't prepared to tell anyone yet.

Back in his office, Ed considered what to do next. It seemed obvious that Russ wouldn't be able to help with his defense but there was still a lot of work to be done. A lawyer prepares for trial in much the same way a warrior prepares for battle. In order to prevail, the lawyer must develop a strategy. The strategy, in turn, must be based upon the evidence that will be presented in a case.

The State will always have its strategy based on the evidence gathered by the police. The police will provide to the defense some, but not necessarily all, of the evidence in its possession. Only foolish lawyers rely on the State for their investigation. The best defense lawyers conduct their own investigations.

Ed was an experienced and crafty lawyer, but before beginning his investigation, he needed to assemble a trial team. He briefly thought about what that meant when he had been a great trial attorney. He would have hit a button on his speakerphone and told his secretary to have one or another paralegal and a couple of associates come to his office. That was no longer possible. He had no paralegals, and he had no associates.

Ed would have to find another attorney to join him. With any luck, he might be able to find a paralegal to work on a temporary basis.

The first call Ed made was to his former protégé, a talented lawyer who had been by Ed's side in more than a dozen high-profile cases. Duane Beecher was now a junior partner with a mid-sized firm in Philadelphia. He was glad to hear from his former boss who, he felt, had been screwed by what had happened. He listened as Ed explained the facts of the case to him but, in the end, Duane had to decline.

He had his own busy practice now and did not have the time to take a low-paying, possibly *pro bono*, case in the middle of nowhere. Ed said he understood and the two talked about getting together for dinner at Del Frisco's the next time Ed was in town, something they both knew would never happen.

Ed tried a couple more of his former associates before realizing that he was barking up the wrong tree. The practice of law is about making money, and defending indigent murderers in faraway counties did not result in revenue production. He next called Dave and told him of the problem. Over the years, he had come to rely on Dave's advice. If nothing else, he was a good sounding board.

Somewhat to his surprise, Dave told him about a local lawyer who'd opened her own practice about two years prior. Dave thought she was good. She had actually taken some cases to trial and Dave thought she might have won two or three. Her name was Shelley Connor. Although she wouldn't make much money off this case, the publicity would likely help her practice. Besides, Dave explained, she was not overwhelmed with work.

"Connor Law Office," she answered on the third ring.

"Ms. Connor," Ed began. "I'm Edwin Reynolds. I've been appointed to represent a guy named Russell Strait in a murder case. If you have any interest in co-counseling the case, I'd like to meet so we can talk about it."

Shelley badly wanted to be involved in the case but she did not want to appear too anxious. Also, she had heard of Edwin Reynold and she considered him to be one of the great trial lawyers of his generation. Sure, there might be some issues as of late, but if she could second-chair a trial with him, especially a murder trial, there was a lot she believed she could learn.

She hesitated intentionally for a few seconds. "Well," she began. "I suppose it wouldn't hurt to talk, but I have a lot on my plate…"

"I understand, and I'm sorry to have bothered you," Ed responded, but before he could say anything else, Shelley cut him off.

"Oh, I see that I do have some time open this afternoon. I can be at your office in a half-hour."

"Perfect," said Ed. Shelley made it over in twenty minutes. Dave arrived about ten minutes after that. Shelley had a 'part-time' paralegal that worked as needed. Her name was Samantha, but she went by Sam. These four people: Ed, Dave, Shelly, and Sam made up the trial team. They were all that stood between Russell Strait and life in prison, or maybe even death.

Chapter 19

There is never enough time for defense counsel to prepare for trial. There are always too many leads to run down, too many facts to double-check, too much legal research to do, and too many motions to write and argue. The government has the resources of the state behind it and can call, when necessary, on the state attorney general for assistance. It can also access the tremendous resources of the state police and the FBI for forensic assistance.

The budget to prosecute a citizen is nearly unlimited. Indigent defendants, however, have only the meager resources allocated to them by state or local politicians. Giving defendants adequate resources to defend themselves has never been high on the list of any politician's list of priorities.

In Strait's case, the early stages of the trial process proceeded routinely. There was a preliminary hearing, a *pro forma* proceeding where the prosecution officer, Detective Jones, provided sufficient information to allow a district justice to find that there was probable cause to believe the defendant had committed the crimes with which he was charged. It was an impossibly low burden, and the district justice held the case over for trial.

He also continued the bail at $10 million. Bail of $100 would have been sufficient to keep Russell Strait incarcerated. Next, the Commonwealth, meaning the assistant district attorney assigned to the case, provided 'discovery', meaning the evidence in its possession that was 'material' either to the prosecution or the defense of the case. Sometimes prosecutors will play games with the information they provided.

In this case, Russell was being prosecuted by the first assistant district attorney, a middle-aged woman named Sarah Barton, who had been a prosecutor for twenty-five years and who had worked under four district attorneys. She knew what she was doing. She also knew there was nothing to be gained by hiding evidence. As the defense team began examining discovery, certain facts were clear:

- There were four victims, each of whom had been violently torn apart by the assailant.
- At each crime scene, evidence technicians had recovered hair that appeared to be the hair of a wolf.
- There were no witnesses to any of the murders—at least the police had been unable to *locate* any witnesses.
- There was no evidence at any of the crime scenes that connected Russ to the murders.
- There was no evidence that Russ knew or had any contact with any of the victims.

The Commonwealth's case rested on the search of Russell's house and on the confession he had subsequently given police. The team realized that without the search, there would be virtually no evidence against Russ. The incriminating wolf suit and the fake mechanical jaws were found during the search. The victims' DNA and several items of the victims' jewelry were discovered during the search, and a wolf skin coat had been discovered.

In addition, the police had found Russell's fingerprints on several pieces of the victims' jewelry that had been recovered. None of this evidence would ever be presented to the jury if the search were illegal. Without this evidence, the Commonwealth would not have sufficient evidence to proceed to trial, and the case would be dismissed.

Shelley volunteered to research the suppression issue and prepare a motion to suppress. According to the Fourth Amendment to the U.S. Constitution, searches can only be conducted pursuant to a search warrant issued by a neutral judge or magistrate, based upon a finding of 'probable cause' by the judge or magistrate. 'Probable cause' sounds like an easy concept to understand, but the jurisprudence surrounding it has grown complex over the years.

Basically, in order for probable cause to exist, there must be reason to believe that a crime was committed, and that evidence of that crime is located in the place to be searched. The evidence presented to the judge or magistrate must be 'reliable'. Reliability is frequently established by showing that the person providing the evidence supporting probable cause is reliable, usually through a proven history of providing accurate information. The evidence may also be deemed reliable if the police are able to verify key parts of the witness's statements.

In this case, however, the sole source for the information contained in the search warrant application was anonymous, and the police had done nothing to verify the information they received from the anonymous source. Shelley was surprised that a magistrate would even grant a search warrant application, but he had. The law was crystal clear, and as she prepared the motion to suppress, she didn't think they could lose. Ed wasn't so sure.

A confession is a particularly strong piece of evidence for a jury to hear, even when it's false. Few people understand the psychological pressure the police can put on a defendant, or how words uttered by a defendant can be twisted or manipulated by police when testifying before a jury. It is difficult to suppress a confession, particularly when, as was the case here, the defendant was provided with *Miranda* warnings.

According to police records, after the search of Russell's residence had been completed, he was handcuffed and taken to the police barracks for questioning. He arrived at the barracks at 1:42 p.m., according to the police log. Two troopers met briefly with him and told him: he had the right to remain silent; anything he said could and would be used against him; he had the right to have a lawyer present when he was being questioned; if he couldn't afford a lawyer, one would be appointed for him; and he could stop the interview at any time.

Russell said he wanted to talk but had some questions. One of the troopers told him he could ask his questions to one of the detectives, but he had to first sign the form. At 2:04 p.m., Russell initialed the form and signed just below the line that said he was giving up all of his rights and speaking voluntarily with the police.

He never read the form. He simply signed where the trooper told him to sign. It was the last time anyone ever talked to him about his rights that day.

The records were ambiguous as to when the interrogation began, and unlike some states, there is no requirement for police interrogations or interviews to be audio or videotaped in Pennsylvania. The interrogation, however, at least according to the detective, resulted in the defendant stating that he frequently used drugs and alcohol, and occasionally had trouble remembering what he did when he was under the influence.

The defendant, at least according to the detective, also said that he might have met at least two of the murder victims in a local bar, although he couldn't remember what happened after he met them. He acknowledged that no one but him had access to his home, and that he could not explain how the murder weapon and jewelry belonging to the victims ended up in his house. He ended the statement by saying that he was sorry for what he had done.

The statement was signed by Detective Jones and witnessed by another trooper, but on the signature line for the defendant was the notation: 'Defendant Refused to Sign'. The time on the statement form was 11:47 p.m. The interactions between Russell Strait had lasted over nine hours, but the resulting written statement was less than a single page. What else happened during the interview?

Shelley and Ed realized there was not an independent basis for the suppression of the statement. Because Russell had signed the form acknowledging and waiving his *Miranda* warnings, the judge would allow the statement to go to the jury. The judge would rule that because Russell had agreed to talk to the police, had never requested a lawyer, and had never stopped the interview, the interview was voluntary.

There was a way to suppress the statement, however. If the search itself was illegal, then it could be argued that Russell's encounter with the police and subsequent statements were tainted by the initial illegal search, what lawyers and judges call 'the fruit of the poisonous tree', then the statement would have to be suppressed, as well. The suppression of both the evidence recovered in the search and the statement from Russell rose or fell on whether there was probable cause for the initial search.

As Shelley toiled away on the suppression motion, Dave focused on the evidence, particularly the wolf suit and the mechanical jaws. They had to be manufactured somewhere, and it was Dave's job to find out where, and then trace the purchase of these items to their owner. In the back of his mind, he was focused on the creature he had seen on the morning after the murder of the first victim, but he understood that the goal was to defend Russ. For now, that was the focus of his efforts.

Chapter 20

As Shelley and Dave went about their tasks, Ed decided to focus on the unique characteristics of these homicides—the *modus operandi*. There were hundreds of crime scene photos that had been taken, as well as video of each crime scene. All of this evidence had been turned over to the defense team. For nearly a week, Ed arrived in his office early in the morning and he stayed until 7:00 or later in the evening. His wife began to think he was becoming obsessive.

The absolute slaughter captured in the videos and still images was horrible, but it was necessary for Ed not only to look at the images but also to study them. He went over each photo and each video multiple times. He then visited the crime scenes to get a feel for location and distances and what the victims must have seen and felt in the last moments before their deaths. He sketched out maps and placed body parts and other pieces of evidence on the diagrams he drew.

As he walked in the steps of the victims and the killer, he thought about Russell with his spindly arms, and wondered how he could literally tear a body apart or rip a car door from its frame. It seemed like only an animal or someone with superhuman strength could visit the damage that had been inflicted on these victims. Maybe someone like Conan, the Barbarian. But Conan was a myth, and these women had not been killed by myth or legend.

Dave still believed something else committed the murders. He became increasingly frustrated by Ed's refusal to consider the possibility that something supernatural had been responsible for the murder. From Ed's point of view, the creature he saw looked like it could be human; that's why he never fired a shot. It moved on two legs and it wore fur like an animal. The more Ed thought about it, the more he realized it must have been a man.

He didn't know it at the time, but he and Dave had seen the murderer. It was a large man, to be sure—a man dressed as an animal. One night, after his wife had gone to sleep, Ed had an epiphany. The killer was a large man, to be sure, but maybe he *believed* he was an animal of some sort.. The unidentified individual tore people apart like he was an animal. Without waiting for morning, Ed jumped back on the computer.

Were there other murders where the victims appeared to have been attacked by an animal? He soon discovered that there were indeed murderers who had attacked victims and inflicted animalistic injuries on their victims. There was even a psychological condition known as 'clinical lycanthropy delusions' (CLD). People who suffered from this condition believed themselves to be werewolves and they acted as werewolves, attacking and killing innocent people.

A Dutch psychologist first identified the delusion in 1852 when a patient he was treating claimed to be growing large amounts of body hair, experiencing a thickening of his jaw, and had protruding fangs. It was clear that the patient thought he was becoming a werewolf. After physically examining the patient, the psychologist could not find any physical changes. Rather, the symptoms the patient described were delusions. Physically, the patient was human, but in his own mind, he was turning into a wolf—or to be more precise, a werewolf.

There were more than a dozen cases in Europe throughout the Middle Ages and into the 1700s where people were tried, convicted, and executed for murder they committed while in the form of a wolf, or so they believed. The condition was exceedingly rare, and Ed didn't think he could use centuries-old crimes to create a case for a more modern instance of CLD, but then he stumbled upon the case of Austin Harrouff in Florida.

In 2017, Austin Harrouff was, by all appearances, a normal teenage boy. He did well in high school and enrolled in a pre-med program in college. After his freshman year, however, he returned home a changed person. To those who would listen, he claimed to be immortal and only half human. The other half was animalistic. Family members worried that he might be suffering from some form of psychological disorder, and even considered pursuing an involuntary psychiatric commitment.

On 15 August of that year, however, neighbors heard screams coming from the home of John and Michelle Stevens in Jupiter, Florida. When the police arrived, they found Harrouff in the house. He had killed both of the Stevens with his bare hands. Harrouff was completely naked and was chewing the face of John Stevens. It took several deputies using stun guns and a number of bites from a police German Shepherd to pry Harrouff off of his kill. He was taken to a psychiatric hospital after his arrest.

The attacks on the various victims appeared to be consistent with attacks by someone suffering from CLD, but the carnage was difficult to explain. More research led to the 'berserkers', Viking warriors who went into battle wearing nothing but the skin of a wolf or a bear. Historical accounts described the berserkers as men having great strength. They were absolutely fearless and, at the time, were thought by many to be werewolves. They were famed for the carnage they left spewed across the battlefield.

If they suffered from CLD, could CLD explain their unusual strength? It took multiple deputies and a police dog to subdue Austin Harrouff, even though he was a small nineteen-year-old boy. There might be another explanation for the extraordinary strength displayed by the berserkers and others suffering from CLD: drugs.

In the case of the berserkers, published stories suggested that a type of mushroom grown in Scandinavia increased pain tolerance and impaired judgment, which might explain the ability of these warriors to continue to fight long after a normal person would either be dead or severely limited in what they could do.

Amphetamines, methamphetamines, and some other forms of illegal drugs might give the appearance of superhuman strength and greatly increased pain tolerance. Police officers had reported encountering people using the designer drug flakka, a type of amphetamine, who displayed superhuman strength, sometimes requiring eight to ten officers to physically restrain a suspect. If a person suffering from the delusions caused by CLD were to come across flakka or some other designer amphetamine, wouldn't that explain the damage inflicted on the bodies of the victims?

At least it was a start. Every defense begins with an idea. Now that idea needed to be molded into a theory.

Ed also thought back to Charles Hunt's manservant, Samuel. If Samuel suffered from CLD, could he be the murderer? He was large enough, and if he was taking some type of drug, perhaps he would have had the strength to inflict the injuries depicted in the crime scene photos and videos. Also, Hunt said he suspected that Samuel might have some responsibility. But how could he have survived gunshot wounds to the chest? Perhaps Dave wasn't as good a shot as Ed thought he was.

Chapter 21

Meanwhile, Dave thought he was making some progress on his part of the investigation. One of the primary pieces of evidence was the wolf suit. The suit was really just a coat made from real wolf skin. There were only a few people in the U.S. that manufactured fur coats, and most of those were located in Manhattan. Armed with pictures of the coat, Dave decided to take a drive east to the city to visit manufacturers of fur coats.

Unfortunately, the manufacturer's tag had been removed, and Dave therefore had to guess which manufacturer had made it. It was the sort of work Dave excelled at, going door to door, talking to people, and finding information no one else could.

He struck out on his first two visits but had better luck with the third furrier. When he shared the photo of the wolf coat, the clerk at the front counter told him to wait a minute and disappeared through a door. Twenty minutes later, the clerk returned with a much older man, who appeared to be the owner of the establishment. He was in his seventies, short, heavy-set, and balding. When he spoke, he had an accent, though Dave could not tell where it was from.

"Ah," he said as he took the photo and stared at it. "My name is Weismann. Come with me." He led Dave behind the counter and through the door he himself had entered minutes before. They walked past several piles of pelts of differing shapes and colors until he came upon a stack of larger furs. They were large and varied in color from light brown to almost black.

"These are pelts from Canadian wolves." He picked one up and handed it to Dave. Dave ran his fingers through the rich fur.

"Not many people appreciate real fur nowadays, or the work that goes into making one of these coats. First the trapper goes out and catches the wolf. He must care for the skin carefully. All fat must be removed and the skin must be stretched and dried."

"From there, the skin is sent to a tannery where the stiff dried pelt is tanned into a leathery consistency. It, too, is a difficult process, and if the tanner is not expert in his trade, the skin will either not be fully cured and the fur will slip from the skin, or if is tanned too much, the chemicals will burn holes in the skin, and it will become useless."

"After the skin has been tanned, I visit the tannery and select only the best products for my coats. You look at the skin in your hand and think maybe the whole skin will be used to make a fur coat. You would be wrong. Only certain parts of the skin are to be used in the finest coats. We cut the pelt into strips and then match the strips so the coat will have fur of consistent color throughout. After the pelts are pinned together using a mannequin to ensure a proper fit, the strips of fur are sewn together to make the coat."

"Sometimes it is necessary to trim some of the fur to make sure it is uniform throughout. Then, at the end, a liner is added to the coat. It takes a long time to create a coat, and I remember every single one I ever made."

This was good news. "Do you remember making this coat?" Dave said, pointing to the photo.

"Yes," the older man said. "I made this coat almost six years ago. It was a very strange order. The man who ordered the coat sounded like he was from the southern part of the country. He placed an order for five coats, all the same size."

"Do you have his name?" Dave asked.

"No, we do not keep records from so long ago. I remember taking the order and speaking to the purchaser, but I do not remember his name. I am not even sure he gave me a name."

Weismann seemed like he wanted to be helpful but there were few details that he remembered after the passage of so much time. His general practice was to keep a file on all coats he made, and then to keep that file for between four and five years. Periodically throughout the year, Weismann would burn the older records. He was certain the records for the coats he made had been burned. He had received the dimensions for the coats by fax, but he had not retained the fax he received.

"Do you recall where you shipped the coats?" Dave asked as he neared the end of his questions.

"The coats were not shipped anywhere. It took me several months to prepare these coats. Several weeks after they were prepared—they were waiting in the back until I received other instructions—a large African-American man came into the shop. He said he was there to pick up the coats. He paid me a large sum of money, in cash, and left. That is the end of the story."

Dave asked one last question. "How much did they cost?"

"What are you, from the IRS?" Weismann asked. He then proceeded. "That has always bothered me. For the five custom-made wolf coats, I charged $97,000. The coats were good coats, of the highest quality, but why wolf? There are much better furs out there, sable from Russia. Lynx, fisher, and martin all make excellent coats. Mink is common. These furs are all warm, soft, and beautiful. Wolf? Its durable but it's a course fur. You wouldn't go to a play or an opera in a wolf coat. And five of them. It never made any sense."

As Dave left, he thought of other things that did not make sense. How could Russell, a man who struggled to make minimum wage and was frequently unemployed, afford a coat that cost nearly $20,000 or more. The coat—one of the ones Mr. Weismann said he made—was at the scene of several murders. It stood to reason that the purchaser of the coat was the murderer, and if Russell was not the purchaser of the coats, then he was not the murderer. There was still more work to be done, but at least he had something.

On his way back to Pennsylvania, Dave thought about that night after the first murder. He had not seen a man in a wolf coat. He had seen a creature he would never forget. He was certain that creature was the killer but creatures did not shop for clothing or buy fur coats. The fur that covered the creature's body was like the fur of a wolf. In fact, it was exactly like one of the furs he observed on the floor during his visit to the furrier.

A creature covered with hair like a wolf wouldn't need to buy a wolf skin coat. A dark cloud drifted over his consciousness as the implications of his thoughts became clear to him. Maybe the creature he encountered, he was sure by now that it was a werewolf, was much more intelligent than he had thought. Dave had assumed that when a man became a creature, it acted as a mindless killing machine independent of the human it otherwise was. The degree of forethought and planning suggested that the creature and the man acted as one.

The plan to frame someone existed before the first murder, and this planning suggested that each of the murders was planned in advance. They were not dealing with an animal acting merely on instinct after it changed from its human form. This was a much more dangerous creature than he first thought.

Chapter 22

The court had scheduled a hearing on the defense motion to suppress evidence for 11:00 a.m. on a Tuesday morning, and allowed one hour for the hearing. Shelley was quite confident about the evidence. The U.S. Constitution was clear. In order for a search warrant to be issued, it had to be based upon probable cause. The search of Russ' apartment was based on an anonymous tip. The tip had come from a burner phone located in the local area at 3:00 in the afternoon.

The police had attempted to identify the individual who made the call but were unable to. The caller had spoken for only two minutes and thirty seconds in a muffled voice. In the call, he said he worked with Russell, and Russell had told the caller that he, Russell, was the murderer. He also said that Russell had the murder weapon in his apartment but was going to get rid of it that night. Then the caller hung up.

The caller had not provided any details that the police could verify. Even though they had no probable cause, they decided to go to a local magistrate to try to get a search warrant. Testimony concerning probable cause was limited to the four corners of the warrant. In other words, the Commonwealth was limited to what was said in the warrant. Shelley had found numerous cases where the appellate courts in the state had found a lack of probable cause even when there was substantially more evidence than the police had provided in this case.

There was simply no way the decision of the magistrate judge to issue the warrant could be sustained. The final ruling on the admissibility of the evidence from the search rested with the trial judge. Shelley had filed the motion and an accompanying legal brief. The state had responded but its response was anemic. She looked forward to this court argument but Ed was not confident. In his experience, judges often went out of their way to avoid letting serious criminals, especially serial killers, off.

It would take some mental gymnastics, but Ed thought the judge might be able to find a way to allow the admissibility of the evidence. Dave attended the hearing just to see what happened.

"All rise," the clerk announced as Judge Watson entered, surveying the courtroom uncomfortably.

"Counsel, do we agree that the evidence is limited to the Affidavit of Probable Cause." An Affidavit of Probable Cause is the document the police sign under oath in order to get the warrant. The judge's statement was legally accurate and meant that the district attorney would not be able to supplement the record. There was nothing the assistant district attorney could do but agree.

"Well, then, it looks like the issue is clear. Is there anything the State would like to add?"

"There is, Your Honor," the district attorney began. "There is an exception to the warrant requirement that we think applies. In the case of *Nix v. Williams*, the U.S. Supreme Court found that a court could consider whether the evidence would have been discovered whether the warrant had been issued or not. It's called the 'inevitable discovery' doctrine. In this case, we can represent to the court that we would have continued to surveil Mr. Strait and, eventually, we would have gathered sufficient evidence to conduct the search of the apartment. The police would have inevitably discovered the evidence."

Judge Watson seemed relieved. "So, you're saying the State was searching actively for this evidence?"

"Yes, Your Honor."

"And you were closing in on this particular suspect?"

"Yes, Your Honor. In fact, Mr. Strait was the only suspect we had after receiving the tip."

The judge thought for a minute. "How do you know that you would have eventually developed probable cause?"

The prosecutor squirmed a little bit. "Well, Your Honor, the investigators in this case were professional investigators with decades of experience. The suspect was known to be in the local area. When the anonymous tip was received, Mr. Strait became the subject of the investigation. The only place to be searched was the apartment where the subject lived, and the police would have inevitably searched it. We certainly would have gotten to it eventually."

"In *Brewer v. Williams*," the prosecutor continued, "the police had violated the defendant's rights by questioning him after he had invoked his right to counsel. In that case, Williams had murdered a ten-year-old girl and disposed of her body someplace in rural Iowa. When questioned illegally by the police, he confessed to the murder and provided police with the location of the body, which they subsequently recovered. The case went all the way to the Supreme Court, and the court sided with the defendant and granted Williams a new trial."

"At the second trial, the State of Iowa argued that the girl's body would have been discovered in any event and therefore should not have been suppressed. The trial court agreed and allowed the body—and evidence recovered from the body—into evidence. Williams was once again convicted of the murder of the ten-year-old girl."

"Again, the case went to the Supreme Court, this time as *Nix v. Williams*. In that case, the court agreed with the trial court and established the inevitable discovery doctrine. That doctrine applies in this case. The police were actively looking for the evidence in Strait's possession and would have found it."

Shelley could wait no longer. "Your Honor," she interjected, "this is preposterous. Basically, what the State is saying is that the Fourth Amendment to the U.S. Constitution has no meaning. If you can search without probable cause because you might someday develop evidence leading to probable cause, then there is nothing to prevent the police searching for anything anytime."

The judge had heard enough, however. "Counsel, thank you for your presentations. I'll look at what you filed and consider your arguments. I think we need to do some research. I'll get an order out probably by the end of next week. Is there anything else?"

Shelley was tempted to say something but she knew further argument would only hurt her—and, by extension, her client. At least she would be able to appeal if the court ruled against her and she lost at trial.

Three days later, Ed and Shelley received an order from the court denying the motion to suppress. If Russ was going to be saved, it would have to be by a jury at trial. In the last paragraph of the order, the judge set the trial date for 4 October. They now had a little under four months to prepare for the trial.

But there was something about the search that just didn't seem right to both Ed and Dave. The police had received an anonymous call, that was certain. The real question was: Who made that call? The police had not identified anyone who had been in Russell's house in the days leading up to the search, and Dave had not been able to identify any friends who might have been at his residence. Russell denied having anyone in the house.

Yet the anonymous caller said he had seen some of the evidence. He told the police that Russ had talked about the murders to him. This anonymous caller must either be the murderer, or he knew who the murderer was.

Chapter 23

Google has changed the world. Whereas Ed had conducted research and found that there was a psychological condition known as CLD, Dave decided to return to his research for large cryptids—unknown creatures—that would match the creature he and Ed had seen. Ed now denied seeing anything other than a human in a wolf skin coat but he had not had the view of the creature that Dave did. His visit to New York had convinced him that there was a human mind behind whatever he saw.

He was looking for something with the strength of an animal but the intelligence of a human. He remembered the Balkan werewolf, and decided to dig deeper into werewolf lore.

Dave's search led him to the old European werewolf legends. Although he was prone to beliefs in UFOs, mysterious monsters, and government cover-ups, he drew the line at vampires and werewolves—the characters of old horror movies from his childhood—but Google revealed a universe of materials on werewolves. These were not the Hollywood creatures who were human most of the time, turning to wolves only on the full moon. They also seemed to be mortal; regular bullets sufficed to kill them.

The historical record was compelling. Nearly every ancient culture contained evidence of werewolves. In Greek history, King Lycaon of Arcadia, seeking to test Zeus's omniscience, roasted his son and served him to the King of the Gods. When Zeus discovered what Lycaon had done, he transformed the human king into a wolf. In the *Epic of Gilgamesh*, one of the oldest stories in human history, Gilgamesh at one point turns down a woman's offer to sleep with him because she had turned a prior lover into a wolf.

There were similar tales in Nordic and Celtic mythology. Even the Bible contains evidence of werewolves. There is the story of Nebuchadnezzar in the Book of Daniel where the ancient Babylonian king turned into an animal covered with hair and possessed sharp claws for a time. Doesn't that sound like a werewolf? And then there are the many verses that talk about false prophets and others being wolves. What if these verses are literally true, like many Christians believe? Are they not proof of the existence of these creatures?

The Roman historian Pliny the Elder wrote of men being turned into werewolves for the act of cannibalism. The ancient Algonquin story of the wendigo is eerily similar to the ancient Roman histories. Then there were the werewolf trials of Europe. From the 1400s through the 1700s, more than a hundred people were charged with, convicted of, and executed for being werewolves.

Werewolves were not the only shapeshifting creature Dave came across in his research. There is a creature in Africa called the were-hyena, that—like the werewolf—possesses the ability to shift between man and hyena. The belief in these creatures is still widespread in the horn of Africa.

Dave then began researching serial killers. There was no shortage of those. He then cross-referenced that search with murders where the victims had been bitten or torn apart. This time, he found a number of murders that were similar to those that had occurred in and around Winter Haven. There was the case of Albert Fish, an American serial killer in the early 1900s, who would rape, murder, and then eat children. He was tried for the murder of three children but claimed to have killed and eaten more than a hundred.

A German serial killer, Joachim Kroll, killed at least fourteen people, and was actually cooking part of a young boy when he was arrested. In 1963, Magdalena Solis, the 'High Priestess of Blood', believed herself to be an Aztec Goddess and reigned over a bloodthirsty cult in Mexico. There were lots of examples of mutilations and murders of people throughout history. And then there were the serial killers that were never caught—Jack, the Ripper, the most famous serial killer—fell into this category.

He next looked at unsolved disappearances and found that in the U.S. alone, more than 600,000 people go missing every year. The vast majority of these missing cases are resolved quickly, but on average, about 17,000 people go missing and are never found. He came across a series of books written by a retired police detective, David Politis, entitled *Missing 411*. As Krell began examining some of these cases, the disappearances were often eerie.

The more he read, the more he convinced himself that a population of large shapeshifting creatures—werewolves—could live in the modern world. He had seen one, and he could believe his own eyes.

Chapter 24

After the denial of the motion to suppress, the defense had a little over four months to prepare for trial. It was not enough time. There was never enough time. Edwin Reynolds was a veteran of hundreds of trials and understood the process of putting a defense together, but it did not become easier with time. When dealing with people and human emotions, things rarely went as expected, and being able to roll with the punches was a skill every trial lawyer had to develop, even if it was never comfortable.

So far, the trial team had been focusing on the Commonwealth's case. The evidence seized during the search would be admitted. This included various items of jewelry from the victims, a fur coat with hair consistent with that found at the scenes of the homicides and a set of steel jaws, which most likely was used to inflict injuries on the victims. Dave had found the guy who actually made the wolf skin coat, and this witness appeared to put a major hole in the Commonwealth's case.

Multiple fur coats had been manufactured for the same person, although the witness did not know who the purchaser was. It could not have been Russell, however. He lacked the financial means to purchase the coats. Also, only one coat had been found in his possession. What happened to the others? If the manufacturer of the steel jaws could be located, they, too, might point to another suspect.

The jaws appeared to be custom-made, but they could have been manufactured in any small welding shop across the country or overseas, for that matter. There were simply too many places to look.

One thing was certain. If Russell did not bring the evidence into the house, then someone else had to, and whoever that person was would most likely be the real killer. There had been an anonymous caller who said he had been in the house, but when Dave and Shelley interviewed Russell, Russell denied ever having anyone else in the house. Interviews with Russell's co-workers confirmed that he had few friends, and the people with whom he was on friendly terms denied ever being at his residence.

Russell had rented the house from a gentlemen who, in turn, had rented the property from the real owner, who was spending the winter in the south of France. The person who rented the pool house to Russell was Charles Hunt. He had been cooperative with the police but had provided no useful information. Ed once again thought back to his dinner with Hunt and the strange manservant, Samuel, the big, lumbering black man who worked for Hunt.

In Ed's mind, he was a plausible suspect. Now there was a connection between Hunt, Samuel, and Russell Strait. It could be a coincidence but it was worth exploring.

Russell Strait's fingerprints had been found on several pieces of jewelry located in his residence. The real killer could have hidden the evidence discovered in Russell's house, but how could he or she have placed Russell's fingerprints on the jewelry? The jewelry was now in police custody and available for reinspection. Fingerprint evidence is not the concrete type of identifying evidence the public thinks it is.

In 2004, Al Qaeda in Iraq staged a series of bombings on the Madrid commuter train system in Spain. Spanish police collected a number of fingerprints from the crime scene. Those fingerprints were shared with law enforcement authorities around the world, and the FBI quickly identified a Portland, Oregon, attorney named Bradley Mayfield as one of the bombers, based upon a 'hundred percent' match of his fingerprints.

Although Mayfield had been home on the other side of the world at the time of the attack and had not been to Europe in more than a decade, he was nevertheless arrested on the strength of the fingerprint evidence alone and held in an undisclosed location for several weeks. The fingerprint evidence turned out to be wrong, but not before an innocent man was arrested and his life upended.

Could that be the case with Russell's alleged fingerprints? The fingerprint evidence was something that needed to be discredited.

There was another piece of evidence that the Commonwealth had disclosed in discovery—an expert report from Rubin Cohen, Ph.D. Dr. Cohen was a chemist and an expert on the effects of certain amphetamines on the human body. According to Cohen, several types of amphetamines could cause an ordinary person to experience unusual and unexpected strength. Alpha-PVP, commonly known as flakka, a newer designer drug, caused anyone taking it to experience an intense euphoria.

Alpha-PVP did this by causing the body to produce large amounts of dopamine that then entered the blood steam. In addition to the euphoria, alpha-PVP made the person using it almost impervious to pain. This also created the effect of unusual strength. A person using alpha-PVP would be able perform acts that appeared superhuman.

In Dr. Cohen's expert opinion, an individual of ordinary strength would have been able to inflict the injuries sustained by the victims if the individual were under the influence of alpha-PVP.

The report from Dr. Cohen seemed unassailable on the surface, but a close reading of the report revealed a couple of potential problems for the prosecution. First, whomever committed the murders possessed almost superhuman strength. Russell would be lucky to manage a push-up with his spindly little arms. Opening a new jar of peanut butter would have been a challenge for him. Tearing a body apart was certainly more than he could accomplish.

The expert report flew in the face of common sense, and Ed knew from long experience that juries were uncomfortable with experts whose testimony flew in the face of common sense.

The drug could explain how someone might have enough strength to cause the excessive damage that had been inflicted on the victim's bodies, but the prosecutors and police had not presented any evidence showing that Russell had ever had access to flakka, or any other amphetamine. The police had searched his residence and not found drugs of any type. There was no evidence Russell ever had any amphetamine in his blood.

In fact, a quick check of local arrests revealed that there had not been any arrests in the past few years for flakka in the area. It did not seem to be a drug that had made it to this isolated rural area in Pennsylvania, at least not yet.

In a criminal case, it is possible to file what's called a motion in limine to prevent a party from offering evidence that would be inadmissible. In some cases, it is better to allow an opponent to offer evidence that would be otherwise inadmissible in order to open the door to other arguments. It was not yet time to decide whether to try to exclude this evidence or not, but it was something Ed kept in the back of his mind.

Ed called a defense team meeting to discuss these issues. Shelley volunteered to look into the fingerprint evidence to see if there was a way to diffuse it. Dave agreed to look into who else might have access to Russell's residence, particularly Hunt or his manservant, Samuel, who sublet the pool house to Russell. He seemed like a possible suspect, but at least from the discovery documents provided, it appeared as though the police had completely discounted Charles Hunt. The police may not have even known of the manservant.

Ed did not share with the defense team his theory that the real perpetrator suffered from CLD. In his mind, it was too preliminary, and he was not yet ready to advance it as a theory of the case. The more he considered all of the facts at his disposal, the more convinced he became that they were looking for a man who thought he was a werewolf. That would explain the brutality of the attacks, the fur recovered at the crime scenes, and the individual he and Dave had seen the day after the first murder.

The government toxicologist also presented potentially useful evidence. If there was no evidence that Russell had ever used flakka, perhaps there would be evidence that someone else did. Dave was actually way ahead of the other members of the defense team, at least in his own mind, in forming a defense theory. This killer was not a human killer at all, or at least not all the time. It was a werewolf, an unknown species that had existed since before recorded history and which now stalked the forests of northern Pennsylvania.

By day, it was human, and that is why no one could find it. Dave, and Dave alone, was the only person who could solve this mystery, and he was well on his way to doing so. He had reminded Ed several times of the creature they had seen, but Ed had inexplicably decided to ignore his own eyes. He lacked the vision and the ability to think outside the box like Dave did.

For now, at least, Dave would keep his thoughts to himself. He would spring the truth on Ed and Shelley when the evidence became unassailable.

Chapter 25

Dave now needed to focus upon the identity of the werewolf he knew was responsible for the murders. What about Charles Hunt? Dave unleashed Google upon Charles, and over the next couple of hours, he began to build a dossier on Charles. He was rich—very rich. He was worth at least hundreds of millions of dollars, maybe as much as a billion. The source of his funds was unclear, although it appeared he had become wealthy at birth and grown richer after the death of his parents.

There was no coverage of him on the social pages. He seemed to avoid the most exclusive parties, and Dave could not find any pictures of Charles like he would have expected with other famous people. He seemed to be a hunter of some note, and Dave was able to locate pictures of him with various animals he had shot. There was no mention of a wife, girlfriend, or love interest. Dave then decided to delve into his business empire. Charles, as he already knew, was born rich.

A century ago, his family was heavily involved in the oil industry. In recent decades, the family operation had expanded to nineteen countries around the globe, and he was a silent investor in many more companies. The *Panama Papers*—the leaked financial records of a Panamanian law firm that exposed the financial misdeeds of thousands of the world's richest people—hinted at other business interests he might have elsewhere in the world.

It was impossible to track offshore accounts and shell companies with nominee directors, especially when they were protected by an army of lawyers and accountants, but it was clear that Charles was heavily involved in these gray-area endeavors. There was another tidbit of information he found. It was only a paragraph carried in a local Louisiana newspaper: 'Local Man Injured in Wolf Attack'. It went on to explain how Charles had been attacked and seriously injured by a wolf while hunting in Europe. There were no further details.

Dave had another idea. Was it possible to correlate Hunt's location around the world with any strange or suspicious attacks? The answer was no; Dave could find no way to track Hunt's comings and goings. But Dave discovered that it was possible to correlate the locations of Hunt's business operations with animalistic attacks on humans, almost always young women. As the sun set, Dave continued into the night.

By the early hours of the next morning, he was able to identify four occasions on which women had been attacked and mutilated in the same way the victims in Winter Haven had been attacked and killed. All of these attacks occurred within twenty-five miles of either a plant or factory that Charles owned, or where he had a significant investment. Was this a pattern, or was it a coincidence? The locations of the murders were diverse: Brazil, Russia, Poland, and Indonesia.

As he looked into the first case he had identified, the one in Brazil, he found that subsequent news coverage revealed that a suspect had been identified but was shot and killed by Brazilian police when they had attempted to apprehend them. The case in Russia had ended in much the same way. Police had identified a suspect, and when police arrived at the suspect's apartment, he had tried to run and was shot by the police and killed.

Dave was not able to determine what evidence the police had in their possession or how strong the case against either of these two individuals might have been. Since these individuals were now dead, there was no one interested in questioning evidence. The cases were simply identified as 'solved' and closed. Investigating these cases further would be difficult.

The case in Poland received significant news coverage, much of which had been sensationalistic. According to media reports, a young man identified as Victor Kowalski, had dressed like a wolf and, over the course of three months, killed four women. The women were between the ages of sixteen and twenty-one. Kowalski had lured his victims to isolated locations and then killed and mutilated them. None of the women had been sexually assaulted.

According to police, Kowalski had confessed to all of the murders. The defense, as one might expect, contended that Kowalski had been beaten until he confessed. The judge who presided over the case, however, determined that the confession was free and voluntary. Press reports also indicated that police had found a murder weapon and items belonging to two of the victims when they searched Kowalski's room. Ultimately, Kowalski was convicted and sentenced to life in prison.

The case is Indonesia presented the least amount of evidence of any of the cases. According to the scant media coverage Dave was able to locate, a drug-addicted Dutch national had been arrested for killing three women between the ages of twenty-one and twenty-nine. Apparently, he attacked these women wearing an 'animal costume' and then engaged in 'ritualistic mutilations'. There were three articles in Dutch newspapers that condemned the Indonesian government for executing this Dutch national. Apparently, he had been shot by a firing squad several months after the conviction.

By the time Dave completed his internet research, it was almost 5:00 a.m. He had a meeting at 10:00 a.m. with Ed and Shelley, and he thought he should get some more sleep before the meeting. He would need to talk to them about the next phase of his investigation. Dave thought he needed to travel to Brazil, Russia, and Poland to look into these murders himself. He was on the verge of cracking these cases wide open.

It was about three months from the start of the trial. Although that may seem like a long time, it is not. The crime of murder is not a complicated crime to prove. It requires the intentional death of a person. In the case of first-degree murder, it requires premeditation, meaning that the murder was planned in advance. There are only a few defenses to murder. These defenses are self-defense, lack of intent--the death was accidental--or the murder was committed by someone else.

From a technical standpoint, the defense has no obligation to present any evidence and can simply rely on the burden of proof. In every criminal case, the defense can simply argue that the government failed to prove its case beyond a reasonable doubt. However, the defense counsel who argues the burden of proof defense is termed a 'loser', and a defendant who relies solely on the burden of proof for his defense is called a 'convict'. In every case that goes to trial, the defense counsel must develop a 'theory of the defense'.

This is the theory that both explains the evidence in a case and leads the jury to the conclusion that the defendant is innocent. Defendants play a role in the formulation of the theory of the defense, but it is a surprisingly small role. He explains where he was and what he did. If the defendant knows anything about the victim or victims, he might be able to provide some insight into a victim that could be useful in formulating the theory of the defense.

If the defense is based upon accident or self-defense, the defendant plays a far larger role. The trial team met that morning to finalize the theory of the defense. It was to be a brainstorming session. Ed was the head of the trial team and he had called the meeting. There were issues unrelated to the case that needed to be addressed. Shelley and Dave had developed an intense dislike for each other. Part of it was a personality conflict.

Shelley had a difficult personality and tended to clash with everyone. Ed had taken over communications with the prosecutors because Shelley had insulted them on several occasions, and they refused to talk to her. Dave also had a prickly personality. In the years they had worked together, Ed had come to accept Dave's moodiness. Dave had graduated from college with lackluster grades. He joined the local police force, and for years talked about becoming a lawyer. It never happened.

Instead, he worked his way up the rungs of the hierarchy until the shooting incident, after which, he would tell people, he left because he couldn't stand the internal politics of law enforcement. Dave often said that he knew more about the law than most lawyers, and he expected his statements to be affirmed. Ed suspected that he actually harbored feelings of inferiority, and overcompensated for those feelings by pretending to know more about the law than he actually did.

Unfortunately, Shelley was not one to affirm anyone, let alone a retired local cop she considered to be a flunky. The relationship had deteriorated to the point where Dave would not talk to Shelley and Shelley would not talk to Dave. Instead, each complained to Ed about the other.

The meeting got off to a rough start. Ed had brought coffee and donuts to the meeting. Shelley made a joke about cops and donuts.

"Guys," Ed began, "we do not have a lot of time left until trial, and we have a lot to do. I can see you two don't like each other—"

Both interrupted simultaneously, each arguing that he or she had no problems with the other. Great, at least Ed had found a common point of agreement.

"Well," Ed said, "we'll skip that topic and get directly to the case. We have all of the discovery and we have all reviewed it. I asked Dave to head down to New York to investigate the fur coat and where it might have come from. Dave, why don't you start?"

Dave was pleased to have the stage. "Sure. I went down to New York and knocked on some doors, and I found the guy who made the fur coat. He made five of them. They were very expensive. There is no way Russ could have afforded them."

"Will the guy testify?" Shelley asked.

"He certainly will."

"The evidence against Russ comes mainly from the search…"

"The search the judge refused to suppress," Dave said as he looked at Shelley. Payback for the donut comment.

Ed continued before more comments could be exchanged. "We have the wolf suit, which maybe we can explain. We also have the steel jaws and the victim's jewelry in Russ' room. How do we explain that?"

"Either Russ is guilty, or he was framed. Obviously, we can't argue that Russ was guilty," Shelley said.

"If he was framed, then who framed him?" Ed asked.

"There were not too many people with opportunity. Russ lived in a room rented from Hunt. Hunt had the ability to buy the wolf suits. He could have framed him," Dave replied.

"Who else?" Ed asked. No other suspect came to mind, but a thorough investigation had not yet been conducted. He mentioned his thoughts about the manservant, Samuel. What did they know about him?

"Maybe it's not a 'who else' but a 'what else'. Let's go back to the beginning. The first murder. At that time, the authorities suspected some type of animal attack." Ed and Shelley were silent as Dave spoke. Dave looked directly at Ed. "You saw it. You saw what I saw."

"I'm not sure what I saw," Ed responded.

"What are you talking about?" Shelley asked. There was a dead silence in the room for several moments. Then Dave began to speak.

"The morning after the first murder, I was driving home from down south on Route 12. I stopped for some fresh air and walked back a short distance to one of the logging roads. I saw a large creature; I'm not really sure how to describe it. It was about seven feet tall, covered in dark hair, maybe black or dark brown or a mixture of both. It walked on two legs. When it saw me, it attacked."

"I drew my pistol and fired five shots into it before it went down. I shot it several times in the chest but those shots did not affect it. Finally, I shot it in the knee just to slow it down. It went down, and I turned and ran. Later, I came back with Ed, and he saw it, too. It was coming from the direction of the murder, and it was headed toward town."

Shelley spoke in a quiet voice. "What was it?"

"I don't know," was all Dave could say.

Ed, of course, had seen the creature, too, but he had seen it from a great distance. Even now, he was not sure what he had seen or how to describe it. In fact, he had tried to push the events of that day from his mind because the rational aspects of his intellect collided with the emotional and superstitious aspects of his emotions. He prided himself on his rational and fact-based worldview.

Ed was the next to speak. "You saw something miles from the murder scene. You don't know what it was. How can we argue that some unknown creature attacked and killed all of the victims when we can't even say what the creature was? How do we explain the wolf suit and the victims' jewelry that was found in Russ' room? We would have to argue that not only was there an unknown creature that attacked and killed all of the victims, but that the creature was intelligent."

"After killing these victims, the creature is able to hide, leaving no evidence behind that could prove its existence. It was also able to frame an innocent person for its crimes. Is there any chance that a seven-foot hairy monster could walk around town, as it would have had to do to plant evidence, without anyone seeing it?"

The comments and questions were not condescending, but real questions that would have to be answered. This would have been an excellent time for Shelley to belittle Dave. In fact, that was what both Dave and Ed expected, but Shelley said nothing. There was a reason why Shelley was not belittling Dave. She had seen something in town on the night of the murder. She wondered in her own mind if she had seen the same creature, but she was not yet ready to share her thoughts. Instead, she sat there and listened.

"Sometimes," Dave said, "truth is stranger than fiction. I have a theory." He waited a few heartbeats before jumping into his theory.

"All of the evidence can be explained if the creature that killed these women was a werewolf. He walks around town in human form and anyone who sees him, sees only another guy. On nights when he attacks, he takes the form of an animal and kills people as an animal would. He possesses human intelligence however, and therefore knows how to frame someone."

"The person he frames, in this case Russ, takes the blame for the murders and the creature's identity remains secret. He moves from location to location and no one ever even suspects his existence."

"I also think I know who the werewolf is. It's Hunt. I have been doing some checking, and I've found that he was attacked by a wolf in Europe. That's probably how he became a werewolf. Also, I've found a series of incidents where murders very similar to the ones we have here occurred around places where he had business interests."

"So, you are suggesting that the seven-foot monster is actually a shapeshifting human?" Shelly asked. There was no condescension or ridicule in her voice, which surprised both Ed and Dave. She seemed to actually be curious.

"Well, yes," Dave replied.

"I'm not sure how far we'd get with the judge arguing the existence of supernatural phenomena," Dave said. "I heard of a case once in Pennsylvania where the defense tried to use a self-defense argument, claiming that the victim was a witch. I also seem to remember a West Virginia case where the testimony was that a ghost identified the location of a murder victim's body. But I'm not sure we can argue that the real culprit to our crime is a werewolf. How could we prove such a thing even existed? It's the stuff of fantasy."

"But what if it's true?" Dave persisted. "What if the facts are that these women were murdered, and that the murderer was not human? Couldn't we prove that the murderer was some animal?"

"You mean like if the victims had been killed by a bear, couldn't we argue that a bear killed the victims?" Ed asked.

Shelley spoke up. "If a bear was the killer, we could clearly argue that the bear was the murderer, and the same rule would apply to a werewolf. If we could prove the werewolf existed, then maybe we could prove that the werewolf killed these women."

Ed looked at Shelley in disbelief. He had not expected her to support such an absurd theory. It was a circular argument. The problem was: How could they prove a werewolf existed? There was Dave's eyewitness account, but it was unlikely that a judge would even let it into evidence.

"Maybe there is a middle ground," Ed began. "There is a psychological condition known as clinical lycanthropy. A person who suffers from clinical lycanthropy believes he is a werewolf. He actually believes that he turns into a werewolf and then goes out to hunt and kill people. It is not uncommon for these people to mutilate and eat their victims."

"But," Dave interjected, "we saw the creature with our own eyes. You saw the creature, as well. It wasn't someone who thought he was a wolf—it was an honest-to-God werewolf."

"For now, at least, let's agree that it was something or someone other than Russ who committed the murder. Later, we can focus either on your theory or my theory as the evidence develops," said Ed.

As the meeting came to an end, Ed began to talk about assignments and how to proceed with the trial preparation going forward. There were some specific tasks that he wanted Dave to do, but Dave had other ideas.

"Ed," he began, "I've been doing some research on the internet, and I think I can establish a pattern of similar murders around the world committed by Hunt. I need to travel to Brazil, Russia, and Poland to look into murders in those cases that were committed within twenty-five miles or so of plants that Hunt-owned companies operate or control. I suspect I will be gone for three to four weeks, but this investigation could blow the case wide open."

Ed and Shelley were both intrigued. "Tell us about the murders," Ed said, inviting Dave to continue.

Dave began explaining his internet research and the animalistic nature of the attacks he discovered. It sounded promising.

As Dave spoke, Ed interrupted when there was a pause. "And none of these cases have been solved?" He asked.

"That's just it," Dave continued. "It's part of the pattern. All of the murders were solved. In Russia and Brazil, suspects were shot and killed. In Poland, a person was sentenced to life in prison. In Indonesia, a Dutch national was convicted and sentenced to death. Hunt committed the murders and then orchestrated the deaths or convictions of innocent people to close the case. I need to prove these people were innocent and set up by Hunt—who is a werewolf."

"Well," Shelley interjected, trying to be helpful. "Can you prove Hunt was in the locations when the murders occurred?"

"Not yet," Dave said. "But I think I can when I go to investigate. I'm telling you, this will blow the case wide open."

However, there was no way the judge would give the defense funds for an international investigation into homicides that had already been solved, and there was no way he would delay the trial to allow for the investigation of a werewolf theory. Ed wasn't even willing to ask. Dave left the meeting fuming.

Chapter 26

Later that night around 2:00 a.m., Shelley came face-to-face with the creature once more. She was walking back home from her favorite bar. As she passed the alcove where she thought she had seen the creature months before, she glanced to the side and saw the creature again. This time, she froze in fear. The creature stepped from the alcove and was fully illuminated by the light of the moon.

It stood seven-foot tall with bulging muscles in its arms and legs. Its chest was massive. The power in the creature was both frightening and mesmerizing at the same time. She looked in its black eyes and could feel it stare into her soul. It snarled, exposing its fangs, which were at least three inches long. Saliva dripped from its teeth. The low growl sent shivers down her spine.

She thought about running, or maybe screaming, but she could not. Her legs felt like concrete fixed to the ground. She wanted to scream but only air escaped from her throat. A thick coat of fur covered its whole body. The black fur was sleek and shiny, wet with sweat or something else, maybe blood. The smell was the worst. A strong musky smell mixed with the odor of decaying blood and flesh. It smelled of death.

In fact, everything about the creature pointed to death. It reached toward Shelley with its long arms. Claws sprung from its thick and blackened fingers. The hair on the arms was matted with dried blood. Shelley knew she was going to die. This was the first time she had ever experienced true fear in her life. Her death would not be peaceful. She was facing the end.

And then she woke up. Shelley was in her bed alone, her room completely quiet. It took several minutes before she realized that she'd had a dream—a nightmare, but still not real. Her racing heart began to slow down. Her sheets were soaked from sweat. After she realized she was safe, she began to relax, but every nerve in her body was tense. She thought back to Dave's statements about a large creature, a werewolf.

In the fog of the middle-night, she tried to reason through what she had learned that Dave and she had seen with their own eyes. What was a werewolf? Were they real? What should she do? Her normally astute reasoning skills were dulled by the chemicals that coursed through her brain in the middle of the night and she could not make sense of anything.

But her sheets and her bedclothes were soaked and she could not find a comfortable spot in the bed. Shelley got up and stripped off everything she was wearing. She normally slept with the bedroom window slightly open so that the temperature in the room was lower than the temperature in the rest of the house. Now naked, she shivered in the cold room. She grabbed a quilt from her bed and headed to the spare room to finish out the night.

That night was only the first. The next evening, she again fell asleep with the help of some pills and some bourbon, but the alcohol- and drug-induced haze that brought sleep did not save her. This time, she was alone in the forest. There was snow on the ground, and as she looked around to get her bearings, she spied a car parked in a desolate parking area on a seldom-used road.

She recognized the car as belonging to Cindy from the crime scene photos of her murder. Now, however, the car was intact, and Cindy sat in the driver's seat. The engine appeared to be off. She seemed to be looking for someone or something.

As Shelley watched in silence, she saw a large creature moving through the night toward the car. It was the same being, large and powerful. Its motions were effortless as it stalked the car. Shelley was an observer. She wanted to scream a warning to Cindy, but there was nothing she could do—no sound came from her mouth. The creature circled the car several times. Twice it came close to Shelley. It looked right at her and wrinkled its lips, exposing its fangs, but did not come closer to her. Once again, she was unable to run or even move.

Then the beast glided to the side of the car. With a single powerful jerk, it ripped the car door from the vehicle and sent it flying into the woods. With its other hand, it grabbed Cindy and pulled her from the car. It sank its teeth into the nape of Cindy's neck, and she screamed, her legs running in midair as the beast held her aloft. After tearing a large piece of flesh from Cindy's body, the beast grabbed her, sank its claws into her, and then literally tore her in two.

Cindy's body, or at least the pieces she could see, went limp. Her screams and cries fell silent. The beast let out a howl and shook the pieces of what had only moments ago been Cindy, throwing blood in every direction. Shelley felt the warm, wet blood her hit cheek. She looked down and saw the blood staining the shirt she wore in her dream.

When the beast was finished with Cindy, it began walking directly toward Shelley. She thought she would be next.

With all her strength, Shelley jumped from the spot where she had been stuck and fell from her bed. She sat on the floor, tangled in sheets, wondering how she could escape. It took a few minutes for her to realize it was a dream, but the realization gave her no comfort. She was again soaked in sweat, but this time, her panties and legs were wet. She could smell urine.

Shelley had wet herself for the first time since she was a child. It had all seemed so real. She washed herself and tried to fall back to sleep but couldn't.

Thereafter, night after night, the creature would return. Sometimes she saw it slinking around town. Sometimes she was in a forest, watching it attack other victims. The strangest thing about the dreams was the smell. She could never remember smelling anything in a dream before, but in these dreams, she smelled the creature as often as she saw him. It was a foul odor, a mixture of musk and decay mixed with blood and rotted flesh.

The thought of the smell during the day made her want to vomit. She was sure that she saw and smelled evil. She had never thought that true evil existed. Over the next couple of weeks, the number of pills she took and the amount of alcohol she drank increased steadily. Sometimes, she needed a drink in the morning to steady her, and then a different pill to pick her up. The only case she now worked on was Russ' case, but she knew she was letting the team down.

She was in charge of the legal research, but she performed very little actual research. Her teammates didn't notice because one can spend a lot of time researching without actually producing a work product. She couldn't talk to anyone at work about what she was going through. Whoever heard of a dream destroying a person? But it was.

She had no friends she could turn to, so she was left with the chemicals that seized control of larger and larger parts of her life. She supposed she might die of an overdose, or she could just swallow a bunch of pills one night and wash it down with a fifth or so of bourbon. It wouldn't be a bad way to go, would it? Her thoughts scared her, but not as much as the creature that stalked her dreams did.

Then, one night after observing the creature's mutilation of one of her friends from elementary school—in her dream, the girl was still of elementary school age—the creature spoke to her.

"You can end this," it said. "All you have to do is leave the case."

Chapter 27

Eleven Years Earlier

Charles Hunt had hunted all over the world. He had hunted lion and elephant in Zimbabwe. He had haunted Marco Polo sheep in the mountains of Mongolia. He was, therefore, looking for a new challenge when he attended a cocktail party in Manhattan. He went to the party thinking it would be the standard boring affair. After all, it was hosted by a classmate of his from Princeton, an individual of inferior breeding, who no doubt was seeking capital for a new investment he was pushing.

It was really only social grace that encouraged him to attend. He arrived a little after 9:00 p.m. and planned to stay for only an hour before heading out to someplace more interesting. At the party, however, he fell into conversation with a gentleman from the Balkans named Dmitri Romanski. It turned out that Romanski was a hunting consultant/outfitter from Macedonia, and before long, the conversation turned to big game in the Balkans.

At first, Charles was interested in hunting chamois, a smaller goat-like animal that usually lives high in the mountains. Charles had hunted another subspecies of the wild goat in Slovenia but he found that harvesting another one in Macedonia might be something he was willing to consider. Although Romanski offered hunts for the chamois, he steered the conversation toward wolf hunting. He explained that Macedonia had a large and growing population of wolves.

These wolves, he said, were decimating not only domestic livestock but also many of the wild animals of the region. He indicated that they had already taken a toll on the local red deer and roe deer populations, and were even reducing the populations of chamois and ibex in the remote mountain regions. Wolves, Romanski explained, were a far greater challenge than chamois or any other grazing animal because of their unique intelligence.

At first, Charles was unimpressed with the concept of wolf hunting. To him, hunting was about one thing, and one thing only. And that one thing who was securing the animal with the largest horns, antlers, or tusks of its species. Money was no object, and Charles was willing to put in the effort to harvest the largest animal possible, if that was necessary. Of course, hunting was not about the challenge of the hunt or the intelligence of the animal he was hunting.

It was about recording a 'trophy' and the photographs he could show to people. On one of his more recent hunts, he had shot a world-record Himalayan tahr in New Zealand. He liked to brag that he had shot the animal at an elevation of fourteen thousand feet and a distance of three hundred and fifty yards. The statement was technically true. What he failed to mention, however, was that he had actually taken a helicopter to the top of a mountain and walked across a mountain ridge for about two hundred and fifty yards before seeing the tahr.

He then fired nine shots at the animal before finally hitting it. Charles had left the base camp at 9:00 that morning and was back at the camp by 2:00 in the afternoon, in time to shower and have drinks before dinner. That, to Charles, was the definition of a successful hunt.

Wolves did not have horns, antlers, or tusks. They were very intelligent and difficult to hunt and, at the end of the hunt, there would be no 'trophy'. As he was about to conclude his conversation with Romanski, he remembered another recent conversation. Because of his station in life, he had decided to become a knight, and in order to become a knight, he had hired a consultant. There were several monarchs around the world that awarded knighthoods, but Hunt had set his sights on a British knighthood. The purchase of a knighthood was not legal, but it was not necessarily illegal, either. His application had hit an unforeseen hurdle, however.

Apparently, the royal family, and perhaps the new King himself, had become suspicious of the number of foreign applications for knighthood. In theory, the leaders of the two major parties would put forth the names of people to be knighted, and the King would accept the list without comment. In recent years, the list had included several corrupt Russian oligarchs who had simply spread money around the political establishment. Now, the King had apparently concluded that the politicians were cheapening the meaning of knighthood.

The consultant had recommended that perhaps it would be useful if Charles could add some sort of charitable work to his application. Charles was appalled. On one hand, he saw the problem associated with granting knighthoods to Russians, whom he viewed as inferior. He was Anglo-Saxon, however, and rich and powerful. His breeding and background entitled him to a knighthood.

He was also not one to share his fortune with the huddled masses or wretched refuse of humanity. They existed to serve the elite. But perhaps this wolf hunt could check the charity box.

"You say these wolves are dangerous and that they are killing the livestock on which the peasants live?" Charles asked.

"Yes," Romanski answered. The term 'peasant' was an offensive term no longer used in modern Europe, but he was willing to let it go for the sake of a sale. "These wolves kill the livestock of the rural population, many of whom exist at a subsistence level. Hunting the wolves would certainly be a humanitarian endeavor."

"And I've read that these wolves are dangerous and kill the villagers."

In reality, there were cases of wolf attacks in Europe and old stories of wolf predation on humans, but Romanski could not think of a single attack in Macedonia. However, if this rich American wanted to hunt man-eating wolves, then what was the harm of encouraging his fantasies? "Oh yes, these are dangerous animals. They have been known to devour women and children, especially in the depths of winter."

With that, the hunt was agreed upon. Charles would travel to Macedonia in a few months to hunt wolves. The King would understand his sacrifice in traveling to a third-world country to save the poor peasants from these wild and merciless creatures.

Macedonia in the winter is a cold and bleak place. Charles landed in Skopje, the capital of the small, landlocked country. It was definitely not up to his standards. The city itself was interesting if a bit odd. There were statutes everywhere. Most had a Hellenistic appearance and were dressed in robes more appropriate to a Mediterranean coast in the summer than the tunics real Macedonians would have worn in the cold winters of the Balkan Mountains.

Many of these statutes featured Alexander the Great, in various poses. Of course, Alexander the Great, never visited Skopje. It wasn't even founded until a couple of hundred years after Alexander's death. Charles Hunt didn't like the city. He was almost insulted by the statuary. To him, modern Macedonians were Slavs who had no connection to one of the greatest military leaders in history. Most countries have national heroes, but the fact that Macedonia reached back millennia to find a national hero seemed to emphasize the lack of recent accomplishments to celebrate.

An ancient Turkish fortress overlooked the city, further obscuring the country's European ancestry. The restaurants were inferior, and the accommodations were second rate. Furthermore, he was stuck in Skopje for four days. His initial itinerary called for only a single evening in the city.

The hunt itself did not start well. Romanski had arranged for a driver to pick Charles up in the morning following his arrival in Skopje and take him to the hunting lodge. He never arrived that day, and it was not until an afternoon three days later that his guide arrived in an old, beat-up Toyota of some sort to drive him to the hunting lodge. Charles took one look at the car and almost canceled the trip, but eventually, the guide was able to convince him to ride in the car. Charles rode in the passenger seat. His luggage rode in the back seat and the trunk.

The mountains were beautiful, but the road through the mountains was rugged and unkept. The sixty-mile drive took nearly three hours. It was still light when Charles arrived, unfortunately. The hunting lodge turned out to be even more disappointing than the Toyota. It was a one-story cinder block building with peeling paint on the outside. The inside of the building was dark, but an old wood stove warmed the interior.

There were a couple of light bulbs suspended from the ceiling by their electric cords, which illuminated the center of the main room to a degree, but light did not reach into the corners of the room. There was a bathroom and a bedroom, more appropriate to a youth hostel than a hunting lodge. An older, heavy-set woman greeted him as he entered the lodge. She directed him to a seat and almost immediately placed a bowl of some sort of wild boar stew in front of him.

It was not the five-star meal he had been promised. Then again, the fine Macedonian wine did not 'rival the best wines of France or Italy' as the brochure had said. He was hungry however, and ate what was set in front of him. In truth, he had eaten worse foods on other hunts, but not by choice.

The chauffeur/guide had carried his luggage into his room and, as Charles prepared for a good night's sleep, his guide told him he would return in a few hours to begin the hunt. As it turned out, wolves are mostly nocturnal and the best time to hunt them is by the light of a full moon. The moon would be full on this night, and the guide explained that it might be the best night to shoot a wolf.

At 10:30 that night, the guide arrived back at the lodge, bringing with him the rifle Charles was supposed to use together with a box of shells. Charles was pleasantly surprised to see that the rifle was a newer Sako, an excellent manufacturer of firearms located in Finland. It was chambered in 7 mm Remington Magnum, an excellent all-round American caliber. The rifle was topped with a ZEISS telescopic sight. All in all, a first-class rifle and outfit.

The guide explained that he would be dropping Charles off at a wolf stand that would be fully enclosed, except for a slot through which Charles could fire his rifle. The stand overlooked a meadow that was now snow-covered. The bright moon and white snow would highlight the wolves as they approached a dead sheep located in the meadow sixty yards in front of the stand. The guide recommended that Charles simply watch the first couple of wolves that came to feed on the sheep.

The smaller juvenile wolves would be the first to arrive, followed by females. The largest male wolves in the pack would not arrive until after the other wolves had begun eating. This was not a chivalrous act designed to ensure that the younger wolves were properly fed. Instead, the older wolves wanted to watch and make sure everything was safe before they left the cover of the forest. Once the largest wolves arrived, the guide told Charles to shoot whichever he preferred.

There was no limit to the number of wolves a hunter could shoot, and the guide told Charles he could shoot more than one wolf if he liked. Under no circumstances, however, was Charles to leave the hunting stand before the guide came to pick him up in the morning. And so, Charles went with the guide. To wait. For a wolf.

Chapter 28

It was cold that night, well below freezing. There was a slight breeze, but Charles could not feel the wind inside the stand. The structure was constructed of wood with barely enough room to move inside. He had entered through a small door in the back, which he had pulled shut and latched behind him. In the front of the stand was a slot about four inches in height that ran the breadth of the structure. He was sat about four feet above the ground with a view of a snow-covered field. He could see the dead sheep that had been placed in the field in the hope of drawing in a wolf.

Another man might have appreciated the moonlit scene, the high mountain peaks in the background, and the mixed pine and hardwood forest surrounding him. It would have been wrong to describe the light as daylight, but it wasn't dark, either. The glow of the moon provided enough light to illuminate everything for a hundred yards or so, but it provided no color. It was like watching a black and white movie.

Charles, of course, was focused on his own comfort and prone to complain under the best of circumstances. His hands were cold and he had temporarily lost feeling in his feet. He could feel the nip of the cold on his cheeks and nose. Charles deemed it too cold for man or beast, but he kept watch over the field. He thought that maybe the next night he would have the guide sit in the stand and shoot a wolf for him.

It would not have been sporting, but if no one knew, he didn't care. He had no innate sense of right and wrong. The hours passed but he saw nothing.

Finally, at about 4:00 a.m., Charles detected movement at the edge of the meadow. As he concentrated, he could see a single wolf standing frozen as it searched for danger. Other wolves materialized in his vision as he focused on the area surrounding the first wolf. Still, minutes passed without any of the wolves taking a single step into the clearing. Charles was no longer cold. That is how hunting is and always had been: hours of tedium punctuated by moments of excitement.

Ever since man's ice age ancestors had strapped a stone spearhead onto a straight ash pole to make a spear, it had been that way. In those days, it might have been weeks before the quarry was actually located—perhaps a mammoth. Once the prey was located, adrenaline would take over, driving the hunter to attack. For those who have never experienced the thrill of the hunt, there is no way to explain it. Hunters, however, from all ages and backgrounds shared a common experience.

Of course, there is rarely the danger of being killed by an animal in the modern world. Even if mammoths still existed, even the most inexperienced hunter would be able to bring one down from a distance of a couple of hundred yards with a heavy-caliber bullet. Modern firearms have created a safe cushion for the hunter, but the thrill of the hunt remains. The surge of adrenaline still remains. Even the sight of an average size buck can cause a new hunter to shake with anticipation.

Charles was feeling that surge of adrenaline now. He wasn't shaking but he was focused. The cold temperatures no longer bothered him.

These wolves were crafty. Half an hour passed as they stood motionless, frozen like statues, searching for any danger. Finally, one moved toward the dead sheep. Then another stepped into the clearing. Charles eased the rifle to his shoulder as slowly as he possibly could so he would not spook the wolves. As the rifle settled against his shoulder and he prepared to look through the scope, a movement at the edge of the forest redirected his focus. He shifted the scope to get a better look.

At the edge of the forest was a wolf of unusual size. It was much larger than wolves are supposed to be. It also appeared to be standing on its hind legs. It had a long snout like a wolf. Charles could make out the beady eyes and the pointed ears. He lowered the crosshairs to the animal's shoulder. Although a shot to the head would be fatal, it was easier to hit an animal in the heart and lung area.

By shooting for the shoulder, the bullet would break the large bones in irs front legs that it used to run. After passing through the shoulder, the bullet would enter the lung cavity expanding as it went. Even if the shot were not immediately fatal, it would be fatal in minutes.

Charles took a breath and held it. The crosshairs were centered low on the shoulder. Slowly, he squeezed the trigger. The rifle went off almost by surprise, the crosshairs still centered on the target. There was an explosion of activity as the other wolves raced for the safety of the forest and then ran to put as much distance as they could between themselves and the rifle shot.

Before Charles let out his breath, the bullet had already struck the animal. In the faded light, Charles thought that he saw the wolf spin and fall. The guide had emphasized that no matter what, Charles was to remain in the stand until the guide arrived after sunrise. Charles was no amateur however, and he had to see his trophy immediately. He marked the animal's location in his mind. There was a sloped tree at the edge of the forest, and the wolf had fallen about ten yards beyond the tree.

It was light enough for him to see the ground. After checking to make sure his rifle was safe, he unlatched the rear door and slid from the stand, took the couple steps to the ground, and then started walking to his trophy.

The animal had been about hundred yards away, and it took him only a couple of minutes to walk to the sloped tree where the wolf had been when he fired. When he looked at where he thought his trophy had fallen, he was surprised to see nothing. Surely, he had hit the wolf but it was too dark to see a blood trail in the dead leaves on the forest floor. He decided to wait there at that spot until it became light enough to trail the animal.

It could not have gone very far. As Charles fantasized about the articles that would be written about him in various hunting magazines about his world-record wolf, someone or something seized him from behind and lifted him off the ground. It tossed him against a tree like a rag doll. His rifle flew from his shoulder and he heard it clatter against some rocks to his right. He was momentarily stunned as the beast walked toward him on two legs.

In the fear that gripped him, Charles didn't know what to do. Should he get up and run? Should he try to find his rifle and fight? Instead, he just lay there on the ground, waiting.

The beast was not a wolf. It stood well over seven feet tall. Its facial features appeared to be those of a wolf but its arms were thickly muscled. Its fingers ended in claws rather than fingernails. It was covered in thick gray hair, dried blood caked around its mouth and neck. As it drew closer, Charles could feel its hot breath and smell the putrid stench of death. It reached down and grabbed Charles again, lifting him completely off his feet and bringing him close.

It was then that Charles remembered his knife. He had never used it before. It was more of an affectation to make him feel more like a real hunter. He unfastened the safety strap that held the knife in place and slowly drew the knife from its sheath. As the beast's teeth closed on Charles' shoulder, he could feel them biting into his flesh.

In one quick movement, he drove the knife deep into the animal's stomach. It roared in agony. With all of its strength, it again threw Charles twenty feet or more. This time, Charles's head connected with the truck of a tree and he was knocked unconscious.

Chapter 29

While in the grip of the beast, Charles did not believe he would live to see another day. He was, therefore, surprised when he awoke with the worst headache he had ever had. He had expected, if he ever awoke, that the beast would be standing over him, waiting for him to come to so that Charles would be conscious when the beast tore him apart.

Instead, Charles awoke in a small shack heated by a roaring fire. He was drenched in sweat. He lay on straw covered with blankets with some other blankets placed over him. Three days had passed since his encounter in the forest. Three elderly men stood over him. They were engaged in an animated conversation in Macedonian. It was probably good that he could not understand them.

"You know there is only one way to deal with this. He was bitten by the *Vrkolak*. If the bite of the *Vrkolak* is not fatal, we must cut the head off the victim, bury it in an iron box, and then burn the body," the oldest of the three said.

One of the other men nodded in agreement. "The legend says that the righteous die from the bite. Only the truly evil survive, and then they themselves become a *Vrkolak*. This man is not pure of heart. If we do not kill him and dispose of his body in the old way, then he will become a powerful *Vrkolak*. We must do it soon."

They spoke in calm voices, as if they were discussing what to have for dinner. Charles tried to follow the conversation but could not understand anything they were saying. He assumed they were talking about his medical treatment.

Finally, the third man spoke. "My friends," he said, "this man is not from here. He is an American, and I doubt the Americans will understand if we cut off his head and burn his body. If he were Macedonian, then your course of action would be wise. But for us to take such action against someone who is not of our own could create even greater problems. If the Americans are provoked by the death of one of their citizens, they might do worse things to us than another *Vrkolak* could."

The conversation see-sawed back and forth for the better part of an hour, but no consensus emerged. Finally, the oldest one spoke again. "We must kill him in the required way. It is the only way to be sure. My axe is outside, and it will only take one blow to sever his head. If we do not do it soon, it will become much more difficult. It grows stronger by the hour."

Of course, Charles did not feel stronger by the hour. To the contrary, he felt as though he had been run over by a freight train. Every part of his body hurt. It didn't feel like it would ever get better. He wondered what the old men were talking about, and gradually grew annoyed when he was not offered something to eat or drink.

It was at this point that Romanski entered the room.

"Romanski," the oldest one said, "he has been bitten by a *Vrkolak*, and is on his way to becoming one. We must cut off his head, place it is a steel box, and bury it." He pointed to a steel box in the corner. Charles and everyone else looked to the corner. Charles wondered what the box had to do with anything. "Then we must burn his body."

"What's he saying?" Charles asked Romanski in English.

"Oh, these are just old superstitious men who believe in treating wounds with herbs and casting spells. Much of what they say makes no sense." Romanski then turned to the old men and spoke in Macedonian.

"You are truly senile. This man is an American—a rich American with connections. Besides, this is the twenty-first century. You can't go around lopping people's heads off. You would be arrested as criminals and executed yourselves. Besides, the *Vrkolak* is a myth. It doesn't exist."

"It does exist," said one of the men in a rising voice. "When I was a boy, there was a *Vrkolak* in this region. It killed dozens of people. Everyone was scared. No one wanted to go out at night. Finally, it was captured by a group of priests. I saw it. It was a man transformed into a wolf. As it snarled and struggled to break its chains, a friend of my father's cut off its head with an axe. Its head was buried in a steel box and its body was burned. There was another, which my father told me about from when he was a boy…"

Romanski grew frustrated. "No one is going to cut off his head. We are going to nurse him back to health, and then we are going to send him on his way. You sound like barbarians from the Middle Ages. Even if the Vrkolak is real, it's not our problem. He will be back in the United States thousands of miles from here."

He then turned to Charles.

"My friend, you are brave if somewhat foolish. We told you to remain in the stand. Wolves are dangerous animals. We were able to tell that you shot a very large wolf. When you went to retrieve it, you were attacked by another wolf, apparently from behind. It bit you on the shoulder, and you killed it with a knife. Both animals are in the cold storage. They will make excellent mounts and even better stories."

In reality, when the guide had discovered Charles, he was unconscious and bleeding badly. There were no signs of the wolf he shot. His bloody knife lay beside his body, but there was no evidence that a wolf had been killed with the knife. Under Romanski's direction, several locals found and killed two wolves. After one of the wolves had been brought back to the lodge, Romanski had stabbed it with Charles's knife, giving the impression that Charles had killed it. Hopefully, Charles would not remember what happened and go along with the story.

"I'm not sure," Charles began. "I remember shooting a wolf, but then something large grabbed me from behind. It was at least seven feet tall, covered with hair. I remember it had hands with claws on them, and it threw me." He paused for a minute. Then he continued: "I know it sounds crazy."

Romanski chuckled. "We have no Bigfoot, no Yeti, in Macedonia. Nothing like what you describe inhabits our forests. You have been suffering from a fever, and I think that maybe the fever has influenced your memory. It was dark and cold. Things must have happened quickly. I am sure that a wolf attacking you from behind must have been traumatic. I can assure you that a giant animal did not attack you."

On its face, Charles had to admit that his story sounded crazy. Maybe it was a dream, or a nightmare, that had bled over into his memories. Reluctantly, he agreed with Romanski and settled back to his bed to fall asleep. He was feeling better already.

Meanwhile, Romanski arranged to stay with Charles through the night. The next morning, they would leave for Skopje, and from there, Charles would head back to the United States. Romanski's real fear was that someone would enter the lodge during the night with an axe and remove Charles' head.

Chapter 30

Charles returned from Macedonia a changed man, or maybe no longer a man. With each passing day, he grew stronger. After he fully recovered, he continued to grow stronger, and his senses became sharper. He felt younger and more handsome. He believed that his intelligence was growing. Charles had grown up as a scion of a blue-blood family, a graduate of Princeton, Yale, and then Oxford. To say that he was born with a silver spoon in his mouth would have greatly understated his wealth and privilege.

Family history held that the younger son of a noble family had migrated to Louisiana during colonial times. They had carved a plantation from the forests and swamps of the Louisiana frontier and joined the ranks of the early American aristocracy. That was the family history, and Charles was the only child of his generation. He was rich when born, but he was worth more than half a billion dollars when his father died.

As is usually the case, family myth was more palatable than reality. In the early days of the American Republic, Charles' ancestor was a maid working in the house of English baronet. After becoming pregnant, perhaps to the baronet, she stole the family silver and jumped a ship to Philadelphia. She gave birth to a son and worked as a maid for a Philadelphia merchant, a man named Hiram Hunt. Eventually, Charles' ancestor and the merchant were married. Hiram Hunt adopted her child.

Later, the merchant passed away, and the child inherited the merchant's wealth in addition to his name. That was Charles I. Charles later became involved in politics, and was able to use his political connections to obtain lucrative government contracts. Of course, the cheaper the contracts could be filled, the greater the revenues that flowed into the family coffers. Each generation became more corrupt than the last.

Charles II increased the family fortune five-fold by supplying defective armaments to the U.S. Army and Navy during the Civil War. Thousands of

Union soldiers died as a result of his corruptions, and there was talk of investigation and maybe even criminal prosecution. It was in the years immediately after the Civil War that the Louisiana Hunts actually made the move to Louisiana. Charles II purchased miles of land from bankrupt plantation owners and then promptly died.

Charles III stumbled upon sharecropping as a means of increasing family wealth. Recently freed slaves, lacking sophistication, entered into contracts with the Clark family where the family would receive sixty percent of all profits. The problem was that all costs were imposed on the sharecropper. All equipment had to be purchased from the Hunt family-owned stores. So, each year when accounts were settled, the sharecropper would be deeper in debt, and the Hunts would be richer.

Having embraced his new homeland, Charles III would frequently turn to the Ku Klux Clan whenever a particularly difficult sharecropper would start to talk about the unfairness of the financial arrangements. Dozens of troublesome individuals were buried on Hunt land.

It was Charles IV who greatly increased the family wealth when oil was discovered in the first decade of the twentieth century on Hunt property. The land the family had purchased for peanuts half a century earlier now produced money faster than a printing press. Since then, no one in the family had to work. Instead, each successive generation focused more on its own comfort. No desire went unmet.

The current iteration, Charles VII, was a narcissist or perhaps a sociopath. People meant nothing to him, except, of course, as a means of serving him. That was before his return from Macedonia. Things were different for Charles when he returned from Europe. As the weeks passed, he felt a new compulsion, a compulsion to hunt and to kill. And at times, he could feel his body transform. He would become taller and stronger. Hair would grow on his body and claws would spring forth from his fingers. His muscles felt like they were as strong as steel.

He could run faster than a horse and jump to the roof of a house with ease. He felt like the creature that attacked him in Macedonia. He was transformed, and he enjoyed the transformation. However, the transformation was only temporary and, after a few hours, he would fall asleep only to awake in human form. He would wake up naked, usually way out in the forest.

At first, Charles thought he was dreaming, but the presence that lurked inside him was real and ever-present. He knew it was no dream. He welcomed the presence and the transformation. He was the creature, and the creature was him. The transformation brought with it an intense feeling of malice. It wanted only to kill. And so it was that after a few months back in Louisiana, Charles decided to let the creature have free rein. He would go out, and he would kill.

He had no particular victim in mind, nor even a location to search for victims. Once the sun went down, he would leave and go wherever he felt like going. The night he decided to grant the creature free rein marked another major milestone in his journey.

The affliction that Charles suffered, as the elders in Macedonia recognized, kills most people. Almost everyone has the capacity to kill another person, but it is a difficult, soul-wrenching thing to do. Most people have feelings of sympathy, empathy, and mercy. The introduction of a malevolent force into the psyche of most people results in internal turmoil that will normally lead to their deaths. There are some people who do not understand sympathy, empathy, or mercy, except as signs of weakness.

To these people—sometimes called narcissists or sociopaths—other people are merely objects created solely for their pleasure. The death of another human being is of absolutely no consequence to them. Charles had always been one of these people. To him, other people were a means to an end. Nothing more. He had grown up in his life of privilege focused solely upon himself. He had never married because he never wanted to be with anyone that long. Women satisfied a certain physical need, but after that, they became wearisome.

He had been brought up with the faux manners of the Southern aristocracy, and so he was able to display a surprising amount of charm. He also studied the feelings other humans showed each other and, although he did not personally experience any of these feelings, he learned how to mimic them and deploy them in order to achieve his goals. He could, therefore, ruthlessly feign love to a woman or friendship to a man. He could come across as caring and compassionate, but did so only when it would lead to something he wanted.

The introduction of the beast, therefore, did not cause any internal conflict, and the damage and death he was about to bring to the world were consistent with what he had always been.

On that night years ago, Charles traveled through the night effortlessly and silently. His travels took him to a small, rural, African-American settlement about five miles from his estate. As he studied the houses, and with his enhanced sense of smell and hearing, he listened to the activities occurring inside the homes of the hamlet. Then he heard two girls walking toward their homes. They were still about a mile outside town. It didn't matter to him but the girls were returning from a church camp.

It was pitch black outside. The swamps and the forest left a slightly musty smell on the almost non-existent breeze. He followed the girls for a couple of hundred yards but they never suspected his presence. As they laughed and talked about the things fifteen- and sixteen-year-old girls talk about, he sprang for the forest onto the road, landing about ten feet in front of them. The terror in their eyes was beautiful. He could smell their fear as they stood frozen in front of him.

He emitted a low growl just to heighten the fear. The feeling he was experiencing now was powerful, far better than any sex he had ever had.

Both girls were quivering. Tears started to run down the cheeks of one teenager. In a movement so fast it could hardly be detected by the human eye, he reached out with his claws and tore the throat out of the one girl. Blood sprayed from her throat as she reached for the laceration with her hand. The blood soaked her yellow dress and sprayed her friend's white shirt. She stood for a moment, dead, before she fell to the ground.

Charles sensed that the other girl was about to run. In a flash, he seized her and sank his fangs into her neck with such force that he tore her head completely from her body, a pleasant and powerful sensation that brought immense joy. Tearing a head from a torso was something he would do again and again in the future. Both victims were dead now but he pulled them into the woods and took his time tearing up the bodies and eating parts of them. It was the best night of his life.

Later, when Charles finished, instinct took over and told him that he needed to dispose of the bodies. Carefully, he gathered everything into a pile, then carried the body parts to a nearby bayou, where he tossed them into the water. Alligators and other scavengers would make short work of the remains. Charles headed back toward his estate, satiated for now but looking forward to his next hunt. It was still dark when he climbed back into his bedroom window.

Chapter 31

The small settlement located so close to Charles's mansion proved to be a productive and convenient hunting ground. Over the next six months, nine young women and one young man disappeared from the village and the area immediately surrounding the village. Lately, however, he had started to sense a change in the settlement. Twice he had ventured out and found no one walking along the lanes surrounding the village. On his last successful hunt, he had to snatch a girl from her backyard and carry her off into the bush.

Then, about a week ago, he had been lurking around the village when he heard the sound of a gunshot and felt several buck shot hit his arm and shoulder. They tore into his muscles, causing extensive pain. He never saw or heard the hunter; the only way he knew of the hunter's presence was from the shot that was fired. He ran quickly from the gunshot, hearing two more shots in rapid succession, but no more pellets hit him. It was a sign that he had become too complacent.

At first, he didn't know how serious his injuries were, but when he got home and was able to look at them in a mirror, he could see they were quite serious—although by now, there was very little bleeding. He couldn't go to a physician or a hospital. How could he explain buckshot in his arm and shoulder? Within an hour, the pain was gone. Within six hours, his body had expelled the buckshot from the wounds. Three days later, the wounds were nearly healed. He was not immortal but he learned that his body could endure severe injuries.

Now, something else unexpected happened. He received a visit from the Parrish Sheriff—actually from two detectives from the Parrish Sheriff's office. As his body was healing, one Tuesday morning, a black sedan drove up his mansion. One of his servants informed Charles that two police detectives wished to see him. He directed the servant to have the detectives wait for him in the study. He then made them wait for half an hour before going to see them.

He was a generous supporter of the elected sheriff and thought he should have received a courtesy call before the detectives arrived. When he called the sheriff on his cell phone, the sheriff professed to know nothing of the visit and assured Charles that his men would not disturb Charles in the future without a very good reason.

When he was ready, Charles walked to the study and met the two men with feigned graciousness.

"To what do I owe this unexpected pleasure?" He asked.

The younger of the two men began to speak. "Sorry, Sir," he said, seeming genuinely sorry, "but we are investigating some missing persons in this area, and we are canvassing the neighborhood to see if anyone might know anything."

"Missing persons?" Charles asked.

"Yes, Sir. Over the past few months, we have received reports that nine young women have gone missing. And one young man, as well. We thought we would stop by and see if you know anything."

"Do you have any idea what might have happened to them?"

"No, not yet. They seem to have all vanished without a trace. All of the missing kids are between sixteen and nineteen. Most of the time when people that age disappear, they are runaways. Sometimes they come back. Sometimes they are never seen again. All of the missing kids are black and, as I said, all but one was male."

"What makes you think that I might know something?" Charles asked. He was trying to see if there was a reason for him to worry.

"Oh, Sir, we don't think you necessarily know something, but we have to be thorough in our investigation."

"I understand," Charles responded. "Obviously, I don't associate with any of the local citizens," he said derisively. "Especially not teenage African-American girls. I'm sorry, but I can't help you." He thought for a second, and then continued:

"If you think it would help, I could offer a reward—anonymously, of course."

The two detectives thanked him for his generosity and indicated they would let him know if a reward was going to be considered. They then apologized again for bothering him. He escorted them to the front door and they left. As they drove down the driveway, he thought about the events of the last couple of days—the gunshot to his arm and shoulder, and a visit by the police. It had been a good run locally but he had been careless.

He had traveled to the same general location too many times. Someone had shot him on his last visit to the hunting ground. Whoever shot him had also most likely seen him. Now the police were looking into the disappearances of his victims. They had no bodies and no clues, and they never would. The fact that they were investigating set off warning bells, however. He would have to find another hunting ground, and he would have to be more careful.

Charles's brush with the law, if you could call it that, made him realize that he needed to be more careful. He was never really in any danger. The detectives who visited him were simply checking a box to make sure they canvassed the area. When they returned to headquarters, they learned that 'troubling' Mr. Hunt with something he clearly knew nothing about was a bad idea. Charles had never been a suspect, and after the detectives were chewed out by the sheriff, Charles would never hear anything else about the case.

But still, he needed to be more careful. His days of hunting close to home were over. From now on, he would pick other locations far away from where he lived. His family had built a business empire that spanned the globe. Although he served as the Chairman of the Board and owned all of the stock in several corporations, he never actually did anything, relying instead on professional managers to make sure his endeavors were actually profitable.

These corporations, however, gave him cover to travel. He would focus upon locations where law enforcement was corrupt or ineffective. He would visit these locations but stay for only a short period of time. There were two other important components to the plan.

First, the victims would have to be throwaway people, people that would not be missed, or at least would not be missed by anyone who cared. The poor, the despised, and disadvantaged—these would be his victims. No one cared if a young African-American girl disappeared, as he had already found out. There are throwaway people everywhere in the world; he just needed to make sure that his victims came from the right class of people.

People with wealth and connections were to be avoided at all costs. When the daughter of immigrant parents dies, only her family weeps. If a daughter of the rich and powerful goes missing, the vast resources of governments, as well as the family's own wealth, can be brought to bear on the case. These realities dictated that Charles avoid those families that might actually hurt or kill the suspect. Instead, he would focus only on the disadvantaged. It was a matter of survival.

The other aspect of his plan involved covering his tracks. After he killed a limited number of people—four was his target number—he would need someone who could take the blame for his murders—a patsy. Whenever he went to a new place, he would first identify his victims. Then he would find someone he could saddle with the guilt for his crimes. It seemed dangerous to him to leave a series of unsolved murders in his wake, even if the victims were people no one cared about.

These murders needed to be solved, and they needed to be solved in a manner that shifted guilt from him to someone else. This person would also need to be a throwaway person—a male that the police would believe was guilty and who would not be able to afford an attorney who could defend him.

Chapter 32

Charles Hunt decided to test his new plan with a visit to Brazil. His research indicated that the Brazilian National Police in the city of São Paulo, where one of his corporations had a small manufacturing plant, were undertrained and underfunded. There were also allegations of corruption in the office covering the area where he intended to hunt. The corruption had benefits, but Charles Hunt was not going to attempt to bribe anyone.

He wouldn't need to. A corrupt organization is an ineffective organization. Charles reasoned that promotions would be premised more on payment and less on competence. It was this lack of competence that made Brazil a good place for Charles to put his new plan into action.

São Paulo is one of the largest cities in the world, a place of vast contrasts. It has some of the most elegant restaurants and clubs anywhere, places where the beautiful, the rich, and the famous went to see and be seen. Just blocks away were the poor and powerless, people who lived by begging and eating the scraps of society. They lived in cardboard homes without running water or indoor plumbing. Sewage ran down the sides of the dirt streets.

People also threw their trash into these same ditches. In the tropical climate of the region, the smell of human excrement, rotted meats, and decay mingled in an indescribable assault on the nostrils. Police rarely entered these areas. Crime was high and murders common; investigations were few and convictions fewer still. The beast that lived within Charles smelled the fear and opportunity in this city.

Werewolves were a common feature of American and European horror films. In the movies, the full moon would summon an uncontrollable transformation in the beast. The reality was very different. The beast was always there, and Charles was always there. Charles could switch from one to the other almost at will by now. He could also resist the transformation, usually with little effort. Charles enjoyed the beast. He enjoyed his power and ruthlessness. Their relationship was symbiotic.

After an afternoon of tours of one of his investments, and dinner at one of the finer restaurants with several of his key managers in the country, Charles turned in for an early evening. His suite overlooked a darkened street. As the minute hand on the clock passed midnight, he stripped and allowed the transformation to take place. He felt the power flow into his arms and legs. He felt a coat of hair cover his body. Claws grew from his fingers and a snout grew from his face as large teeth sprang from his jaws.

More significant than the physical transformation was his heightened senses. His vision was sharper, and he could hear a human heart two city blocks away. His sense of smell was even more sensitive. Like a bloodhound, he could track a particular human being for miles, even if the trail were cold.

Once the transformation was complete, he opened the window and dropped from his darkened bedroom into the ink black of the streets to begin his hunt. He would return through this same window in a few hours.

He quickly made his way through the better part of the city until he found the slum he was looking for. He sniffed the air. Though it stank to the human nose, he was able to separate the hundreds of odors, and picked a particular smell to hunt down. The victim was a young woman, fifteen or sixteen years old. There was a certain innocence to her smell. The creature's heart quickened as he began the hunt.

The victim had no idea she was being hunted. She lived in a better residence than most—a single room she shared with two brothers and two sisters. It was a small room but it was in a building. Her parents had long since vanished. That night, she went to visit a cousin who lived about a hundred feet down the street. She decided to make the visit because she was bored.

The beast followed her scent, first to her room, where he was able to discern that she had stayed there for some time before leaving and was now located in another residence. He could hear her heartbeat, the light and quick beat of a young women's heart. As he concentrated more, he could hear her breath enter and exit her lungs. The Portuguese language she spoke was indecipherable to him but her words were melodic. He imagined she spoke of love or some other juvenile emotion.

The excitement built as he imagined what would happen when she left. His own heart started to race as he anticipated her terror. But it seemed like it took forever for her to leave. All the while, he stood silently, waiting motionlessly in the shadows. It was the life of the predator—hours of waiting before a sudden and violent attack.

And then she left.

She was small, no more than five feet tall, no more than ninety pounds. She walked as if she had not a fear in the world. He followed her for about a block, waiting for just the right moment.

When the moment was right, he sprang from the shadows and landed a mere four feet in front of the girl. Her happiness evaporated, replaced by the terror he craved. Her eyes grew wide and her bowels loosened as she smelled the creature's foul breath. She inhaled, preparing to scream, but before she could fully inhale, the creature reached over and tore the trachea from her throat. The swipe severed her jugular vein and carotid artery.

Blood poured from her throat as she reached for the wound. A second later, her head was completely torn from her body and he pulled the remnants of the corpse back into the shadows where he continued to feast on her. When he was done, he picked up a locket that lay in a pool of blood and took it with him back to his hotel room.

It had been a glorious night.

Over the next three weeks, three more murders followed. Each was similar to the first. As Charles suspected, the horrific nature of the crime did attract police attention, but there wasn't even a story in the local paper. He thought about continuing his killing spree; it was easy. Ultimately, however, he decided not to deviate from the schedule he had previously set. Four deaths. Now it was time to put the remainder of his plan into action.

As he murdered women at night, Charles searched during the day for a suitable suspect to take the blame for the murders. He settled on Raul, a simple-minded mechanic who worked at the factory where Charles had been spending his time. Raul was a giant of a man, well over six feet tall with powerful arms. He had suffered a traumatic injury in his youth that had arrested his mental development at about the level of a ten-year-old. That same accident had crushed several of his facial bones.

Inadequate medical treatment left him scarred and deformed. Although gentle and harmless, he appeared dangerous and menacing. He was perfect for the remainder of Charles' plan.

To frame Raul, Charles had one of his employees report Raul to the local National Police station for the theft of cash from the company. The police officer who arrived was a full head shorter that Raul. When the police officer directed Raul to empty his pockets, several pieces of bloody jewelry fell from his pockets.

Raul looked confused as the officer reached for the jewelry. Someone—no one could remember who—later whispered, "I bet that's the jewelry from those dead girls."

Both Raul and the officer were afraid. The officer reached for Raul to handcuff him. Raul tossed the officer across the room. Knowing that he was no match for Raul, the officer drew his pistol and fired three quick shots into Raul's chest from a distance of six feet. Raul was dead before he hit the ground.

From that point, the investigation moved quickly. The police were able to determine that the jewelry in Raul's pocket belonged to some of the victims. Raul's attack on the police confirmed his guilt. Because of his death, there would be no more investigation and no trial. A press release carried by all of the papers reported the death of a serial killer, killed by police as they attempted to arrest him. The police report noted that he had the blood-soaked jewelry from two of the victims with him at the time of his death.

The animalistic attacks and strange hair recovered at the scene were soon forgotten and ultimately lost. So, too, was the statement of a local drunk who had described a giant upright walking dog-like creature, at least seven feet tall, walking from the scene of one of the murders.

The plan had worked flawlessly.

Chapter 33

Four to six times every year, Charles would travel to new locations around the globe to 'hunt', as he called it. Almost always, this would involve trips to locations associated with his various business interests, but occasionally, he would hunt in a location where he had no connection, no real reason for visiting. Often times, he picked these locations on a whim, but no matter where he went, his plan worked in the same way, with one exception. It jarred his sense of reality—his new sense of reality anyhow—where he was all-powerful.

There was a small village in Guatemala, a speck on a map, unknown or forgotten by anyone important. San Miguel was the name of the town, an ancient town that began its existence hundreds of years before the Spanish conquest of the region. Its inhabitants were still largely Native American, and most still spoke the language of their Mayan ancestors. The town was cut off from any roads by a steep mountain range. There was a path that many in the region called a 'jeep trail' that led from the main road to the village deep in the jungle.

Charles had visited this village years before while hunting jaguars. At the time, and even to the present, jaguars were a protected species in Guatemala, as they were everywhere in the Americas, and both federal law and international treaty prohibited Americans from killing or possessing jaguars. The laws of Guatemala also prohibited the hunting or killing of jaguars, but Charles wanted one. Laws frequently bend for the ultra-rich, and Charles fell into that category.

By spreading enough money around, he was able to find out that Guatemala had a healthy population of jaguars. Jaguars are not actually 'endangered', but no country in their range has prepared the necessary studies to prove populations sufficient to allow sport hunting. Throughout their range, estimates of jaguar populations vary greatly, usually without any scientific basis.

His hunt was successful, but it was the town of San Miguel that interested him more. It had a certain appeal to him, although he could never tell exactly why. With his newfound powers, he decided to visit San Miguel again to hunt. His quarry this time would not be jaguars or any other animal; this time, it was humans he sought. He remembered a healthy population of younger women, teenagers mostly.

He knew there was no effective police force. In fact, there was almost no police force at all. It would be a beautiful place to try his skills.

The first night in town, he started his hunt earlier than usual. Darkness arrived a little after 7:00 p.m., and his hunt started at about 8:00. This time, his suite was on the ground floor. Once he transformed to the creature, he slid out the bedroom window into the night. The moon was full but the tropic jungle created a level of moisture that clung to the ground, obscuring the moonlight.

He immediately caught scent of a girl about fourteen years old. She had the same sweet and innocent smell of other girls he had killed. He tracked her to the Catholic church, the oldest and largest building in this ancient town. The creature had slight trepidation about hunting in a populated area, but he could move silently in the shadows. People would walk within feet of where he stood and never see him—unless he wanted them to.

He found a nook between two buildings about a block from the church and waited for her to leave. As he waited, he savored the anticipation.

It was just after 9:00 p.m. when the girl left to begin her journey home. She was small, as he had anticipated, and dressed in rags. As he followed from a distance, she left the village proper and began walking on a trail through the jungle to her home somewhere in the distance. The creature knew she would never make it. Never again would she see her mother or her two brothers. Her life would be snuffed out in an instant of terror.

His senses told him there were no other humans in the vicinity. Perhaps he would let her scream so that he could hear the terror in her voice.

Silently but swiftly, he made his way around her and found the perfect place for the ambush. It was a wide spot in the trail. He crouched behind a large tree and waited. Moments later, he heard her footsteps about ten feet away. He sprang from his hiding place and landed squarely in front of her.

But then something very strange happened.

She just stood there and looked at him. Her heart did not race and he could tell she had no fear of him. No matter. It was a little bit disappointing that there was no bloodcurdling scream, no physical reaction at all, but she would die just the same. He would still enjoy the smell of her blood and the taste of her flesh.

As he looked, however, he saw something else. Just behind her was another being, something he could not smell and had not detected before. It was humanoid in form but not human. It stood a foot taller than the beast, with an immensely powerful chest and huge arms. A sword hung from its belt. It had form but was at the same time translucent. Its arms were folded across its chest. Its eyes, brighter than the sun, bore directly into him.

This being stood over the girl but said nothing.

For the first time since the creature had fused with Charles, he felt fear. Not trepidation about being caught. Not a momentary worry that he might be seen, but real fear. He knew without doubt that this creature could and would kill him.

All thoughts of his intended victim disappeared, and it was the creature that fled quickly through the night to the relative safety of his hotel. As he retook human form, he tried to reason though what he had seen. No explanation came to mind.

This might be surprising in view of the transformation into an unknown creature he himself had become, but Charles Hunt did not view himself as a 'werewolf'. He believed that the condition he experienced had existed since the beginning of time, completely misunderstood by science. Perhaps it was a virus or some other unknown microbe that caused the transformation, he didn't know.

He was aware of the ancient stories of werewolves and other shapeshifting legends—well, he knew they were not legends now—but he realized that these were myths created by ancient man to explain the condition he now experienced. These legends were based upon real life experiences. He was proof of that. But over the centuries, as evidence of shapeshifting beings never materialized and the truth behind the myth was lost, only myth remained. In Charles's own mind, however, his existence was not proof of the paranormal. He was just one of many mysteries science had yet to unravel.

This being standing behind the girl was beyond his ability to comprehend. It did not appear to have substantial physical form, but at the same time was clearly physically present. Charles', or rather the beast's, instinct—that historic, deeply rooted collection of historic memories passing from generation to generation in an animal's DNA—had screamed for him to flee, and flee he had. In fact, he was not yet done fleeing. He would abandon his hunt in Central America and be back in Louisiana before the sun set again.

The rational part of Charles' brain could find no explanation for what he had seen. As a child, he had heard the stories of angels and demons but his Christian faith was more an affectation than any real religious belief. The Episcopal Church had been a major part of his family's history. Indeed, he had an uncle who had been an Episcopal bishop until his death. He learned early on that the church provided a venue for connections and social advancement.

The stories he had been taught as a child were, in his mind, just that—stories. The being he had encountered resembled the stories of angels and fit in with the concept of a guardian angel, but if his brain allowed for the existence of angels, then he would have to consider the whole panoply of the heavenly realm, including the existence of God. It could be a life-altering event.

He quickly discounted the possibility of God or any type of heavenly being. What surprised him most was his feeling of fear—a deep fear that triggered a fight or flight response, although he never for an instant considered fighting the being. Until that night, he was the apex predator. Everything feared him, and like the demigods of legend, he was near immortal. Now he had to contend with the possibility that there were other creatures out there. Maybe he was not alone at the top of the food chain. It was an unsettling thought.

Chapter 34

As the years passed, the encounter in Guatemala receded into some of the deeper recesses in his mind and, after a while, he wasn't sure that it had ever occurred. The bodies piled up as his unquenchable thirst for blood only seemed to increase. It was not, strictly speaking, the flesh and blood that fed him. Certainly, he enjoyed tearing his victims apart and drinking their blood and eating their flesh. But it was the emotion, the fear, the sheer terror that he most sought.

As the creature visited dozens of locations around the globe, leaving carnage in his wake, never did Charles or the creature come under suspicion. His plan of leaving a suspect behind always deflected attention from the real killer and left a perfect suspect with no loose ends. It was best when the police shot and killed the suspect. When that happened, there were no defense attorneys and no courts to question the prosecutor's open-and-shut case. News outlets dutifully reported the death of the local serial killer.

Even when defense attorneys were involved, they were public defenders, overworked and underpaid, or court-appointed attorneys who worked for free. In much of the world, the duty an attorney owed to his or her client was not as strict as it would be in the U.S. Often, defense counsel would simply agree with the prosecutor and acknowledge his or her client's guilt. Not once had Charles or anyone from any of his companies ever been questioned.

There were sporadic sightings of a large hairy beast in close proximity to where victims had been discovered, but descriptions of the beast were conflicting and deemed by authorities not to be credible. They never made it into police reports. In fact, the conclusion that a report was 'not credible' became self-fulfilling. The fact that the witness was reporting a monster meant that the report was not credible. The killings were becoming almost too routine. The thrill of the escape was gone but the enjoyment of the hunt and the kill remained.

While in Saint Petersburg, Russia, Charles and the beast killed four women, the usual carnage. They committed these particular murders in the dark alleys of one of the poorer sections of the city. In several cases, local media arrived before the police, and photographed scenes of indescribable horror: A severed head, viscera spread the length and breadth of the alley, blood pooled on the ground and splashed twenty feet up building walls.

Many of the photos showed twisted, human-like piles of visecera, matted hair, partial torsos, and broken limbs. The murders made worldwide news with many in the west comparing the murderer to Jack, the Ripper, who terrorized London in the 1880s. Jack was never caught.

For some time, Charles toyed with the idea of allowing these murders to remain unsolved. There was something enticing about letting an entire city live indefinitely in fear. He also looked into the comparison with Jack, the Ripper. There was no comparison. Jack had killed some women and mutilated some bodies, but he was an amateur compared to Charles and the beast. Jack's notoriety probably came from the fact that he was the 'first' known serial killer.

In the end, he decided to put his plan into effect and left an anonymous tip for the Saint Petersburg police. This particular patsy, like many of his patsies, was a large, mentally challenged man in his thirties. He was unemployed and his criminal record showed a long history of violence.

To their credit, the Saint Petersburg police tried to take the suspect alive, arriving at his apartment at 8:00 a.m. to make an arrest and search the apartment. The suspect broke the jaw of the first police officer. He broke at least four ribs and punctured the lung of the second. The suspect had the third police officer on the ground and was choking him when the fourth police officer shot him four times. The suspect died at the scene.

The subsequent search of his apartment revealed that the suspect had four small pieces of jewelry in an envelope in one of his bedroom dressers. Each piece of jewelry was from a different victim. The city breathed a sigh of relief at news of the suspect's death.

But to Charles, it was all becoming too easy. Maybe it was time he tried a more sophisticated hunting ground, one where there might be a real investigation by a competent police agency. He didn't want to challenge the FBI or Scotland Yard, but maybe it was time to return to the United States to try his vocation there. Perhaps the thrill of the chase would return.

He recalled that one of the investment bankers who worked for him had recommended an investment in the northeastern United States. Charles couldn't remember for sure, but maybe it was in New York or Pennsylvania. As he tried to bring the details to mind, he recalled that it was a privately held ski resort. The analyst from the investment banker indicated that the resort was not producing the revenue it could. When he returned to Louisiana, he found the report and started to read through it in depth.

All businesspeople deal with bankers. Bankers provide normal banking services: checking and savings accounts, loans, lines of credit, etc. Investment bankers are different. They do not provide normal banking services. Instead, they focus upon investment opportunities, looking for ways to help the rich become even richer. Charles Hunt's investment bankers were very good, ensuring that he became wealthier and wealthier through no effort of his own.

In this particular case, they identified a ski resort in Pennsylvania that was now in the second, soon to be third, generation of family ownership. The analysis showed that the resort was underperforming and that there was a belief that the remaining family members would 'sell cheap'. The resort itself was somewhat dated, and the family that owned it had done almost no marketing over the past decade. It was still a fine resort but business was declining slightly every year.

The investment banker estimated that by putting about four million into the resort, it could be fully modernized. A relatively modest advertising budget, marketing experts reported, could double the number of people coming to the resort and double the revenue. The plan would be to take the company public in about three years, producing a return of nearly two hundred percent in that time for Charles. Charles called the investment banker and told him he was intrigued by the opportunity.

But there was actually another opportunity in Winter Haven that intrigued Charles more.

Chapter 35

There was a diner called O'Malley's on Main Street in Winter Haven, and every morning at 7:00, Dave appeared at the diner to start his day. It was part of his personal ritual. Usually, he would join someone he knew. Occasionally, he would sit at the counter by himself. Dave was, by nature, a social guy, which fit in with his view of himself as a private investigator. An investigator had to develop sources in order to know what was going on in the area.

Dave would talk to the people at the diner in the morning to see what he could learn. Later in the evening, he might stop by a bar or two and see what he could learn there. This case with Russ, though, had cut into his normal routine. Rather than sit in his favorite breakfast restaurant, Ed was asking him to do this and that, without even seeking Dave's advice concerning the case.

And there was the rub. Dave understood the case inside out. He had seen the real murderer. He had determined that the murders were not committed by a human, but rather by some shapeshifting being, probably a werewolf. He had researched werewolf lore and hundreds of real cases of werewolves, and now knew the subject probably better than anyone else in the world.

He had discovered that there were a vast number of missing persons in the United States, and probably more in the rest of the world. Undoubtedly, at least a small portion of these unexplained disappearances could be attributed to predation by a super predator, which was, again, the werewolf.

Dave had even figured out who the werewolf was. Charles Hunt. He found the other murders that were probably connected to Hunt. All it would have taken was a couple of trips to ferret out the details. He already knew what happened; it was just a matter of proving it. But no, Ed stopped him in his tracks. As the 'lawyer', Ed acted as though he was in charge. He barked orders and focused on a theory that he knew was wrong.

If only Ed was half as smart as he thought he was, he would see the merit of Dave's argument. But he was too stupid to understand the truth right in front of his eyes.

That was the way it always was. Lawyers who lack his intelligence, insight, and experience were always telling him where to go and what to do. They were only glorified mouthpieces who went into court and asked a few questions. They wouldn't even know what questions to ask if it weren't for Dave Krell. His whole career, they had been suppressing him and taking credit for his work.

Dave was too busy brooding to notice that Charles Hunt had entered his favorite diner. He didn't even notice when Hunt walked over to the counter and sat next to Dave. It took a full five minutes for Dave to realize he had company. When Dave noticed he wasn't alone, Charles looked at Dave and smiled but said nothing else. If Dave was correct, he sat beside a monster and a serial killer, but Dave had become accustomed to representing the worst of the worst. He was not about to show fear.

"Sir," Dave said in the politest way he could.

Charles looked at him. "Have we met before?" He asked. "You're Ed Reynold's assistant of some type, aren't you?"

Dave bristled at the remark. He was definitely not Ed's 'assistant'. If anything, he was Ed's superior, at least intellectually. After silently taking a moment to calm down, he began to speak. "Actually, I am a private investigator. I have my own firm and my own clients. I do some work from time to time for Ed, but I'm not his employee."

"Sorry," Charles said. "I meant no disrespect. In fact, I've heard you're the best investigator in this area, perhaps in the whole state."

Dave was pleased by the recognition. Charles invited Dave to join him in a nearby booth where they would have more privacy. Dave thought this was an excellent development. Now, even without Ed's authorization, he could begin to conduct his investigation into Charles Hunt. There was a lot he wanted to learn. Now by sheer luck, he was able to interview the key witness in the case.

"So," Charles began. "I hear that you and Ed make a pretty good team."

From there, Charles asked Dave how he became an investigator. He then coaxed several stories out of Dave about his past cases. Then subtly, the conversation turned to Russ' case.

"I'm sorry," Dave explained, "but I really can't talk about that case today."

"Oh," Charles replied. "I didn't mean to offend you. It is just a fascinating case, and all of us are a little bit afraid of the dark now. Isn't there anything you can say about the case?"

"It *is* a fascinating case, but I can't say anything."

Charles continued, "I understand, but everyone says you're the smartest member of the team, that you've always been responsible for Ed's success. I hear you're the one who is putting everything together, am I correct?"

Dave didn't say anything but he was pleased to know his involvement in the case was noticed. There was more to this conversation than met the eye. Dave knew that Charles was the murderer. He believed that Charles was a werewolf. He had never met Charles before and found it odd that he would pick this particular diner at this particular time for breakfast. Clearly, Charles was trying to find out what Dave knew. In a way, he was flattered that this incredibly rich and powerful man would seek him out.

"What are you having for breakfast?" Dave asked.

"I don't know, maybe just a bagel."

There you go, Dave thought, but said nothing. This wasn't a random meeting in a diner. Charles wasn't even hungry. *Two can play at that game*, he thought.

"So," Dave began, "what brings you to our town?"

"Purely business," Charles answered. "I am thinking about putting some money into the resort. I spent some time with the books but, to me at least, it's always important to visit the investment to get a feel for it. Numbers only tell you so much."

"What have you decided?" Dave asked.

Charles smiled. "You don't want to share information about your case. I'm the same way when it comes to business decisions. The trouble with investments in tourist businesses is that tourists are fickle. Like in the movie *Jaws*, you have a beachside town dependent on tourists. A shark shows up and the economy collapses. The numbers from the year before don't matter if it becomes a bad investment."

"One good thing about the mountains," Dave replied, "is that there are no sharks."

"No, but you do have something out there killing people, don't you? The first stories in the media talked about some wild animal that had torn people to pieces. That animal would be like a shark, wouldn't it?" Charles looked Dave squarely in the eyes. "Tell me, have you ever seen such a creature?"

Charles's gaze was intense and Dave found that he had to look away. "Have I ever seen a wolf or a mountain lion in this area? No. None of the animals native to this area are dangerous. I don't think you have anything to worry about in terms of your investment."

"What about something not native to this area?"

Dave said nothing.

"Just because science has not yet discovered something doesn't mean it doesn't exist," Charles continued. "Suppose there was a creature that was large and powerful and intelligent that hunted humans as humans hunt deer, for example. Suppose this creature could avoid detection and live in the shadows." He paused for a moment before proceeding. "Even if someone saw such a creature, he couldn't really say anything to anyone, could he? I mean, who would believe him?"

"Do you mean like a Bigfoot or a Sasquatch?" Dave asked.

"No, eventually evidence of a Bigfoot or Sasquatch would surface. A population of large ape-like mammals would certainly be discovered. But what about an animal that could shift form between human and animal, kind of like a chameleon? Something that could hide out using the form of a man during the day and then assume another form at night. That way, this large animal could exist and strike and then completely disappear, never to be discovered."

"You mean like a werewolf?" Dave laughed a little to show the ridiculousness of the idea.

But Charles continued in a serious voice, "Stories of werewolves, or other shapeshifting animals, go back to the very beginning of human history. Lycanthropy, the concept that humans can turn into animals, comes from the name of an ancient Greek king. These stories were known in all ancient civilizations, even the ancient Egyptians. The oldest known poem, *The Epic of Gilgamesh*, is about a creature that is part man and part beast."

"Stories abounded about creatures that were half man and half god, and these stories were widely believed. Even the Bible contains the story of Nebuchadnezzar, who God turned into an animal for seven years." Dave was about to ask a question but Charles started laughing. "But the police caught the murderer, didn't they?"

"Well," Dave said, "we don't think so."

"Maybe, then, the creature is still out there. It's a pity you don't have an eyewitness." Charles took a sip from his coffee. "Or maybe you do?"

"What do you mean?" Dave asked.

"Oh, nothing really. I just thought that maybe somebody had seen something. With all the people out and about, driving through the forest, I just thought that maybe someone—perhaps a man who stopped to relieve himself or something like that—walked a short distance down a logging road and saw something. I just thought that in your interviews with witnesses, maybe somebody said something. But I am not a detective."

Dave didn't know what to say. "That sounds a little crazy. Are you suggesting that I start asking people if they saw a large hairy creature walking on two legs? I'd lose my license."

"Sometimes my imagination gets ahead of me," Charles replied.

"Well, let me ask you this," Dave said. "Do you know anything about any large, undiscovered predator that hunts women and mutilates their bodies?"

Charles looked as though he wanted to say something, but after a long pause, he merely said that such a creature could only be a myth. He had seen and hunted some of the world's top predators. He had shot lions and leopards. He had never seen or heard of such a creature personally, but that didn't mean they didn't exist.

Charles stood up to leave. He took a twenty-dollar bill and laid it on the counter. It paid both his bill and Dave's with a generous tip. There was more Dave wanted to ask, about Brazil or Russia, but he let it go. Charles Hunt was friendly enough, but deep down, Dave knew he had the intelligence, power, and cunning to kill him. It would not be wise to ask too many questions that struck too close to home.

Dave also noted that Charles had brought up the topic of werewolves. It was an obvious ploy to see how Dave would react. Dave hoped he had passed the test. This morning, he had come face-to-face with his adversary. He suspected the man's charm covered evil and malice. He would have to be very careful. Charles was a cunning adversary, but in Dave's mind, he was superior.

Chapter 36

As the trial drew closer, Ed became more imperious in his attitude toward Dave, at least in Dave's opinion. He'd summon Dave to his office at a moment's notice and dismiss him when he was done. Dave had always viewed Ed as almost a partner, but now Ed treated him as a servant or maybe an errand boy. Ed had little to no interest in Dave's theories or thoughts, and Dave, in his own mind, was the one who understood the case.

He had figured out that the murderer was a werewolf, and he was the only one who had uncovered any evidence whatsoever. Ed, and to a lesser degree Shelley, would receive all the credit. The reporters would not seek out Dave for his opinions. No one would know that he was the one who broke the case. It was infuriating.

There had been an argument. Dave mentioned that he had been approached by Charles Hunt, and Ed responded by 'ordering' him to have no further contact with Hunt. Dave was incensed, first by the fact that his supposed partner would order him to do anything. They were supposed to be equals and, in reality, Dave knew that he was the one who knew most about the case. Dave was also offended by the fact that Ed did not trust him to talk to Charles.

Dave had been a professional investigator all of his professional life. He knew how to talk to people and how to get information from them. He'd show Ed. He would get some admissions, possibly a confession, from Charles Hunt.

That night, Dave was at a local bar drinking his favorite whiskey, Jameson. He was not a heavy drinker and normally limited himself to two drinks, but tonight he didn't care. He had arrived early, and after three of four drinks, he had tried to engage one of the bar's other patrons in conversation, but his attempt flopped. He tried to talk about his career as a detective but the younger man didn't seem to care. He was more interested in the basketball game on TV. Imagine that—a basketball game! Screw him!

That had been a couple of hours ago and he had another three or four drinks since then. The voice in his head, the only voice he cared about, kept reviewing and amplifying the grievances he felt.

There are seven deadly sins: pride, greed, lust, envy, gluttony, wrath, and strife. The sins are deadly because they involve an aspect of one's character and they spawn other sins Dave was a prideful man, and Ed had wounded his pride. Ed, of course, was oblivious to the many minor slights he inflicted on his old friend. He was caught up in the stress of trial preparation and paid little attention to Dave's feelings. Well, Dave would show Ed!

When Dave ordered his ninth Jamison, the bartender asked him if he was sure. Incensed, told the loser that he certainly knew how much he could drink, and he was just fine. Besides, Dave assured the bartender that he wasn't driving home anyhow.

"So, tell me: What's on your mind?" Dave turned to see Charles seated next to him. Dave had been planning a ruse to arrange a meeting with Charles but now he didn't have to. His adversary was playing right into his hands.

Charles looked at Dave's near-empty glass and ordered another drink for him. Dave drained his drink and picked up the new one. Charles lifted his glass to toast.

"To your future," said Charles. Dave looked puzzled but started on the drink anyhow.

The interesting thing about alcohol is that the more one drinks, the more impaired the person taking the drink becomes. However, the more impaired one's judgment becomes, the more difficult it becomes for that individual to see his own impairment. Dave was spiraling down that path but he thought he was completely in control. He was having trouble concentrating, and he realized he was speaking louder, but he told himself that was to cover the background noise.

Instead of exercising caution, he decided to charge ahead. He was sure he was in complete control.

"Well," Dave said, a slight slur on his voice, "since you asked, I, and I alone, solved the murders." Dave took another sip. He was sure this comment would peak Charles' interest.

"You did?" Charles asked.

"Yes, I did!" Dave said.

Charles looked around the bar. They sat alone, and the bartender was on the other side of the room. He looked Dave in the eyes.

"Well, then, would you care to enlighten me?" Charles asked.

Dave stared at Charles. "You already know," Dave said. Charles said nothing. He knew Dave wanted to tell him what he knew, and if he was only quiet, Dave would tell him. Dave, on the other hand, thought he had complete control over Charles.

After a moment, Dave leaned toward Charles and spoke in a low voice. "It was you," he began. "You killed all of those women. And you've killed other women around the world. I know it. I figured it out. You're a serial killer."

"And how did I kill them?"

"Well, that was the hardest part to figure out, but I figured it out. You're a werewolf or something like that. You can change into an animal, can't you? The night after the first murder, I shot you, didn't I? But it didn't kill you because…I haven't figured everything out yet. But I know." Dave took another drink. A smile formed on Charles' face.

"You know what? You are absolutely correct. I am a lycanthrope—that's the term I prefer—but some people call lycanthropes 'werewolves'. The fact is, I am not a wolf at all. I'm actually more like a god. You did shoot me. The shots in the chest stung, kind of like a bee sting to me. The shot to my knee did do some damage and it took nearly a week for it to return to normal. That was smart thinking of you. You might have died that night if you hadn't thought of that. No one else has ever figured that out."

Dave just looked at Charles. He thought about saying something but the word 'lycanthrope' was beyond his ability to say. Anyhow, he was getting his confession. It had been much easier than he thought.

Charles paused for a moment. "The question now is: What are you going to do with that information? You could go to the police but they would never believe you. They'd probably call you a crackpot. You could never convince them there was a such a thing as a werewolf. They'd call you crazy. You told your best friend, Ed, about me, didn't you? I doubt even he believed you. They might even suspect you of the crimes, or decide that you're crazy and involuntarily commit you."

"There is also your safety and that of your family to consider. Sometimes some knowledge can be harmful or even deadly. It makes me shudder to think about it."

"Or," he continued, "you could be my friend. I have a tremendous capacity to reward friends, just as I have a tremendous ability to punish enemies. I have had enemies in the past. None of them exist any longer. Most have died a very unpleasant death. It would be a shame if someone as intelligent and capable as you…well, there's really no reason to contemplate that, I hope."

"Most of my friends, the people I like and choose to work with, become fabulously wealthy. I appreciate intelligence and the ability to solve problems. Someone with your talent could have unlimited potential with me."

Dave was surprised at his own thoughts. Here he was, facing the most dangerous man he had ever met. Heck, he wasn't even a man; he was far more dangerous than a man could be. This thing standing before him should have been an enemy, something to be destroyed, but he felt somehow drawn to the creature—maybe he was a god of sorts. The creature saw the greatness in him that no one else saw—at least that's what Dave thought.

Dave had always seen himself as a great man thwarted by life's circumstances. He should have been a great lawyer, winning multi-million-dollar verdicts, living in a mansion, and flying in a private jet to vacation spots around the world.

In his mind, his failure to be accepted by a decent law school stemmed from the unfair actions of one of his college professors who had given him a C in one course and a D in another. Dave lacked the insight to see that the grades were the result of his own laziness and that even without those two particular grades, his GPA was still too low to be admitted into law school. This same pattern followed him through his police career.

He was passed over twice for promotions he should have had. In one case, the office chosen over him was a woman. Dave saw himself as the victim of reverse discrimination. He could not see that this particular woman worked harder than he did and achieved better results. Then there was the shooting. His actions were completely justified, but other law enforcement officers, no doubt professionally jealous, had used the shooting as a way to get him out of the way.

To Dave, it was always someone else's fault.

Dave listened to what Charles had to say, and when they were finished, Charles gave Dave a ride home—Dave was too drunk to drive himself. The next day, Charles told Dave that he had some business in Chicago. If Dave could make it, he offered to have his driver pick Dave up, and then they would fly to Chicago for the day. Charles had a proposal to make. They would discuss it over dinner, and whether Dave accepted or not, Charles would pay him $1,000 for his time.

For a moment, Dave thought about what he needed to do before the trial. But Ed was there, and Ed thought he knew everything. *Screw him,* Dave thought.

A black SUV picked Dave up at his house the next morning.

Chapter 37

They were only two weeks out from the trial. Normally by this point, Ed would be prepared for trial. He would know what witnesses the State was going to call and what evidence it was going to present. He would also know what witnesses he was going to call and what evidence he was going to present. In just two days, he would have to file his pretrial memorandum, listing his witnesses and his evidence. The pretrial statement also required him to identify any legal issues that might arise.

The problem was: He was older and tired. He lacked the energy he had twenty years before. He thought his team, Shelley and Dave, would make up for that deficit. Shelley had turned out to be a disappointment. She started out strong, drafting some excellent memoranda and doing some top-quality legal research. God only knew how many hours she was putting into the case. Something had happened a month before, however.

She started coming to meetings late or sometimes not at all. She would agree to take assignments and then not finish them or turn them in late. Her work product went from excellent to unacceptable. Her physical appearance deteriorated. Dark circles developed under her eyes, and her conversation became disjointed. She had always been a sharp dresser, but lately, her clothing was wrinkled. She smelled like she was not bathing as regularly as she should.

Sometimes, she came in with the smell of alcohol on her breath. Ed was worried about her, and with growing frequency, he would ask if there was anything he could do. He suggested she might want to see a therapist. Ed didn't know if she was religious, but he suggested that she might want to see a priest or a minister or a rabbi to help her through whatever trouble she was experiencing. Shelley had been offended by these suggestions, so he stopped. Not everyone is cut out to be a trial attorney.

In fact, most lawyers are not cut out to make their careers in the courtroom. Probably the stress and strain of preparing for a major case had gotten to

Shelley. They would just have to muddle through, and then after the trial, he would talk to her about another vocation.

Then—three weeks before the trial—she had come in and said she couldn't do the trial. She quit. Ed was mystified and tried to explain that he needed her. The plan had been for Ed and Shelley to split the examinations of the witnesses equally. He tried to tell Shelley that he could not do the case on his own. She pointed out that he had Dave. Obviously, Dave wasn't working out, either. Now, Ed was going to have to do all of the examinations himself.

Worse yet, he had no other lawyers to bounce ideas off of. His relationship with Dave was even worse. Shelley at least felt bad about abandoning Ed. In Dave's mind, he had solved the case and had no desire to do any further investigation. The key to the defense was the furrier from New York who would identify the fur coat the State had in evidence and explain that he made the coat along with four others. He would also testify as to the cost of the coat and how it was picked up.

Ed had obtained a subpoena from the court a month before to be served on the furrier, requiring his appearance and his records. Service of a subpoena meant that it had to be hand-delivered to the recipient, in this case the furrier. Dave had delayed serving the subpoena for some reason, and now the furrier seemed to have disappeared. Worse yet, the records Dave claimed to have seen were now missing. For some inexplicable reason, Dave did not even get a copy of the records when he had first seen them.

When Ed expressed frustration that the subpoena had not been served, Dave said that it should not be his job to serve subpoenas, anyhow. Ed escalated the disagreement and an argument ensued. In short order, Dave stormed out of the office, saying that he was done. That had been three days ago—three crucial days in the limited time available for preparation.

Now, Ed was essentially alone, without evidence or support. But to a certain extent, trial lawyers, and especially criminal defense lawyers, were always alone. Sure, there were sometimes other team members, but in the final analysis, the lead defense counsel made the important decisions and lived with their consequences. There were witnesses to be cross examined, but Ed had cross examined thousands of witnesses in his career, and deep down, he knew that even unprepared, his cross examinations would be better than most other lawyers.

The opening statement and closing argument—as he thought about it, he knew what he wanted to say.

The missing furrier was problematic but he seemed to have just disappeared. This was definitely a negative development, but there were things Ed could control and things he could not control. Fretting over things he could not control did not help the case. He had to focus on the things he could control. The missing witness was something that was beyond his control.

He knew from his long experience in the courtroom that there would be other developments in the case that would not be helpful. He would just have to adapt as they arose.

One of those potential developments was the discovery of human remains at the ski resort about six weeks before the trial was about to start. The remains consisted of fragmented skeletal remains. DNA tests had recently been conducted, and the victim had been identified as Katie Neuman, a ski patroller who had disappeared during the previous winter. The coroner had concluded the cause of death was homicide, and local and state media outlets identified Ms. Neuman as yet another victim of the serial killer.

Early in the morning, the prosecutor had stopped by Ed's office to drop off discovery the prosecutor said she had only recently received herself. This discovery consisted of the police and medical examiner reports related to Ms. Neuman. At first, Ed believed that the State was going to attempt to add the Neuman homicide to the indictment, but the prosecutor assured him that was not the case. It was too late to add charges without delaying the trial, something the State did not want to do.

The current four homicides would be sufficient to obtain the death penalty. If for some reason Strait was not convicted of the current charges, the prosecutors would indict him later for Katie Neuman's murder. The prosecutor assured Ed that she was providing the information to Ed just to make sure that all relevant evidence had been given to him.

Ed's first thought was that he would give the information to Dave to review, but Dave had gone silent. He thought next about Shelley but then remembered she had quit. He would have to review the information himself, on top of everything he needed to do to prepare for trial. He doubted there was anything there, but he needed to make sure.

For most of the rest of the day, Ed worked on his closing argument and opening statement. Around 3:00 p.m., he turned his attention to the reports the prosecutor had dropped off. This time, there were no bloody crime scene photos. There were about a hundred and sixty photos of the where the victim's remains were discovered together with some white bone fragments and small pieces of clothing.

Mice and other rodents had apparently chewed on many of the bone fragments. Police and the medical examiner noted that most of the victim's bones had been carried away, probably by the woodland scavengers that inhabited the forest.

A time of death could not be determined with the limited remains available; however, police interviews determines that she had last been seen on Thursday, 22 February. After completing her daily shift, she never showed up for work again. Subsequent interviews with Neuman's landlord indicated that when he entered her apartment on 5 March after the she failed to pay her rent. The landlord reported there was no personal property belonging to Neuman in the apartment.

Several members of the ski patrol were also interviewed, but none of the people interviewed had any relevant information. Finally, when police ran her vehicle information through the NCIC system, they discovered that her vehicle had been located in long term parking at Logan Airport in Boston. There was no evidence that Neuman had booked a flight. That was it.

By the time he finished reviewing the file, Ed was tired, too tired in fact. He reviewed the file with an eye as to how it could impact his case and was relieved to see there was nothing connecting Russell Strait to the homicide. He was confident there was no information the police could use in the upcoming case.

If he still had a team, Ed would have asked Dave and Shelley to review the discovery. He thought about calling Dave, but his last three calls had gone directly to Dave's voicemail. Dave hadn't returned the calls, and Ed thought another call would simply be a waste of time. He moved the file to the corner of his desk and forgot about it.

This was a mistake. Further investigation would have been valuable. As it turned out, one of the pieces of jewelry belonged to Neuman linking her deaths to the other murders that winter. In addition, if one were to drive from Pennsylvania to Logan Airport near Boston, that person would take Interstate 84 to the Massachusetts Turnpike. Although automated, cameras located at the entrance to the Turnpike photograph every vehicle that passed through the toll gates.

Had anyone bothered to check, they would have discovered that Ms. Neuman's vehicle passed through the toll gate at 4:09 a.m. on 23 February. This discovery would have been significant because Russell Strait had suffered a concussion that night from a fall and was under observation in a local hospital when Neuman's car was passing through a toll gate six hours away.

A more thorough investigation would have uncovered a surveillance video at a rest stop in Connecticut. Had the video been watched, a larger African-American man would have been observed exiting Neuman's car and walking into the rest stop. Another video inside the rest stop was clearer. Anyone familiar with Charles Hunt's manservant would have recognized him as the individual who was driving Neuman's car.

But the investigation that would have shown, at the very least, reasonable doubt as to Russell Strait's guilt never occurred. The police had already solved the crime and saw no reason to investigate further after the murder had been solved. If there had been more time before the trial and if Ed had his trial team, Ed might have requested an investigation. But as it was, the lack of time and the lack of resources conspired to deprive Russell Strait of this defense.

The truth was that it had been decades since Ed had tried a homicide case, and as he went to bed that night, he wondered if he was simply too old or too beaten down by life. He began his career as a criminal defense lawyer because that was what he wanted to do. He wanted to represent the despised, the poor, the forgotten members of society.

In his naivete, he wanted those who could not afford a lawyer to have the same shot at justice as the wealthy. He discovered quickly, however, that doing things for the right reason does not pay the bills.

Ed's career as a criminal defense lawyer did not last long. He was paid $2,500 for that case, which was difficult and stressful. He might receive a fee of $20,000 from a private client for a major felony, but that was about the maximum. About two years into private practice, a friend asked him to try a personal injury case, an uncomplicated traffic accident where the client had suffered serious injuries.

After a three-day trial, the jury awarded the plaintiff $600,000. The fee for the case was 33-1/3 percent of the award, which Ed's friend shared equally with him. In that one case, which was far easier to try than a criminal case, Ed pocketed $100,000. Soon thereafter, Ed was only trying personal injury cases.

Chapter 38

Ed filed his pretrial memorandum on time but only listed three witnesses. All of the other witnesses who would testify would be called by the State. His fact witnesses were the furrier, who remained missing, and Dave, who was still not talking to him. His third witness was an expert who would testify about lycanthropic syndrome. He summarized Dave's testimony as follows:

Mr. Krell will testify that on the morning following the first murder, he was returning from an assignment on Route 74 when he stopped and walked into the forest a short distance. While there, he observed a large creature, possibly a large human wearing some type of fur coat, which the defense believes to be the actual killer. Mr. Krell will testify to his observations that day.

He summarized the expert's testimony as follows:

Melissa Saunders, Ph.D., holds a doctorate in clinical psychology and has published extensively on the psychology of lycanthropic syndrome, a recognized condition where the patient actually comes to believe that he is a werewolf and will attack victims in a matter consistent with an animal attack. Dr. Saunders will testify that the attacks of the victims in this case are consistent with attacks committed by someone suffering from lycanthropic syndrome. Dr. Saunders will further testify that she has examined the defendant and he does not suffer from lycanthropic syndrome.

The State had objected to the testimony of both Dave and Dr. Saunders, and the judge had scheduled a hearing on the State's objection. The trial would begin the following Monday. There would be a pretrial conference on Friday, and then he would have only the weekend for final preparation before the trial started.

At the pretrial conference, Ed sat at the defense counsel table with his client seated next to him. They rose as the judge entered the courtroom. After the clerk called the case, the judge began the hearing.

"Will the State place its reasons for its objection on the record," the judge began.

"Your Honor, the defense proposes to call Mr. Krell as a witness to testify that he saw some sort of large, unidentified animal in the woods the morning after the murder of the first victim. There is apparently nothing tying this sighting, whatever it was, to the murder in this case. The State believes this evidence to be completely irrelevant."

The judge turned to Ed. "Counsel, your response."

"Your Honor, first of all, we did not say the creature was an animal. It was something very large and fur-covered, possibly a human. It is the defense's theory that this thing, whatever it was, was actually responsible for the death of all of the victims. Its location with respect to the first victim indicates that it was more or less on a straight line from the scene of the murder to Winter Haven."

The judge frowned. "First, let me ask: What was this creature your witness alleges he saw?"

"As I said, Your Honor, we aren't sure. It might have been a very large human, Your Honor," Dave responded.

"Now you say it was on a direct path from the murder scene to Winter Haven?"

"Yes, Your Honor." Ed could see where this was headed, and he felt a little ridiculous.

"Is it your position that the animal in question lives in Winter Haven?"

There was a chuckle in the courtroom. "Or human. Perhaps, Your Honor," was all Ed could say.

"I see," the judge said as the prosecutor began to rise.

"Your Honor, the State has learned that Mr. Krell believes the creature he saw to be a werewolf—a shapeshifting creature that, when the moon is full, turns into a wolf and attacks innocent people. The State notes that only one of the murders occurred on a full moon." There was a certain glee in the prosecutor's voice as he spoke.

The judge turned to Ed. "Is this true?"

"Well," Ed began. He wondered where the State had obtained its information but there was no point in bringing that up. "First, Mr. Krell does not believe that the transformation occurs only when there is a full moon, but yes, Mr. Krell has said something about the creature being a werewolf."

There were more snickers in the courtroom as the judge's face became red. This was not going well. "Counsel, are you trying to turn my courtroom into a circus?" The judge asked.

"No, Your Honor," Ed responded quickly.

The judge took only a moment to consider his ruling before giving it. "I don't think the evidence has much relevance but I am going to allow it. Mr. Krell can testify that he saw something and the location where he saw it. He can describe his interactions, if any, with whatever he saw. He cannot speculate as to what it was or where it was going."

The judge paused for a second before continuing.

"I expect this testimony to be very short and controlled. If there is any mention of a werewolf, the word 'werewolf', or any other mythological or mythical being, spirit, monster, or anything similar, both the witness and the attorney offering the testimony will be going to jail. Is that understood?"

Ed nodded.

"Now," the judge said, "let's turn to the expert witness. As I read your proffer, Counsel, we're talking about werewolves again."

"No, Your Honor," Dave said. The prosecutor started to stand but the judge waived for him to sit down.

"But your witness, as I understand, is going to testify that there are some people who think they are werewolves?"

"Yes, Your Honor," Ed acknowledged.

"Now, this isn't a diminished capacity or insanity defense, is it?"

"No, Your Honor."

"Tell me, Counsel, are there murders where the victim has been mutilated and the defendant does not suffer from this psychological condition you mentioned."

"There are, Your Honor, but…"

Ed wanted to respond further but the judge had heard enough. "Thank you, Counsel, for your arguments. As I said before, Mr. Krell will be permitted to testify, albeit in limited fashion. The expert, Dr. Saunders, will not be permitted to testify. Is there anything else?"

Ed knew the answer to the next question but he raised it anyhow. "Your Honor, our only other witness is missing. We would respectfully request that the trial be continued for ninety days so that the defense can locate the witness."

The judge turned to the prosecutor. "What is the State's position?"

"Your Honor, this case has been pending for months, and Commonwealth's witnesses and the victims' families have already made arrangements to attend the trial on the date scheduled. We oppose any continuance."

The judge looked at Ed. "I understand your dilemma, but witnesses disappear all the time. If we continue the trial, we don't know if you'll find your witness or not, even if I granted a ninety-day continuance, which I'm not going to do. Besides, the State has already planned for its witnesses and the victims' families to be here. I'm going to have to deny your motion. Is there anything else?"

No one said anything. "Good," the judge said in closing. "I will see all of you for jury selection and trial on Monday morning. Have a good weekend."

Chapter 39

The weekends before trial are a difficult time for trial attorneys. Rather than relax and rest during the lead-up to trials, lawyers must spend these hours reviewing and re-reviewing evidence, checking with witnesses to make sure they are still on board, and writing and re-writing their opening statements. If there is a trial team, the weekend before the trial is not as bad. There is a shared sense of purpose and no member of the team is alone.

They can talk about the case among themselves and, occasionally—occasionally—someone will think of something new that can turn the case around. Ed, however, had no teams. He would spend the weekend in his office going over everything one more time.

Ed called Dave four times that weekend but all four calls went to voicemail.

Charles had invited Dave to spend a long weekend with him fly-fishing in the Bahamas for bonefish. They had left on Thursday evening on Charles' private jet and would not be back until Sunday evening, Monday morning at the latest. Charles assured Dave that he would be back for the start of the trial on Monday afternoon. Dave might miss jury selection but that was it. Dave decided to go with his new best friend.

His new best friend? Strange, this attraction Dave felt toward Charles. Charles was a murderer, someone who killed and mutilated women, and Dave had been the one who figured it out. He should have been repulsed, but he wasn't. Evil attracts some people, perhaps most people, and Dave was inexplicably drawn to Charles, just as the ancient Babylonians were drawn to their bloodthirsty gods, or as Nazis had been drawn to Hitler. There was something irresistible about the raw power and the fantastic wealth that drew Dave in.

There was a part of him that feared Charles and the beast that he became. He knew that he was defenseless if Charles wanted him dead. There was nothing he could do. But if he served Charles, if he were indispensable, then he reasoned that he would not only be safe but would also be protected and rewarded. He viewed the trip to the Bahamas as a test—a test he wanted to pass.

Charles' driver picked Dave up at his home Thursday evening while his wife was out running errands. Dave told her he would be gone for the weekend because he had some last-minute witnesses he had to interview in New York. It was important to Dave that his wife knew he was in charge of the case. Besides, she probably wouldn't understand this last-minute trip to the Bahamas. The driver deposited Dave at the local municipal airport.

In fact, he presented ID at the gate and drove onto the tarmac, right up to the sleek Bombardier business jet. Charles leaned out the door and waived him in. The stewardess pulled the door closed and locked it as the pilots started the engines. The ordinary configuration of seats Dave had seen on previous flights—coach—were absent. In their place were a couple of large, overstuffed chairs that reclined into beds.

The interior walls, bulkheads in aviation terms, were trimmed in mahogany like the walls of a suite in a five-star hotel. As they taxied to take off, the stewardess brought out two flutes of champagne. It was a middle-grade Don Pérignon, but it was better than anything Dave had ever drank. They followed up the champagne with a tray of hors d'oeuvres, which tasted even better than the champagne. Charles watched as Dave took in his new environment and marveled at how easily people were seduced.

Dave had already agreed to do what Charles needed him to do, but he needed Dave to be all in, at least for another week. The cost associated with this seduction was minimal from Charles' standpoint, and the gratitude and loyalty he was purchasing were invaluable.

"Dave," Charles began. "I cannot begin to tell you how impressed I have been with your investigative skills. You have figured out what no one else ever has—my true identity and, in the process, solved a series of murders. Fortunately for me…" He chuckled. "You are my friend, and I am completely safe."

Charles raised a glass and clinked it against Dave's.

"I believe, however, that there is more you can do for me," said Charles, continuing the seductions. This is what Dave had been waiting for.

"As you know, I have business interests throughout the world. So many business interests that it is difficult for me to keep track of everything. For some time, I have been thinking that I need a head of investigations. The trouble has been that I have never been able to find the right person, but now I think I have. The position would be a vice-president level position. The pay is negotiable, by I am thinking maybe $300,000 per year."

Charles knew this was four times more than Dave had ever made before. He continued, "Of course, there are down sides. I would need you to travel around the world, sometimes for weeks at a time. I would pay all expenses, and you could have this jet or one of my others for the travel, but I know that it is a terrible imposition to be away. Do you have any interest, or should I keep looking?"

Dave was hooked but he thought he should not seem too eager. "Well, it is definitely something I would consider. I have my own thriving practice now, and I would have to give that up. I need some time to think about it."

"Of course," Charles replied, but he knew he had Dave exactly where he wanted him. "I should also mention that loyalty to me, and only to me, is an important part of the job. Sometimes we operate…" He paused for a few heartbeats before continuing. "…in legal gray areas. I need to know that whomever I am going to hire isn't going to run to the authorities the first time someone says something might be illegal, if you know what I mean."

For someone trained as a law enforcement officer and trained in the law, Dave was surprisingly dexterous when it came to any sort of personal morality or commitment to the law. In fact, one of the things that made him a successful law enforcement officer was his ability to bend the truth to meet his needs. He had learned years ago that investigations were easier and more productive when he simply made up an informant to get a warrant. He knew when he testified under oath that he would be believed.

Deep down, he knew that the magistrate and the prosecutors knew he was lying, but they wanted to get the suspect as much as he did. To Dave, the entire justice system was based on a system of lies. Charles was not asking for anything he hadn't done before. Only this time, he would make a lot more money.

Dave was, of course, wrong, at least about how the system worked. It was simply another lie he told himself to justify his actions. Other officers held much more firmly to the truth, even when it made investigating harder. And while prosecutors and judges frequently gave Dave the benefit of the doubt, it wasn't because they wanted to get a suspect at any cost; it was because they gave Dave Krell, a sworn law enforcement officer, the benefit of the doubt. In any event, Dave could use his moral flexibility to Charles' advantage.

Chapter 40

The jet landed on a small, private island entirely owned by Charles Hunt. It did not clear customs or immigration—it just landed on a small runway. There would be no record of Dave Krell's entry or departure. When the door opened, Dave emerged into a tropical paradise. Although it was dark by the time they landed, the temperature was just about perfect, a far cry from the cold weather he had just come from.

A porter retrieved his luggage from the jet and followed Dave and Charles to a small bungalow about thirty yards from a larger building. He showed Dave the bungalow where he would be staying. He then told Dave that dinner would be served in about an hour. It was the best dinner Dave had ever had.

The ostensible reason for traveling to the Bahamas was to fish for bonefish. Bonefish are sleek, torpedo-like silver fish that can weigh several pounds. They inhabit an area known as 'the flats', the shallow waters on top of a sandy sea floor. Oftentimes, the water will be six inches deep or less, and the bonefish will work these shallow waters in search of shrimp and other small crustaceans to eat.

A skillful fisherman would cast his fly, a small lure, immediately in front of the bonefish, hoping the fish will take it. When it does, it attacks with ferocity. It is one of the most exciting experiences a fly fisherman can have.

Saturday morning after breakfast, Dave headed to the flats with a guide Charles had assigned to him. Dave was not a fly fisherman, and he proved so that day. When Charles met him wading on the flats, he marveled at Dave's ineptitude. He almost never saw the fish and could not cast more than twenty feet when the closest fish were at least twenty yards away.

Dave looked at Charles with an uncertain eye. "Don't worry about it," Charles said. "You're doing well for your first time."

But Dave didn't catch a single fish that day or that weekend.

Saturday evening, Dave again met Charles for dinner. They talked about the Bahamas and the day on the flats fishing. Ordinarily, when Charles entertained on the island, there would be anywhere from eight to twenty guests. Now, it was just Charles and Dave. "What did your wife think of the trip?" Charles asked.

"I didn't tell her about it," Dave replied. "Yeah," Dave continued. "I'm not sure she is going to be part of my new life. She is older now, set in her ways, and not as attractive as she used to be."

"Oh," Charles replied. "You don't love her?"

"To tell the truth, I'm not sure there is such a thing as love. We used to talk about love, but for me, she was just sex, and to her, I was just a meal ticket. I think it's time for both of us to move on."

"Well," Charles continued. "If you ever have trouble with her, let me know. I can probably help."

Dave wasn't sure what Charles meant but this, but he didn't want clarification. He told Charles everything would be okay and that he didn't need any help. He feared what might happen to his wife if he said the wrong thing. It sent a chill up his spine.

In the back of his mind, Dave realized how vulnerable he was as well. No one knew where he was or what he was doing. If anyone attempted to check into his travel, they would find nothing. Any witnesses who could testify about his whereabouts were employed by Charles, and they all seemed to be very loyal employees. As he sat there dining on fresh lobster that had been on the reef only an hour before dinner and washing it down with an $800 bottle of wine, he wondered if this was his last meal.

Charles could kill him in a heartbeat if he wanted. But Dave suppressed these thoughts, hoping he would be worthy to join Charles' employ.

After dinner, a skiff arrived from a neighboring island with four scantily clothed young women, girls really. They seemed to range in age from about fourteen to maybe seventeen. They appeared to be Hispanic or mixed race. They were all beautiful, with caramel-colored skin and dark eyes.

"These are for you," Charles said.

For a second, Dave was mortified. He asked in a low voice, "Are you going to kill them?"

Charles laughed. "That's funny. I rarely kill people, and when I do, it is only selectively. You see, the beast inside me, the one you discovered, kills for compulsion, not for pleasure. I am careful about the victims I select. They are all bad people—drug addicts and criminals. Their removal from the earth is a benefit to humanity."

"It's like the process of natural selection, like when a mountain lion kills a deer. It selects only the weakest, those who are diseased or deformed. Its actions make the herd stronger. It's the same way with me."

Of course, it was all a lie. But it was a lie Dave wanted to believe, so he didn't delve into the matter more. Instead, he turned his attention back to the girls.

"They appear so young," he said.

"They are," Charles replied. "But one of the benefits of being really rich is that laws don't really apply to you. Feel free to enjoy them."

And Dave did.

Chapter 41

The trial started on Monday with jury selection. Ed had received the list of potential jurors on Friday afternoon. There were hundred and forty names on the list, which would be whittled down to twelve jurors and two alternates. Ed sent the names to Dave by email about ten minutes after he had received them. Dave was supposed to do a background search on each juror to identify potentially prejudiced or unfavorable jurors that would need to be struck.

While Ed was putting the final touches on his case, Dave would research all of the potential jurors. Dave didn't respond on Friday afternoon or Saturday morning. Saturday afternoon, Ed began calling Dave on his cell phone, but all of his calls went to voicemail. This continued through Sunday. Sunday evening, Ed decided to do some of his own research but he didn't have access to the databases private investigators use, and his efforts were cursory at best.

Ed gave a final call on Monday morning before heading to court. Dave again failed to answer. As that Monday morning call came in, Dave was enjoying his final breakfast in the Bahamas before returning to the U.S. He looked at his cell phone as it rang but never contemplated answering it.

As one would expect in a high-profile case, jury selection proceeded slowly, with the judge being particularly careful about the jurors that were seated. He allowed what is known as 'individual *voir dire*'. Ordinarily, attorneys will question the prospective jurors as a group. In this case, the jurors were left in an assembly room and the judge would call each juror into a conference room one at a time and allow the attorneys to question the juror.

When the questioning was over, the juror would be excused, and each attorney would place any objections to the juror on the record. The judge would then decide whether the juror could be fair and impartial. The parties also had thirty 'peremptory challenges', meaning that each lawyer could remove up to thirty potential jurors for no reason at all. After the judge determined that a potential juror could be fair and impartial, each side then had an opportunity to strike the juror.

This lasted until all sixty peremptory challenges had been used. It was a laborious task.

As Monday closed, only eight jurors had been seated. Jury selection commenced again on Tuesday in the same slow, plodding manner. Finally, after lunch on Tuesday, there were only two jurors and two alternates left to be picked. That was when Dave finally showed up. He seemed to be in good spirits and appeared to Ed to have a tan. "Where were you?" Ed asked Dave.

"You know, you're not my only client. I had things to do," Dave replied.

"I needed you for jury selection."

Dave stared at Ed for a moment, with something that looked like contempt in his eyes. "Ed, sometimes you just have to do your own work."

There was no time to continue the conversation since the judge was anxious to finish jury selection. The final juror was selected just after 3:00 p.m. With that, the judge decided to call it a day. Ed asked Dave to come over to his office to discuss a few things but Dave declined. Ed then asked Dave if he had time to swing by the jail and see Russ. Dave said no. It made no sense. Dave was initially enthusiastic about the case.

He was the one who first believed Russ to be innocent. Just weeks before, Dave was putting his heart and soul into the case. Now, he didn't have time to talk about the case with Ed, or even see Russ. Ed could understand Dave's issue with him, but for Dave to abandon a defendant made no sense. Dave said he would be there the next morning and then turned and walked out of the courthouse.

The prosecutor was the first person to give an opening statement. She did a commendable job, focusing on victims, referring to each by name and talking about their young ages, their dreams, the children and parents and family and friends they were leaving behind. From there, the prosecutor moved into the vicious and unprovoked nature of the attacks. Then she discussed the strength of its evidence, focusing on the fact that the police had searched 'the defendant's' room and discovered the murder weapon, a fur suit the defendant had worn during the attacks, and the property of the victims discovered in his room.

The murder weapon was a set of handmade jaws with steel teeth. According to the prosecutor, the defendant had carefully cleaned the jaws, but traces of the victims' blood had still been found in several seams in the device. The fur suit had the victims' blood on it and the defendant's DNA inside the suit. He had taken jewelry—trophies—from each of the victims. The defendant's fingerprints were found on the jewelry he had taken from each victim. As the prosecutor closed her opening statement, she left no doubt as to the defendant's guilt and referred to the conviction as a foregone conclusion.

After the prosecutor finished, Ed sat in his chair for a minute, collecting his thoughts. Studies showed that the opening statement was the most important part of the trial. Most jurors make up their minds after the opening statements and it is difficult to get a juror to change his or her mind once it is made up. Ed had to at least give the jurors something to think about. Otherwise, the case was over before it even started. When he was ready, he stood and approached the podium the clerk had set up in front of the jurors for the statements.

Ed smiled and looked at each juror in turn.

"Ladies and gentlemen of the jury," he began. "The prosecutor makes a compelling argument. Fingerprints, DNA, a confession—or at least 'admissions', whatever that means. But what does this evidence really tell us? Precious little. There was a search of Russell Strait's house, the room where he was staying. A set of steel jaws was recovered, a fur coat was recovered, items from each of the victims were recovered."

"That is all true. But is it enough to say with certainty—or even more, beyond a reasonable doubt—that Russell Strait killed the four women he is charged with killing?"

"I will submit to you, ladies and gentlemen, it is not. All of the State's evidence taken as a whole does not point to Russell's guilt beyond a reasonable doubt. Now please permit me to go back and explain why. It's 27 November last year, just a few days after Thanksgiving. Cindy Johnson has been lured away from her home, from her family to a remote location. There is a light snow falling. It's cold outside, and Cindy is waiting to meet someone. Who?"

"That is the first question the State cannot answer. Was it Russell? If you listen carefully, you will hear no evidence that Russell and Cindy ever met. Cindy was a local girl. Russell from elsewhere. They didn't work together. There is no reason their paths would have crossed. Also, as you will see throughout the trial, Russell is not the type of guy a woman like Cindy would be attracted to."

Ed turned and looked at Russell. He knew the jury would follow his lead. There before them sat a small, diminished man. The thought of Cindy traveling into the woods to meet him seemed unreasonable. Ed continued. "Even if Cindy and Russell were to meet somewhere, why meet deep in the woods? There would be no reason. It was cold and uncomfortable. Both Cindy and Russell were single, and there would be no reason to hide their meeting. They could have met at any number of establishments in town. But they never did.

Cindy would only have met someone where she did because the person she was to meet did not want to be seen with her. Perhaps he was married. Returning to that horrible night, Cindy sits in her car, awaiting her suitor. We don't know what she sees. We don't know what she hears. All of a sudden, someone or something smashes the driver's side window, grabs the door, and rips it from the car frame, throwing it away like a used piece of trash. You will hear from police officers that it was located at least twenty-five yards from the car."

Ed paused, and once again turned toward Russell. Russell could not afford a suit and the county wouldn't buy him one for trial. Instead, he wore a blue dress shirt buttoned at the collar. If he had biceps or triceps, they were hidden within the wrinkled fabric of his shirt. It was clear to everyone that Russell was weak and powerless.

"Whoever tore the door from the frame of the vehicle possessed tremendous strength. How could anyone, let alone Russell Strait, tear a car door from its frame? That is the second question the State cannot answer. Could Russell have torn the car door from its frame? It would have been impossible."

"After Cindy Johnson's death, a series of other murders occurred as the prosecutor outlined. The murders were committed with extreme violence. Bodies were literally torn apart. What was the reason? That is the third question the prosecutor cannot answer. Did Russell have a reason to commit these murders? If you listen carefully, you will hear no evidence of motive. Russell had no reason to commit any of these crimes."

"In fact, Russell was born in the Midwest. He dropped out of school and left home early. He works as a ski instructor when he can, and anything else when he cannot. His earnings are meager, living from paycheck to paycheck. In fact, there is nothing in Russell's background that would suggest he could commit the heinous acts you will hear about today and over the next few days. Nothing at all."

Ed paused again to give the jury time to catch up. Then he continued.

"Serial killers are among the most difficult criminals to catch. They are also some of the scariest. The thought of a serial killer in a community is unsettling, and pressure is focused upon the police to solve the case. In this case, the police were under intense pressure to make an arrest."

"And then when the police had exhausted all of their leads, an anonymous call came in. What a coincidence." Jurors had watched enough police dramas to be suspicious of coincidence. Conspiracy theories were more in vogue. "And this coincidence, if that's what it was," Ed said, and paused yet again, "came in the form of an anonymous call. One afternoon someone called the state police barracks and said they had been in Russell's home and seen the murder weapon and the fur coat."

"Who was this anonymous caller? This is the fourth question the State cannot answer. The police, as you will hear, attempted to do everything in their power to identify this anonymous witness and could not. They would not even determine if anyone had visited Russell in the days leading up to the search of his house. Why is the identity of the anonymous witness important? Because he knew of the evidence in Russell's residence. If Russell did not commit the murders, then this anonymous person did.

"Now let's look at the evidence that was seized from Russell's house more closely. The police found a fur coat, a vital piece of evidence. Where did it come from? Fur coats like the one recovered from the search of Russell's home are expensive. Russell could not have purchased it. This is the fifth unanswered question. The State cannot show where the coat came from, who purchased it, or how it ended up in Russell's house. Could it have been placed there by someone else? The anonymous caller, perhaps?"

"Listen carefully to the evidence as it unfolds. There are more questions than answers, more smoke than fire. Once you hear all of the evidence, you will see that it does not prove Russell Strait guilty beyond a reasonable doubt."

With that, Ed thanked the jury and sat down. He looked over and saw a confused look on the prosecutor's face. The prosecuting officer, Detective Jones, looked angry. Ed hoped that he'd planted a seed of doubt in the jury's mind. That was the most he could have hoped to have accomplished. Later, Dave would tell him the opening state was 'lackluster'.

After court, Dave did not come to Ed's office. By this time, Ed wasn't surprised. He would go back to his office and prepare for the next day's events.

Chapter 42

The first witness the State called was the woman who initially came across the scene of the first crime. She was driving home from a neighboring village where she had been visiting her sister. She noticed something odd as she passed by the crime scene. She noticed an open door and the dome light in the car illuminating the scene. As she pulled over to try to help, she saw the victim's body and then left, driving down the road about a half mile until she could get a cell signal.

She called 9-1-1 but did not return to the scene. The prosecution's examination of her took twenty minutes. It was then Ed's turn to cross-examine the witness.

"Ms. Jenkins," he began. "You say that the door was open. Did you see the car door lying in the snow about twenty feet from the car?"

"Yes, I did."

"And did the door appear to be torn from the car?"

"I can't really say. I didn't look at it closely."

Ed changed the subject slightly. "Now, you indicated that you saw a body. Did you see the whole body?"

Everyone in the courtroom could tell this was difficult for her. "Well, I saw pieces of the body. I didn't look that close."

"Was it snowing?"

"Yes, it was," the witness replied.

"But you could see the red blood in the snow, couldn't you?"

"Yes."

"So, you must have arrived soon after the murder?"

The witness began to tremble. "I guess you're right," she said.

Ed paused for a second. He wasn't sure what the witness would say but he decided to ask, anyhow.

"Did you observe any tire tracks near the victim or her vehicle?"

The witness gave the question some thought and then said, "No."

"Did you observe any footprints near the victim or her vehicle?"

"Yes," the witness replied.

"Where did they lead?"

"They went from the front driver's side of the vehicle and into the woods. They were headed toward town."

"Did you take a close look at the footprints?"

"I'm sorry," the witness said. "I just wanted to get out of there."

Ed thanked the witness and she left the witness stand. The next witness to testify was the state police detective first called to the scene. Most eyewitnesses who testify are intimidated by the courtroom and nervous about being questioned. They tend to be careful in their answers and default to the truth. Police witnesses are different. They are professionals, and part of their job is testifying before judges and juries.

They are relaxed, and because of the uniform they wear, they have a lot of credibility with judges and juries. They also know that their testimony is unlikely to be challenged by anyone other than the defense counsel. Most police officers have testified so often that they have lost their fear of the questions a defense attorney might ask. They also know how to stick to the State's theory of the case.

This detective was not the prosecuting officer. He had merely gone to the scene to oversee the collection of evidence. He was simply a link in the chain of events that would eventually lead to the search of Russ's apartment. The prosecutor's questioning was short and perfunctory. Two patrol troopers had arrived at the scene before him, observed the victim in several pieces, and then stretched yellow crime scene tape around the area. They then waited in their patrol car until the detective arrived.

Evidence techs came and gathered evidence from the scene. They then took photographs. About ten minutes after the detective's arrival, the county coroner showed up and collected the body for transport to the medical examiner who would conduct an autopsy. The detective then took possession of the evidence gathered at the scene and logged it into the evidence locker at the local state police barracks. That ended his involvement in the case.

"Detective," Ed said, beginning his cross, "did you observe the car door?"

"I did," the detective said.

"How far was it from the car?"

"About twenty-four feet." The detective wanted to show the exactitude of his observations.

"Did you examine the doorframe to determine how the door had been removed from the doorframe?"

"No, I'm not an engineer, and not really qualified to speculate on how things might have happened," the detective said with a slight smile.

"Did it appear to be torn off?" Ed asked.

"I'm sorry, but I can't speculate. I have no idea how the door was removed from the car."

"Now, turning to the area around the car, were you able to observe any footprints?"

The detective continued in an even tone. "Yes, I observed a lot of footprints. The responding troopers had walked around the crime scene. The paramedics who first arrived at the crime scene had walked around the area. After I arrived, the coroner walked around the area. I think it's safe to say there were a lot of footprints."

"Were there any that led into the woods?" Ed asked.

"Not that I saw," replied the detective.

"Had it been snowing before you arrived?" Ed asked.

"Yes."

"How much had it snowed between the time the crime was called in and the time you arrived?" Ed asked.

"I don't know," the detective replied. "Maybe a couple of inches."

The State next called one of the paramedics to describe the scene when he arrived. It was truly gruesome. The victim had been torn into several pieces and scattered around the area. There was blood everywhere. Ed had no cross-examination.

The next witness was the medical examiner. A short, rotund woman with closely cut gray hair. She described the cause of death as blunt force trauma and exsanguination. The victim had been beaten, torn apart, and died of blood loss. The State offered several photos of the victim, or at least some of the pieces of the victim, and seemed surprised that Ed had not objected to the pictures. The prosecutor also seemed surprised when Ed said he had no questions for the medical examiner 'at this time'.

He might have some questions later, after the State had introduced more evidence, but he didn't want to give the State anymore insight into his defense that he had to. He could call her later in his case and chief if he thought it necessary.

After the medical examiner concluded her testimony, the judge called it a day and warned the jurors not to discuss the case with anyone. Dave had appeared in the audience for a short period of time and then he left.

Trial practice is a lonely practice, and Ed spent the evening in his office, alone, preparing for the next day. By now, he knew this was the way it was going to be. He reviewed his notes for the next day's witnesses and then turned in early.

Chapter 43

The next day, Thursday, the State presented the heart of its case. The star witness was Detective John J. Jones of the state police. He took the stand confidently, smiled at the jury, and swore to tell the truth. His testimony of direct examination was just about perfect.

He had not been on duty the night the first murder occurred. He reported to the scene as quickly as he could but did not arrive until an hour and a half after the initial call came in. When he arrived, he thoroughly examined the crime scene. He did not see any footprints leading from the crime scene into the forest, but it had been snowing and he wouldn't have expected to see any. It was obvious that there had been a homicide.

They were able to identify the victim preliminarily from the vehicle registration and the driver's license the police had found in a purse located on the passenger's seat of the vehicle.

The driver's side door had been removed from the vehicle and positioned about twenty-five feet from the car. Crime scene techs had taken fingerprints from the car door, but were unable to match them to any known suspects. Thereafter, he began interviewing friends and relatives in an effort to identify a suspect.

When the second and third victims were discovered, Detective Jones realized they were dealing with a potential serial killer. He explained that serial killers are particularly difficult to capture because they tend to select their victims at random and have no prior significant history with the victim. Also, since Winter Haven was a resort town, it attracted a transient population. People came and left without establishing firm connections to the local area, and it was therefore difficult to track the movements of people like detectives in more settled areas might be able to.

Detective Jones explained to the jury that they received a major break in the case when the police received an anonymous call. Because of the hearsay rules, he was not able to tell the jury what the witness had said, but he was allowed to mention the call and explain what the police did after receiving the call. Based upon the phone call, they obtained a search warrant for the residence of Russell Strait.

Initially, they had considered surveilling Strait to obtain more evidence, but ultimately, the police decided it was too risky to leave him on the street. They thought he might kill again.

Russ' residence was essentially a pool house on a larger estate. The estate itself had been leased by a Charles Hunt but he sublet the pool house to Strait for the winter skiing season. At precisely 5:57 a.m. on a Tuesday morning, Detective Jones accompanied a SWAT team to the residence because they feared Strait might be armed and dangerous. They knocked and announced their presence as the law requires. Upon receiving no answer, they broke the door down and entered the house.

The building was small and there were only three rooms in the residence. These included a bedroom, a large room with a small TV and couch on one side, and a small kitchenette with a table and four chairs on the other. There was also a bathroom and two closets.

Russ was asleep in the bedroom when the SWAT team entered. He was 'secured' and allowed to dress before being taken to the kitchenette area for the duration of the search. Detective Jones explained that all searches are conducted pursuant to a plan to ensure that nothing of 'evidentiary value' was missed. As the investigating detective, it was Jones' job to supervise the search. He did not actually do any searching himself.

Rather, he sat with Strait, and observed his men searching the residence. As they located each item that might have evidentiary value, they would bring it to Jones who would catalog the evidence. All members of the search team wore rubber gloves and protective booties to prevent contamination of the evidence and the crime scene. As the search proceeded, one of the troopers located a tool in Russ' dresser that appeared to be constructed of stainless-steel.

It had the form of a set of animal jaws with artificial teeth welded to the frame. Jones placed the tool into an evidence bag, sealed it, and had the trooper who found the item sign it. Jones then countersigned the bag to preserve the chain of custody. The prosecutor handed the jaws to Detective Jones, who identified them as the tool discovered at Russ' residence and taken into custody.

The State, through other witnesses, would establish that the tool had traces of all three victims' blood in the interior parts of the mechanism. Also, the tool had Russ' fingerprints on it and no one else's. It was a damning piece of evidence.

The detective next testified about the fur coat that had been pulled from the closet in the main room of the house. He actually watched the recovery of this piece of evidence. As he looked across the room, he observed another trooper pull the fur coat from the closet. It was a dark gray or black color. It seemed odd that someone like Russ would have a full-length fur coat in his closet. The trooper who found the coat brought it to Detective Jones who, in turn, bagged it. Again, the trooper who recovered the bag signed it and Detective Jones countersigned the chain of custody document.

Finally, Detective Jones testified about the 'trophies' of serial killers. A trophy is actually a memento of a crime. It is used by the serial killer to form an emotional bond to the crime, as opposed to the victim. Sometimes, these trophies will be parts of a body or an intimate piece of clothing. In Strait's case, however, the perpetrator had collected property—specifically, jewelry from each of the victims.

In a shoebox located in the bottom of the bedroom closet, another trooper found three rings, two bracelets, and two necklaces. These items, like the fur coat and tool, were turned over to Detective Jones, who bagged and signed them together with the trooper who found them.

Later witnesses would identify Russ' fingerprints on the two bracelets. Blood on the fur coat would match the blood of three victims. With the admission of the exhibits, Detective Jones' direct examination came to an end. It was mid-afternoon and the judge could have continued with the cross-examination, but he decided to recess the case early. Ed left the courthouse at 3:30, and went to his office to prepare for the cross-examination the next day.

He was already prepared for the cross-examination but there was always more that could be done. Once again, Dave was nowhere to be found.

There was something about Detective Jones' testimony that bothered Ed, but he couldn't put his finger on it, until he awoke at 2:10 a.m. It was the fingerprints, the most damning pieces of evidence. There was one small table in the residence. Detective Jones sat there, wearing gloves. Russell Strait sat there, not wearing gloves. The evidence gathered by the detectives sat on the table, as well.

According to Detective Jones, the evidence was brought to the table and bagged immediately. If that were true, then Russell could not have touched the pieces of evidence as they sat on the table. *If* that were true.

But the search had been photographed while it was underway, and Ed thought he remembered a photograph of the table with Russell and Jones sitting at it. Did the photo contain a picture of the evidence? Ed didn't remember but he was soon in his office, in his pajamas, to find out.

Chapter 44

The next morning, Ed arrived at the courthouse early. The cross-examination of Detective Jones would be perhaps the most pivotal part of the trial and he wanted some time in the courtroom to collect his thoughts. When he arrived, Jones was already there. They exchanged pleasantries, sizing each other up. The relationship between defense attorneys and police is not as acrimonious as one might think. Most defense attorneys have good friends who are cops. Sometimes their best friends are cops.

Many police officers likewise count criminal defense attorneys among their best friends. This is not to say that either would jeopardize a case or endanger a client because of some out-of-court friendship. Rather, it is more like the relationship between Ralph Wolf and Sam Sheepdog in the old *Looney Tunes* cartoons. These two characters would punch a clock at the beginning of each episode, battle ferociously throughout the day, and then return to being friends after the clock was punched at the end of the day.

In reality, the vast majority of defendants in the modern American criminal justice system plead guilty. Trust between the prosecution and the defense is therefore essential. Likewise, if the police have arrested the wrong person, most would prefer to do the right thing. Being receptive to defense counsel can therefore further the ends of justice.

But it's not always that way. Some police officers hate all defense counsel, just as some defense counsel believe that all cops are corrupt racists. These police officers see the questioning by defense counsel as attacks on their integrity. They shy away from accountability and blame attorneys when defendants are found not guilty. Detective Jones was one of these sorts of police officers. He cut corners when necessary and saw the Bill of Rights as an unnecessary obstacle to police officers doing their job.

In his mind, criminals had no rights. Jones also had a huge ego, which was already bruised. He wasn't going to let this attorney pull anything over on him.

When the judge called the court to order, Detective Jones took the stand. Ed wasted no time in going after him.

"Detective Jones, you were at the scene of the first homicide, were you not?"

"I was."

"And did you observe the driver's side car door?"

"I did."

"How far was it from the vehicle?"

"About twenty-five feet."

"Did the door appear to have been torn from the car?"

"No." Detective Jones' answer was direct. Ed waited for a moment to see if the detective would continue, but he did not.

"Was the car door removed from the car?"

"Yes."

"Were you able to determine how the car door was removed from the car."

"No." Detective Jones, however, felt a need to explain some more, so he continued. "It appeared some sort of tool might have been used to pull the bolts holding the car door to the door frame from the frame."

"Were you able to determine what type of tool was used?"

"No," the detective answered.

"Why do you think a tool might have been used?" Lawyers are taught never to use open-ended questions on cross-examination, especially of police officers, but Ed thought this was a good time to break that rule.

"I don't know exactly…maybe professional instinct," Jones responded.

"Professional instinct. Isn't it true, Detective, that you thought a tool must have been used because no human can rip a car door from its hinges?"

Jones didn't know what to say. He repeated, "Professional instinct," but it sounded lame and disingenuous to everyone in the courtroom, especially the jury.

"Detective," Ed asked, trying to pin the detective down a bit more. "Do you know of any tool that could be used to pull the door from the doorframe the way it was done on that night?"

"I'm not a mechanic," the detective responded.

"Did you examine the car door yourself for any tool marks?" Ed asked.

"Yes," the detective replied.

Now was the time to be very direct and leading.

"And when you examined the car door, you didn't find any evidence of tool marks, did you?"

"Like I said, I'm not a mechanic."

"But you didn't see any tool marks, did you?" Ed was not about to let this line of questioning go, and Jones knew it.

"No," he answered.

"Did you submit the car door to the state police forensic unit in Harrisburg for analysis?"

Jones was secretly livid. How did this defense attorney know he had submitted the door for forensic analysis? He hadn't even told the prosecutor because he was afraid the prosecutor might turn the report over to defense counsel. He thought he'd better stick with the truth. Ed, however, did not know whether the car door had been submitted or not, but he surmised that it might have been.

"Yes," he answered.

"And they didn't find any evidence of tool marks either, did they?" Again, this was a guess but a safe one. Had the forensic investigators found anything, a report surely would have been produced.

"No," Jones answered. Jones was shedding credibility and Ed wanted to prolong the exercise.

"I take it, then, you don't know of any tool that could have removed the car door?"

"No," the detective responded, a bit reluctantly.

"Now, the car door that was lying in the snow twenty-five feet away, how much did that weigh?"

"I don't know," the detective responded, showing just the slightest hint of hostility in his voice.

"Would a hundred a twenty pounds sound about right?"

"I don't know," the detective responded in the same clipped voice.

"You never weighed the door or contacted the manufacturer to see how much the car door weighed?" Ed said with feigned disbelief.

Jones glared at the attorney for just a moment, careful not to be seen by the jury. Then he answered, "No."

Ed walked over to the defense counsel's table and gestured toward Russ. "Does Russ look like the kind of guy who could tear a car door from its hinges and toss it twenty-five feet?" Russ looked even more diminutive at that point.

Both Ed and the detective knew the jury wouldn't think Russ would be able to throw a car door twenty-five feet.

Detective Jones paused for a minute. "Maybe he carried the door to that location and put it down, or maybe he had an accomplice," the detective speculated.

"Now, Detective, you've been a state trooper for over thirty years, haven't you?"

"Yes," the detective said, unsure as to where this was going.

"And you've been a criminal investigator for close to twenty years, correct?"

"Eighteen, actually." The detective was uncomfortable ceding too much to the defense attorney.

"Now, with all of that experience, were you able to identify an accomplice?" The defense attorney asked.

"No."

"Have you identified anyone you suspect of being an accomplice?"

Detective Jones thought about saying something like, the investigation was still open and the police were looking at other leads, but that would have been a lie. After a pregnant pause, the detective simply said, "No."

"Now, you speculated that Russ could have carried the door to its location; did you observe any footprints leading from the vehicle to the car door?"

"No," the detective replied, but felt he should explain. "It was snowing and the snow would have covered up any footprints."

"So, you're telling us you got there too late?"

"No. I got there as soon as I could."

"But it was too late to see any footprints that might have been left behind."

"Yes."

"Did you see any indentations in the snow where footsteps might have filled in the holes?"

"No."

"Did anyone report to you the presence of footprints leading from the car to the door?"

"No."

"Now, a prior witness reported seeing tracks leading from the crime scene into the woods behind the vehicle. Do you recall that testimony?"

"Yes, I do."

"Were you aware of that before the witness testified yesterday?"

"No."

"That would be pretty important evidence, wouldn't it? I mean, if there were tracks leading from the scene of a homicide, you'd want to follow them, wouldn't you?"

There was no graceful way out of the box the detective now found himself in. "Yes, that would be information I would have liked to have had."

Ed next turned to the search of Russell's residence.

"Now, Detective, you were also in charge of the search of Russ' residence, were you not?"

"Yes, I was," the detective answered.

"That search was based upon an anonymous tip?"

"In part," Detective Jones answered.

"Was there anything other than that tip that led you to the residence?" The defense counsel asked.

"No."

"Were you able to identify who this anonymous individual was?"

"We were not."

"Did you try?"

"We did."

Ed thought about the exact way to phrase the next question. "But this anonymous tipster was able to tell you about evidence located inside the residence?"

"Yes," the police officer answered.

"So, this tipster must have been inside the residence?"

"I suppose so," the detective replied.

"Did you collect fingerprints from inside Russ' residence?"

"No," the detective answered.

Ed had set the stage to suggest that the anonymous tipster could have been the murderer. Based upon the testimony he had adduced from the detective, he could argue that the tipster had knowledge of the murders and access to the residence. Furthermore, he could point to the failure to take fingerprints as sloppiness on the part of the police.

Ed walked over to the evidence table and picked up the set of steel jaws that had been admitted as State's Exhibit 47. He walked over to the witness stand and set it in front of the detective.

"Now, Detective Jones, are these the steel jaws that you found at Russell Strait's residence?" Ed asked.

Detective Jones was relieved to be back on safe ground. "You know that they are, Counselor," he answered, and then said, "They have your client's fingerprints on them."

"We will get to the fingerprints in just a few minutes, but for now, we just need you to confirm that you recovered this piece of evidence."

"We did," the detective replied. Then went on to say, "They had DNA from all three victims." It was another gratuitous remark but Ed decided to ignore it. He didn't want the jury or the court distracted by petty disputes.

"Is it your theory that this…" He paused for a second before continuing, "Tool is the murder weapon?"

"Yes," the detective responded.

Ed walked over to the evidence table once more and picked up a report. He then walked over to Detective Jones again and handed it to him.

"Detective Jones," he began. "This is the autopsy report from the medical examiner concerning victim number 3. Do you recognize that document?" Jones admitted that he did.

"Could you then turn to page 9, paragraph 3 and begin reading at the beginning of the paragraph?"

Jones did not like this but he was stuck. "On the victim's upper-right leg, which had been severed from the body, there were a series of four horizontal lacerations. These lacerations were identified as lacerations 37, 38, 39, and 40 on the accompanying diagram." Jones tried to keep his voice steady so as to betray no emotion. He paused to see if he could stop but the lawyer told him to continue.

"Laceration 37 was measured to be two-point-nine inches deep, laceration 38 was located two-point-two inches from laceration 37. Laceration 38 was measured to be three-point-two inches deep. Laceration 39 was two-point-two inches from laceration 38 and was measured to be three-point-two inches deep. The fourth laceration, laceration 40, was also two-point-two inches from laceration 39 and was three inches deep."

"You can stop there, Detective." Ed looked at the device that sat on the table in front of Detective Jones. It appeared to be a steel replica of some type of animal jaws, maybe a bear or a wolf. It was a hideous contraption that appeared to be designed to inflict pain.

"Incidentally, Detective Jones, were you able to determine where the tool was manufactured?"

"No," the detective answered. It was a recurring theme.

"And I suppose you weren't able to determine how much it cost, were you?"

"No."

"Now, Detective, please take a look at the teeth—the steel teeth—on Exhibit 47. How long are those teeth?"

Detective Jones was about to say he didn't have any way to measure them when Ed pulled a ruler from his suit pocket and handed it to the detective. Jones thought about protesting but he knew he was stuck. Jones measured the longest tooth; it measured a mere two inches. Ed then asked Jones to measure the distance between the two parallel rows of teeth. That distance was just over three and a half inches.

"Now, Detective, this device with its two-inch teeth could not have produced three-inch lacerations, could it?"

The prosecutor objected in an effort to help out the detective but the judge overruled the objection without waiting for Ed to say anything and ordered the police officer to answer.

"I suppose not," the detective said.

"And these lacerations that are two-point-two inches apart could not have been made by this device where the rows of teeth are three and a half inches apart?"

"I don't know," was the best the police officer could muster.

"Counsel," the judge asked, "are you almost through?" The judge had lost track of time and had failed to call a mid-morning recess. They were now into the lunch hour. When Ed said he had more questions, the judge called a lunch recess. Ed didn't leave the courtroom for lunch. Instead, he stayed in his chair, thinking about the afternoon's questions.

When court reconvened, Ed struck quickly. He walked over to the evidence table, picked up the fur coat and handed it to Jones.

"Do you recognize this?" He asked.

"Of course," the detective responded, apparently having regained some strength over lunch.

"Do you know where this coat was made?"

"No."

"Do you know *when* the coat was made?"

"No."

"Do you know who made the coat?"

"No."

Ed walked back to counsel table and picked up a piece of paper. Turning back to the detective, he said, "Would it surprise you to learn that this coat was made by a Saul Weismann in New York about five years ago?"

There was an immediate objection from the prosecutor. These were facts not in evidence but the judge decided to permit the question, anyhow.

"I don't know," was all Detective Jones could say, but he hated admitting there was so much he did not know.

"Would it surprise you to learn that it cost $12,000?"

This question precipitated another objection. The judge decided to issue a cautionary instruction to the jury.

"Ladies and gentlemen of the jury, sometimes when an attorney asks a question, that question presumes certain facts to be true. Such questions are proper; however, I am instructing you that you may not consider any fact contained in a question to be true just because the attorney asked the question. You may only consider the fact to be true if the witness agrees that the fact is true."

When the judge finished, Ed paused until the judge told him to proceed. Ed asked exactly the same question.

"I don't know how much a coat like that costs," the detective answered.

"When you were searching Russell Strait's home, did you find anything that would indicate he could afford a $12,000 coat?"

Detective Jones decided it was his turn to take a shot. "Maybe he stole it," he answered, pleased with himself. He knew there would be an objection and he would be admonished by the judge, but he didn't care.

But there was no objection. Instead, the attorney followed up on the question.

"Did you check to see if a coat matching Exhibit 52 had ever been reported stolen?"

"No." Again, the detective was back in uncomfortable territory.

"Did you send a description of this coat to any other police agencies?"

"No."

"Do you know if a wolf skin fur coat has been reported stolen anywhere in the country?"

"No."

"Did you contact the FBI about the coat?"

"No."

"Is it fair to say that you have no evidence to suggest the coat was stolen?"

Jones was once again trapped. He paused for a few seconds trying to find a way out, but he couldn't. "Yes," he said finally.

"So, you accused Russell Strait of stealing an expensive fur coat, even though you had no evidence?"

Jones knew he had stepped into another trap. "I never accused him of stealing anything. I said 'maybe'." It was an anemic response, and the detective knew it. It was time for Ed to move on to his next line of questioning.

"Now, Detective Jones, on the morning of the search, you stationed yourself at the dinette table, correct?"

"Yes."

"And Russell Strait was also sitting at that table?"

"Yes," the detective answered.

"Was he handcuffed?" The attorney asked.

"No." In fact, Russ was not in custody at this time and it would have been improper to handcuff him.

"So, his hands were free?" Ed asked for emphasis.

"Yes," the detective responded.

"And you were just sitting there as the other officers searched the residence?"

"Well, I was keeping an eye on the suspect," the detective responded.

"You mean Russell?"

"Yes."

"Now, as the various pieces of evidence were brought over and put on the table, did you touch them?"

Detective Jones was not sure where this was going. "Of course, but I was wearing rubber gloves so that the evidence would not be contaminated."

"Because contamination of the evidence could be a major issue, couldn't it?" Ed asked.

"It could," the detective responded.

"Was Russell wearing rubber gloves?" Ed asked.

The detective paused for a minute before answering, "No."

"Did you show the items of evidence, which were on the dinette table, to Russell?" Ed asked.

"No," the detective responded.

"Could Russell Strait have touched any of the items of evidence as he sat there at the table?"

"No, the suspect could not have touched any of the items of evidence," the detective answered.

"Why not?" It was a question that might give the detective an opportunity to hang himself.

"Well, Counselor," Detective Jones began. "Each piece of evidence was brought to me separately. Once it was brought to me, I sealed it in a plastic bag. I signed the evidence bag and so did the trooper who found the particular piece of evidence. You heard that from the other troopers who testified. Strait could not have touched any item of evidence."

"And that is the way it's supposed to be," Ed asked.

"Exactly."

"And I suppose that's because if the evidence were not immediately bagged—if it were simply allowed to lie on the table—the defendant could touch it and contaminate it?"

"Exactly," Detective Jones said.

"And you're sure that on the day of the search, no piece of evidence was left unbagged on the table in front of Russell Strait?"

"I'm sure," the detective said confidently.

Ed walked back to his table and picked up something. He turned and said to the judge, "Your Honor, I'd like to show Detective Jones Defense Exhibit 19."

Immediately, the prosecutor was on his feet, objecting. "Your Honor," she said, "this exhibit was not on the defense exhibit list. We object to its use."

"Counsel?" The judge said, inviting a response.

"Yes, Your Honor. We only learned of the significance of this exhibit last night. It was provided to us by the State, so they were clearly aware of it. It's not a surprise. Besides, we are using it for impeachment purposes."

It was exactly the right thing to say. Evidence that is being used for impeachment purposes does not need to be disclosed to the opposing party. The reason for the disclosure rules is to prevent unfair surprise. Since the evidence came from the State, the State could not argue that it was unaware of the evidence. The judge overruled the objection and allowed Ed to proceed.

Ed walked up to Detective Jones and laid the picture in front of him. In a series of responses, the detective explained that there had been a police photographer at the scene of the search to document everything that had happened. He had taken hundreds of photos during the course of the search. This was one of those photos. Jones immediately saw the problem.

"Now, Detective Jones," Ed started. "Who all are in the picture?"

"I'm in the photo and the defendant is in the picture."

"And where are you at?"

"Seated at the dinette table."

"Who else is at the table?"

"The defendant."

"Is there anything on the table between the two of you?"

Detective Jones just wanted to get through the rest of the questions. "Yes, there is jewelry on the table."

"And that jewelry, is it the jewelry seized in the search on Russell's home?"

"Yes," the detective said.

"And that jewelry, is it in evidence bags?"

"It doesn't appear to be," the detective continued.

"Why not?"

There was not a good answer. Jones just sat there.

"How far are Russell Strait's hands from that jewelry?"

"Maybe six inches."

There were only a few more questions Ed asked, although none of them were questions of consequence. When Ed finally finished his cross, the State had no more questions for Detective Jones. They wanted him off the stand as quickly as possible. They did not want to give Ed a chance to ask any more questions.

Chapter 45

After Detective Jones' testimony, the rest of the government's case was anticlimactic. An expert in fingerprints—a forensic technician—testified that he had a bachelor's degree in biology and had taken a five-day course on fingerprints. The bachelor's degree had nothing to do with fingerprints. Basically, the kid fed the fingerprints into a database to see if there were any matches. There were not.

Then he compared the fingerprints to Russell Strait's fingerprints, which had been taken at the local police station, to fingerprints off of the tool with the teeth in it and the jewelry the police recovered. There were a number of matches. That was it.

Next came a DNA expert to talk about DNA and explain that the victims' DNA was locate on various pieces of evidence. Few things are as boring as a DNA expert. Three jurors and the judge fought drowsiness; two of them lost. In the end, the government proved the victim's DNA was on the items located in the defendant's residence. The last witness the State called was Charles.

He had been called by the State to say that he had rented the pool house on his property to the defendant and that no one other than Strait had access to the property. He was not an important witness, and he said nothing that directly implicated Russ, but Ed felt compelled to ask a couple of questions.

"Of course, you had a key to the pool house?" Ed asked.

"Of course," Charles answered.

"You also have a servant that lives in your house?"

"Yes, Samuel."

"Did Samuel have access to the key?"

Charles thought for a moment before answering. "I keep the key in a drawer in the kitchen. I guess Samuel would have access to it if he wanted, but he wouldn't have had any reason to go there."

"How would you describe Samuel?"

Charles took another moment before answering. "He's a large man, maybe six feet six inches tall. I would guess he weighs somewhere around two hundred and sixty pounds or so." Ed waited a moment as he contemplated his next action. After deciding what he wanted to do, Ed picked up the fur coat the State had entered into evidence. He handed it to Charles.

"Do you recognize this coat?" He asked.

"No," Charles answered.

There was no point in going further.

The final three witnesses were relatives of each of the victims. Cindy's mother identified one of the rings found in Russ' house as belonging to Cindy. She also identified one of the necklaces as one she had given to Cindy on her fifteenth birthday. She could not hold back tears as she held the necklace in her hand, knowing she would never see Cindy again.

Susan, the mother of Megan, testified about the bracelet she and Megan's father had purchased for her the previous Christmas. Holding back tears, she identified one of the bracelets that had been recovered from Russ' room. Maria, the sister of Danny, identified another necklace and a ring as belonging to her sister, who had left Mexico two years before. There was another ring that no one identified.

The State rested at 2:00 p.m. on Thursday. The judge told the jury they could go home and then held a conference to see how long the rest of the case would take. Ed informed the judge that he had only one witness and possibly Russell—defense counsel never liked to commit to calling the defendant until the last possible moment. When Ed finished, the judge announced that the testimony would close on the following day, and that after the jury was sent home for the weekend, counsel and the judge would review the jury instructions in the afternoon.

Ed went back to his office before returning home for the evening. He called Dave and asked him to come in to review his testimony. Dave, however, said that he couldn't. He also told Ed that he should be well aware of Dave's testimony. Then, without saying goodbye, Dave hung up. Ed sat on his deck, trying to figure out what was wrong with Dave. They had been friends and worked together for twenty years and, although Dave could be moody, his behavior in this case was difficult to understand. Ed wasn't even sure if Dave would show up to testify the next day.

Ed decided to visit Russell at the jail. He didn't think Russell should testify, but he needed to confer with the client. The decision to testify or not ultimately belonged to Russell.

Chapter 46

Jail cells possess an odd quality of both sterility and filth. They are sterile because of the lack of life or hope. Iron bars and concrete wall and floors, all painted the same steel-blue color, create an intentionally drab atmosphere. There is no cleaning service, and the inmates assigned to clean the cells care little about cleanliness. There are no large items of trash, no crumpled papers or empty Styrofoam cups. There is only the accumulated dust in the corners and under the benches and beds.

To complete the feeling of powerlessness meant to control inmates is the lone stainless-steel toilet in the corner of the cell that strips away any sense of human dignity that could remain. Russell had now lived in this place for over seven months and had adjusted to his new environment. Truth be told, he expected to never leave these surroundings, or surroundings similar to them. Other prisoners who passed through the county jail told him that the state penitentiary was better. There was more to do.

You could read and develop friendships with other inmates with whom you would spend your life with. Russell knew he faced the death penalty, but he also knew that the State had not actually executed anyone in more than thirty years. He knew he was innocent, but he also knew that things never worked out for people like him.

He appreciated Ed's efforts, although he suspected they would not come to anything. For a long time, Dave had come to see him the most. He liked Dave and thought Dave understood him best. Dave's visits stopped about two months earlier. Russell didn't know why. He suspected Dave had better things to do. Ed still came but not that often. Ed had never come that often. Ed explained that his time was better spent working on Russell's case. Russell didn't know what that meant but he appreciated the visits when they did occur.

"Tomorrow is going to be the last day of the trial," Ed began.

"I know," Russell replied. "Thank you for everything. You did a really good job."

Ed smiled. "We will see. I need to know if you want to testify."

"Well," Russell said. "I suppose not. I get confused and scared. I don't think I would help."

"Probably wise," Ed said.

The two talked for another forty minutes about all sorts of things, but they didn't talk about the trial. Only one witness remained, and then it would be for the jury to decide. Russell said that he trusted Dave. Ed hoped that trust was not misplaced.

Chapter 47

Ed had given up on trying to talk to Dave, and he was mildly surprised when Dave actually did show up in court. He was wearing a blue suit with a blue tie. As Ed tried to talk to Dave, the judge entered the courtroom.

"All rise," said the clerk of courts. When the judge was seated, the clerk continued, "Please be seated." It was an ancient ritual but one still followed in American courts. Then the judge in his long black robe looked at Ed and told him to call his first witness. Of course, the defense only had one witness. Ed announced David Krell's name, and Dave approached the witness stand. He took an oath to tell the truth, the whole truth, and nothing but the truth.

Then he entered the witness stand to the right of the judge and took a seat. The clerk asked for his name and address, and then it was Ed's turn to start asking questions.

"Mr. Krell," Ed began, "what do you do for a living?"

"I am a private investigator," Dave answered.

"How long have you been a private investigator?"

"Oh, let me see," he said as if counting the number of years required some effort. "I guess about twelve years now."

"And what did you do before you were a private investigator?"

Dave hesitated a moment and then said, "I was a detective for the Scranton Polce Department. In that capacity, I investigated serious felonies and was involved in the investigation of over ten murders."

Ed was not certain this answer was correct but he continued with his line of questioning. "What does a private investigator do?"

"Basically, the same thing," Dave started. "One of my duties involves investigating crimes, usually for criminal defense lawyers. I interview witnesses, collect documents, and put the defense of the case together for lawyers."

It was a gross exaggeration of what Dave really did and the answer irked Ed. He decided, once again, to let it go.

"Mr. Krell," Ed said, "you remember the night that Cindy Owens was murdered?"

"Yes," Dave answered.

"Where were you the morning after?"

"I don't remember," Dave replied. Ed was stunned by the answer.

"Well," Ed said, trying to get the examination back on track. "Do you recall anything unusual happening that morning?"

"No," Dave answered. That morning had been the only thing Dave had wanted to talk about for the previous nine months.

"Do you remember coming to my house that morning?" Ed asked.

"No," Dave answered.

"Let me refresh your recollection. This would have been the morning after the first woman had been murdered. Does that refresh your recollection?"

Dave hesitated for a minute and then said, "I'm sorry, Ed, but I can't lie. I know you want me to say I saw a big hairy monster, but I didn't. I investigated as much as I could, but all of the evidence pointed toward Russell. I kept telling you that but you wanted an acquittal, no matter what. Even after Russell told us he was the murderer…"

Dave's voice trailed off as the observers in the galley began talking and the judge started pounding his gavel. As the jury was taken from the courtroom, Russell leaned over to ask why Dave would lie. The judge's face was red as he took over the questioning of the witness.

"Are you saying the defense counsel is suborning perjury?" The judge asked after the jury left.

"I don't know; I'm not a lawyer," Dave answered. "All I can tell you is that we rehearsed this story many times over the past couple of months. It was a lie, and I told defense counsel that I didn't want to lie. But he told me I had to. There were other things he wanted me to do. He wanted me to falsify a receipt for the fur coat the police found."

"Why did you agree to do it?" The judge asked.

"We've been friends for decades. Ed is, or was, my best friend. He vouched for me when I got my detective license and he has been my biggest client over the years. I felt like I owed him. But I've also spent a life in law enforcement. The State had offered the defendant a plea agreement that I thought was very generous. It would have saved his life but Ed wanted the glory. In the end, I'm a servant of the law. I couldn't lie under oath."

Ed was stunned and speechless, but he felt the need to say something. "Your Honor—" He began, but the judge cut him off.

"Mr. Reynolds," the judge began. "You have a Fifth Amendment right to remain silent. Here is what is going to happen today. First, I am declaring a mistrial and dismissing the jury. There is no way that the defendant can get a fair trial after these revelations. In addition, Mr. Krell disclosed attorney-client privileged information on the witness stand, which he should not have done. I am going to file a report with the state licensing agency."

"He owed a duty to his client, and he flagrantly violated that duty. Uttering a private conversation where a client admits guilt, allegedly, in a public form— a courtroom on the record no less…it's unbelievable." The judge glowered at Dave, and Dave was a bit taken back. He had expected to be treated as a hero for revealing Ed's dishonesty. He couldn't believe the judge was being critical of him. Reporting him to the licensing board?

It didn't matter, Dave said to himself as he sat in the witness chair. After all, he was about to be rich—richer even than the judge, so who cared what this old man in a black robe thought. The judge continued, "Next, defense counsel is disqualified from further representation in this case and is directed to have no further contact with this defendant. I am appointing the public defender to represent the defendant."

"Furthermore, I am ordering the district attorney to re-offer any plea agreements it had previously offered. It does not sound like the defendant received accurate advice concerning the plea offer."

"Next, I am finding defense counsel to be in direct criminal contempt and ordering him to be taken into custody immediately. He will spend at least this weekend in custody. Monday morning, I will hear from defense counsel after he has had an opportunity to confer with his own counsel. I am also reporting this matter to the state bar for investigation. Court adjourned."

The testimony of the private detective had caught the judge completely by surprise. Never before in his career had such a thing happened. He knew and liked Ed Reynolds, even after he became aware of his previous professional problems. He suspected there might be more to the private detective's testimony than met the eye, but the sensational events of the morning required decisive action. He would sort things out over the coming weeks.

Chapter 48

The day after the trial ended, at about 10:00 in the evening, Charles Hunt paid Dave Krell a visit. He would have liked to have visited in his animal form but that would have been too risky. This visit required more subtlety.

The driveway was empty as he came up the sidewalk. He had walked the nearly three miles from his chalet to Dave's ranch house, careful not to be seen. He watched the house for a further half hour to ensure no one was at home. When he was satisfied that Dave was there alone and that no one had seen him, he approached the door on the side of the house and knocked. A minute later, Dave answered the door and motioned for Hunt to come in.

"Are you alone?" Hunt asked.

"Yes. Just like you said, I sent my family to New York for the weekend. They think I am at my hunting cabin in New Hampshire and out of cell phone range. They won't bother us."

"Perfect," Hunt responded with a smile. He had brought with him a briefcase and a cardboard box.

Hunt walked over to the table in the breakfast nook and removed a small laptop from his briefcase. "What's your login?" He asked.

Dave told him the login information for the Wi-Fi. In a few moments, Hunt was online. As Dave watched, he logged into a bank account for a bank in Cyprus and transferred $1,000,000 to a bank in the Bahamas. The account had been set up in Dave Krell's name. He then handed Dave a piece of paper with the login into the Bahamian bank—the username was Dave's initials. With that, Charles stood and turned around.

"Go ahead and change the password," he said. "The money is yours."

With a couple of keystrokes, Dave had more money than he had ever had before. After he changed the password, Hunt shut down his laptop and placed it back into his briefcase. He then opened the cardboard box and pulled out a bottle of wine.

"Perhaps we should celebrate," he said.

Dave went to retrieve a couple of wine glasses. He didn't actually have wine glasses but he went for the best glasses he could find. When Dave returned, Hunt said to him, "I really appreciate your help. Reynolds seemed to be making headway with the jury. I even started to fear that the jury might find that Strait kid not guilty. Then, they would have opened the investigation and who knows what would have happened."

"I am fortunate that you decided to come with me. You really saved the day. Tell me, how long have you and Ed Reynolds known each other?"

"It must be twenty years by now."

"And yet you had no qualms betraying him?"

"Well, you know, it really wasn't like we were best friends. He always thought that he was better than me. I would do all the leg work and he would take all the credit and all the money. I pretended we were friends. He thought we were friends but I never really liked him."

"And lying to the court so convincingly. That didn't bother you?"

"Well, sometimes there are more important things that need to be considered." Dave didn't add that this was not the first time he had lied to a court, nor did he expect it would be the last.

Hunt poured some wine into each of the glasses. It seemed uncouth, almost a sin, to pour fine wine into water glasses, but sometimes one has to make sacrifices. He raised a glass and proposed a toast.

"Here's to the future," he said. With that, the two men clanked their glasses together. They thudded together like two blocks of wood.

The wine was a fine wine that cost about $400 a bottle, not the most expensive wine but acceptable. Hunt thought that wine like this would be wasted on Dave, anyhow, but he needed to maintain an illusion. He was correct, of course. Dave couldn't tell the difference between this wine and the $25 bottle his wife sometimes picked up at the local wine and spirits store.

As Dave gulped the wine, Hunt almost stopped him to explain that fine wine was for sipping, but then he thought, *why bother?* Hunt then removed another document from his briefcase and sat it on the table in front of Dave.

"I've taken the liberty of having my lawyers draw up an employment contract. I will leave it here for you to read over, but basically, one of my companies in New York is hiring you as the Head of Corporate Investigations. Your salary will be $500,000 per year for a minimum of two years, but I hope much longer. You will report only to me and you will take orders only from me."

"The company is located in New York but you are free to live anywhere you want. However, you must be available to me at all times. If you're interested in relocating to New Orleans, I can have someone arrange suitable accommodation for you. The contract provides that you will start work in sixty days, but we can adjust that date if you like. Do you have any questions?"

Dave was unsure what to say. He thought he should ask something but he didn't know what. He asked about vacation and health insurance. *He's just been given a million dollars, and he asks about health insurance,* Hunt thought.

He paused for a moment, turning to look at Dave. "Where does that door lead?" He asked, pointing to a door on the interior wall.

"Oh, that goes to the basement," Dave responded.

"Do you mind if we take a look?" The request puzzled Dave but he felt he should accede to his guest's request. He smiled when he saw Dave's hesitation. "Oh, please let me explain. I will be leaving the area in a few days. I have a case of rare burgundy that I don't want to take with me," he said, pointing to the box he brought with him.

"I was hoping I could store it here, if you don't mind and if the space is suitable. As you know, wine needs to be stored in a specific environment, someplace cooler and with the right humidity, like a basement. That's where the term 'wine cellar' comes from."

"Sure," Dave said as he walked across the room. He opened the door to give Hunt a tour of the basement.

In a flash, however, Hunt seized Dave by the neck and, with a flick of his wrist, severed Dave's spinal cord. In his years of killing, Hunt had become an expert at the application of just the right amount of force. He knew how much force would kill a person and how much would leave them alive. He wanted Krell alive, at least for now. He allowed the private detective to fall like a limp rag to the bottom of the steps.

Dave had no feeling in his body; he felt no pain anywhere. Strangely enough, he was still conscious, but he could not command a single muscle in his body to move.

Hunt slowly walked down the steps and knelt over Dave's broken body. "In layman's terms, you have suffered a broken neck. Whoever finds you will conclude that you fell and broke your neck. These injuries are always fatal but sometimes it takes hours for a person to die. You may live for five or six hours. If you are very lucky, you may not die until tomorrow morning. It doesn't matter. Your wife won't arrive for another two days, and it will likely take some time for her to check the basement. By that time, you will be long dead."

"You should thank me for this mercy. You see, you now have to time to make things right with your creator, if you think you have one. You might want to think about the fact that you are a fraud, a liar, and a fool. You know what I am and what I've done, and yet, for very little money, you were willing to serve me. I suspect your heart is as black as mine, but who knows. You can ask for forgiveness, even though you don't deserve it."

"As your life slowly ebbs from your body, think about the fact that you have no hope. You can't call for help. No one will come looking for you. You are alone. You can't even ask why, but you know your end is certain. All you can do is lay there and wait for that end to come."

"All I can tell you for certain is that you are going to die here alone. You will never see your wife or your daughter. You'll never enjoy the money you received for betraying your best friend. You will lie here in the dark until your heart ceases to beat. This is my final goodbye."

There was more Hunt could have said but he was growing bored lecturing a corpse. He turned away from Krell, slowly ascended the stairs, shut off the light, and shut the door. He probably should have mentioned that Krell would die in the dark, as well, but he forgot that part. He spent the next half hour wiping down everything he could possibly have touched. He left behind no evidence that he had ever been there.

He washed the water glasses and put them back in the cupboard Dave had taken them from. When he left, he took the laptop he had brought with him. There had never been any money transferred. It had all been fake. He also took the case of wine and the wine bottle he had opened for himself and Krell. There was no evidence that he had even been there.

Chapter 49

Ed had not expected his legal career to end in prison, but that was where he sat now. He had visited prisons in the past, most recently to see Russell Strait, but he always knew he would be leaving in an hour or two. He had been brought over from the court in handcuffs, and once at the prison, had been 'processed', meaning he had been fingerprinted and photographed. The photo would be released to the media and he would no doubt make the front page.

Another lawyer once told him that there was no such thing as bad publicity. He wasn't so sure.

He was forced to strip naked upon arrival and then provided with a one-size-fits-all yellow jumpsuit. Two guards escorted him to his cell. They seemed embarrassed by the situation. When he got to the cell, one of the guards geastured for him to enter the cell, showing him where to go. The other whispered to him, telling him not to worry, that he would probably be out soon.

Because the local county jail where Ed was placed was not crowded—and because of Ed's age, status, and lack of any criminal record—he was given a cell to himself. Later, when he was allowed to leave his cell for a break, one of the guards allowed him to call his wife. He hated to make the call; he feared what this further humiliation would do to her.

She was surprisingly sympathetic and seemed more concerned about Ed than she was about herself. When she came to visit Saturday morning, Ed could see the worry on her face. They talked for hours. It was the best conversation they'd had since early in their marriage. They talked about retiring and moving away. His legal career seemed to be over but there was still a lot that they could do. Money would be a problem but Ed could probably find something to do.

Ed's wife left a couple of novels for him to read, and after she left, he returned to his cell to read them. It was surprisingly peaceful in prison, and the crushing weight of being a criminal defense lawyer was now gone. There was also a liberating feeling in knowing that he was no longer in control. A judge would now decide his fate and Ed accepted the fact that he would be here as long as the judge wanted him here. He suspected it could be a couple of months, but deep down, he believed he would be cleared.

Now at the end of his career, Ed looked back to contemplate his successes and failures. He had soared to the heights of his profession, renowned within bar associations, sought out by the best lawyers in the world, flying around in his own private jet. He had now been laid low, imprisoned, broke, without a friend in the world. His best friend, or the person he thought to be his best friend, had been the source of his ultimate demise. Strangely, however, he was at peace.

He remembered a line from Rudyard Kipling's poem *If*: 'If you can meet with Triumph and Disaster and treat those two impostors just the same…you'll be a Man, my son'. He was the same man he had been when he was rich, and he was no less a man now. His greatest regret, he realized, was that as he contemplated his life, he considered at first only his professional life. He had long neglected his wife and his family, and that was his greatest failure. Maybe it would not be too late to change.

He began reading one of the novels his wife had brought. Normally, he would not have had time to read a novel, but now he had more time than he could have contemplated. As darkness approached, he fell into a deep and dreamless sleep.

Chapter 50

Things had not gone as Charles Hunt had planned. The hunting had been good but he had been seen by three people. Krell was now dead, or soon would be. Shelly was debilitated, and it was unlikely she would say anything. And then there was Edwin Reynolds. The crux of Hunt's plans always centered on leaving a fall guy. In his case, it was Russell Strait. The police followed the clues and arrested Strait, as they were supposed to.

Reynolds had come very close however, to derailing the whole plan. If it hadn't been for Krell, Strait could have been acquitted, upending his entire scheme. But the lawyer's spirited defense had caused other complications. He had been forced to kill Krell, not that he had any qualms about that. He was no more significant than a gnat to him. But it was a death that would have to be explained.

He felt sure any investigation would end with the obvious conclusion that Krell fell down the steps and broke his neck, but there was a possibility, however slim, that someone might look deeper.

The other loose end was Edwin Reynolds himself. Hunt had procured a poison on the black market in Russia using several intermediaries, at least one of whom was now dead. The poison was fast-acting, simulated a heart attack, and was not detectable. He planned to inject Ed with the poison over the weekend.

Some people might think that it was too coincidental that two people involved in the same case would die on the same weekend—one by heart attack and the other by accident—but there would be no evidence to the contrary. It wasn't ideal but it would have to work.

The judge had thwarted that plan by putting Reynolds in jail. He was now beyond Hunt's reach. Hunt contemplated trying to smuggle the poison into the prison and injecting him there, but he couldn't make the plan work. There was a significant risk the syringe would be discovered when he entered the prison.

Even if he were successful in smuggling the syringe through prison security, he found out that he could not have an in-person meeting with Ed.

Since he was not a relative, he could only meet through a plexiglass window and speak over the phone. There would be no way to administer an injection.

Charles thought about staying longer, until Ed was released from custody, but he had no idea when that would be. Besides, he thought he had already stayed much longer than he should have. No, he was going to leave, but that still left a loose end. It was just the way it would have to be.

On Sunday morning, he decided to visit Edwin Reynolds in the local jail. There was a conversation he wanted to have with the lawyer.

He was surprised at how much time it took to pass through security before he was finally able to meet with Ed. After a little over an hour, he was ushered into a long room with a bunch of dividers separating one station from another. There was a single stool in each station affixed to the floor and facing a thick plexiglass window. A phone, the old commercial kind businesses used before cell phones, hung on the wall. This morning, no one else was in the room.

Charles Hunt was escorted to one of the stations and told to sit on the stool and wait. After about fifteen minutes, Ed arrived in his yellow jumpsuit. Hunt and the lawyer picked up the phone simultaneously. There was no phone network. They could only talk to each other.

"What can I do for you?" Ed said, beginning the conversation. When he had been told there was a Charles Hunt there to see him, he initially considered refusing the visit but ultimately decided to see him. He had nothing else to do and there might be a chance he could learn something.

"It brings me no joy to see you in this position," Charles replied.

"Me neither," said Ed.

Charles chose his next words very carefully. "I will make this brief. I believe you may have stumbled into some things you may not understand. It would be unfortunate if you were to inadvertently come across information that could jeopardize not only your life, but the lives of everyone dear to you."

He paused to let the words dig in. Then he continued, "At this time, you have nothing to fear. You and your family are safe. I can guarantee that. Enjoy your life and enjoy your family. Just don't look any further."

With that, Charles stood and hung up his phone. Ed hung up his phone as well. His decision to hunt in the United States had been exciting. It had given him all the thrill he could have imagined, but the danger he encountered wasn't worth it. He would never visit this town again, and he hoped never to see this town, or even this state again. Hopefully, he would never hear the name 'Edwin Reynolds' or see his face again. If he did, there would be no more Edwin Reynolds.

By 3:00 that afternoon, Hunt was on his private jet, headed for Louisiana. He would take a few weeks to contemplate his next hunting trip, but for a while at least, he would confine his hunting to third-world countries.

Chapter 51

Over the weekend, the judge decided that Ed's conduct was probably more indirect criminal contempt than direct criminal contempt. This meant that he would have to hear from that private detective under oath, and any other witnesses Ed Reynolds wanted to call. He would have a lawyer by now, and maybe Ed would want to tell his side of the story. First thing Monday morning, he issued an order releasing Ed from custody and scheduling a hearing for 3:00 that afternoon.

When 3:00 arrived, Ed Reynolds and his lawyer were in the courtroom. So, too, was Shelley Connor. She had heard about what had happened to Ed and was there to support him and testify if necessary. She had been shocked when she heard that Ed had asked Dave to lie. To the contrary, it had been Dave who insisted on the creature's existence. She was prepared to testify to what she saw.

The one person who was not present was David Krell. The prosecutor indicated that both she and the state police had called and texted and left messages for the private investigator but had been unable to reach him. One of the troopers had reached his wife on her cell phone early in the day. She had been in New York but was on her way back. His wife said he might be in a hunting cabin in New Hampshire but wasn't sure.

The judge told everyone to wait in or around the courtroom until they found Krell. They would then plan the next steps.

Krell's wife arrived home just as a state police SUV (they no longer used cruisers) pulled into the driveway behind her. Dave's pickup was parked in the driveway where it normally was, so he obviously wasn't in New Hampshire. The side door to the house, the one they normally entered, was locked. That was unusual. Normally that door was kept open unless they left for an extended vacation.

Samantha Krell entered the house, her daughter and the trooper right behind her. She called Dave's name but there was no answer. The house was not large, and it took no more than five minutes to determine that Dave was not there. Perhaps he went for a walk, the trooper suggested. Samantha was suspicious; Dave never used any unnecessary energy. There was no evidence of foul play or anything unusual, and so the trooper started to leave.

It was then that Samantha noticed something unusual about the basement door. It was shut, but not completely latched. They seldom visited the basement and the door was always latched.

Samantha asked the trooper to wait a minute as she walked over and opened the door. She flicked on the light switch and screamed as the light illuminated the broken body of her husband. The trooper rushed past the shocked woman and down the steps. He placed his fingers upon Dave's carotid artery but there was no pulse. The skin was cold and clammy. Rigor mortis had settled in. The trooper called for an ambulance and the coroner on his radio, and then secured the scene.

There was nothing mysterious, however, about what happened.

The judge called for everyone to assemble in the courtroom around 4:00 p.m.

"I've just been informed by the police that Dave Krell is dead. The preliminary information indicates that he fell down his basement steps this weekend and suffered a serious injury to his neck that proved to be fatal. There is no suspicion of foul play."

None of this sounded right to Ed. He suspected foul play, and as he thought about the events of the past few days—Dave turning on him and then the visit from Charles Hunt—he believed he might be catching a glimpse into what happened. *What if*, he asked himself, *Krell changed his testimony at Charles Hunt's urging? What if Krell then became just another loose end that needed taking care of?*

He wasn't in a position to offer theories, or even question anyone's conclusion about Krell's death, but he thought there might be more than meets the eye.

The judge continued, "At this point, we need to decide what to do with respect to the contempt charge against Edwin Reynolds. I heard the testimony under oath from David Krell before he died, but I'm not sure what weight to give it. Mr. Reynolds was not represented by counsel at the time and didn't have an opportunity to cross-examine the witness."

"Let me turn first to the State. Does the State have any evidence that would substantiate anything Mr. Krell said?"

The prosecutor spoke directly, "No, Your Honor. We have reached out to the defendant, who is now represented by the public defender. Mr. Strait will be entering an *Alford* plea later this week, but our information is that he disagrees with Mr. Krell's testimony. We do not have any other information to present."

An *Alford* plea is a guilty plea where the defendant maintains his innocence. "I see," the judge said, turning to defense counsel.

Ed Reynolds had retained an old friend, Joshua Myers, to represent him. 'Retained' was not really the right word because Josh was representing Ed for free. He was about Ed's age and had been around for a while.

"Your Honor," he began. "These charges are preposterous. I hate to speak ill of the dead, but David Krell is—I mean, was—a liar. There was another attorney, Shelley Connor, who was intimately involved in the case for many months. She was forced to withdraw for personal reasons. She is here today and prepared to testify that David Krell, on multiple occasions, told both her and Ed Reynolds that he saw a large creature the morning after the first victim was murdered."

"In fact, she would say that Ed was skeptical of the story but Krell insisted it was true. Never once did Ed Reynolds ask Krell or anyone else to lie. Ed would also testify that he never asked Krell to lie. This is a man who has been practicing law for over forty years. Now, here at the end of his practice, why would he suborn perjury? This needs to be dismissed immediately."

The judge looked back to the prosecutor. "Does the State anticipate opening a criminal investigation into this matter?"

"It does not," the prosecution answered.

The judge looked back to Ed. "Mr. Reynolds, the contempt charge against you is dismissed. I am sorry that you spent a weekend in jail. I may have reacted too hastily. The prosecution has indicated that it will not be opening a criminal investigation and I am not going to refer this matter to the disciplinary board. I am of the opinion now that the statements of Mr. David Krell on the witness stand last week were a complete fabrication."

"I wonder why he would say such things, but I think we will never know. He's dead and, in my mind, the matter is closed. Please go with the court's thanks on the *Commonwealth v. Strait* matter. It sounds like that matter is now going to be resolved as well. Good luck, Mr. Reynolds."

Chapter 52

Later that night, Ed sat with his wife in their family room. The TV was not on but soft music played in the background. Everything had turned out better than he could have imagined forty-eight hours earlier when he sat with his wife in the prison visiting room. He could continue with his practice. He could even maybe work his way out of the debt he was in and claw his way back to the top of his profession.

Ed might be older, but he still had a lot to offer. But as he sat there talking to his wife, he realized it was over. The practice. The clients. The cases. He didn't want to deal with any of it anymore. He had neglected his family for far too long. He suggested to his wife that they go to Philadelphia and have dinner with their son and daughter-in-law. Ed didn't know her well but thought he should learn more about her. She seemed like a nice girl.

They would go down, that is, if his son could find time for them. It was a lot to ask. He never had time for his son when he was younger.

There was something else nagging at him. A murderer had escaped justice and an innocent person was behind bars. Was he going to do anything about it? He didn't know.

Meanwhile, Lagos had proven to be a productive hunting ground. Charles had killed four young women already, and no one seemed to notice or care. It felt good to be back in action. Anna Okon was a pretty sixteen-year-old who relished seeing the handsome older American she had met at the café outside her school. He could be her ticket from poverty, she thought. Charles Hunt's intentions were otherwise.

Tonight, she would become victim number 100, and in the morning, what remained of her would not even be recognizable as human. Nothing could stop him.